About the Author

Michael White has been a professional musician, a science lecturer, a newspaper columnist, science editor for *GQ* magazine and a series consultant for the Discovery Channel's *The Science of the Impossible*.

First published in 1991, he is now the author of 25 books including the international best-sellers *Stephen Hawking: A Life in Science, Leonardo: The First Scientist* and *Tolkien: A Biography*.

He was awarded the Bookman Prize in the US for best popular science book of 1998 for his biography of Isaac Newton, *The Last Sorcerer*. In 2002, he was short-listed for the prestigious Aventis Award for *Rivals*, and his book *The Fruits of War* made the long-list in 2006.

An Honorary Research Fellow at Curtin University, he lives in Perth, Australia with his wife and four children. This is his first novel.

For more information visit Michael White's website at: michaelwhite.com.au

D0001962

BOOKS BY MICHAEL WHITE

Non-Fiction
A Teaspoon and an Open Mind:
The Science of Doctor Who
C.S. Lewis: The Boy Who Chronicled Narnia
The Fruits of War
A History of the 21st Century (with Gentry Lee)
The Pope and the Heretic
Tolkien: A Biography
Rivals
Leonardo: The First Scientist
Super Science
Isaac Newton: The Last Sorcerer
Life Out There
The Science of the X-Files
Asimov: The Unauthorised Biography
Breakthrough (with Kevin Davies)
Darwin: A Life in Science (with John Gribbin)
Einstein: A Life in Science (with John Gribbin)
Stephen Hawking: A Life in Science (with John Gribbin)

For Children and Young Readers
Alien Life Forms
Mind and Matter
Newton
Galileo
John Lennon
Mozart

Memoir
Thompson Twin: An '80s Memoir (Time Warner, 2000)

Equinox

Michael White

arrow books

First published by Arrow Books in 2006

10

Copyright © Michael White 2006

Arrow Books
The Random House Group Limited
20 Vauxhall Bridge Road, London, SW1V 2SA

www.rbooks.co.uk

Addresses for companies within The Random House Group Limited can be
found at: www.randomhouse.co.uk/offices.htm

The Random House Group Limited Reg. No. 954009

A CIP catalogue record for this book
is available from the British Library

ISBN 9780099505235

The Random House Group Limited supports The Forest Stewardship Council
(FSC), the leading international forest certification organisation. All our titles
that are printed on Greenpeace approved FSC certified paper carry the FSC
logo. Our paper procurement policy can be found at
www.rbooks.co.uk/environment.

Typeset by Palimpsest Book Production Limited, Polmont, Stirlingshire
Printed in the UK by CPI Bookmarque, Croydon, CR0 4TD

For the guys:
Lisa, India, George, Noah and Finn

Prologue

Oxford: 20 March, 7.36 p.m.

He cuts the fuel line to the girl's car while she enjoys an early dinner at her friend's house, and then watches the petrol spatter onto the tarmac and run down the hill away from the car, the residue evaporating slowly.

Minutes later he sees her emerge from the house and he follows the car for a quarter of a mile into the country, observing silently as she pulls the dying vehicle to the side of the road.

Flicking off the lights and turning his ignition key to 'off', he allows his own car to glide to a quiet halt fifty yards along the lane behind her. He listens as the girl tries in vain to fire up the parched engine.

He steps out of his car and walks slowly along the lane, keeping out of the moonlight and staying in the tessellated shadows.

She is a mere silhouette, as the lemon lunar

radiance spills across the car roof and lights up the branches of trees and the leaves overhead.

The plastic covers over his shoes squelch against the soft turf. He can hear his own steady breathing, which hits the inside of the plastic visor covering his face. He quickens his pace.

The girl stops turning her ignition key and looks around her through the windows, but she doesn't see him in the deep shadows as he walks towards her car.

He sees her pick up her mobile phone from somewhere on the passenger seat. Two more paces and he is at the door. Opening it, he thrusts inside, scalpel first.

The girl screams and her fingers loosen on the phone, letting it slide down her front and onto the floor of the car. In one seamless movement he leans in close and raises his arm. She cannot see his face, obscured as it is by perspex.

The girl starts shaking involuntarily, her mouth open, speechless with terror. As she is about to scream her attacker's free hand comes down hard over her mouth. His face is only a few inches away from hers now – she can see through the visor that his black pupils are huge.

Her pain starts as a pinprick, but in an instant it swells into her chest. In disbelief, she feels liquid spill out of her, soaking her blouse. The metal of the blade feels like it is rearing up inside her neck, pushing on to pierce her brain.

She shudders and a roar comes from her throat. It hits dead air and is swallowed up.

The next thing that flies from her mouth is a stream of blood. Arterial spray flies over the front seat and hits the windscreen.

Seconds later she is dead.

Chapter 1

Chapter 1

Laura Niven was led to the door of the Bodleian Library by her old friend, the Chief Librarian, James Lightman. They had been seeing a lot of each other during the past three weeks – her first visit to Oxford in four years. They descended down the steps leading to the street. Laura kissed Lightman on the cheek and he held her at arm's length, considering her. She was tall and slender, dressed in a wide-lapelled crimson jacket, faded blue jeans and suede loafers, her blonde hair done up in a loose bun.

The Chief Librarian shook his head slowly and appreciatively. 'It's been wonderful seeing you again, my dear,' he said. 'Please don't wait so long for the next visit, will you?' His croak of a voice was almost a whisper.

Laura smiled at him, studying the wrinkled, benign face. Lightman looked for all the world like an ageing tortoise, his shell the Bodleian, home to the most magnificent collection of books in the world. She placed a hand on his shoulder before turning and continuing on down the steps. At the bottom she stopped and looked back, but the old man had gone.

Laura loved this city and felt a twinge in her abdomen at the thought that she would soon be heading home. Oxford had seeped into her blood when she had been here as a student more than twenty years earlier. It had become part of her, just as in her own tiny way she had become part of it, part of that vast, complex human tapestry that was the history of the city.

She turned along Broad Street, strode past the Sheldonian and started to cross over. But she hadn't looked each way: a young woman in subfusc pedalling an ancient black Hercules bike almost ran her over. The cyclist swerved at the last moment, ringing her bell furiously. Laura, feeling strangely exhilarated, watched her wend her way towards St Giles. Twenty years ago that would have been her, deliberately intimidating American tourists.

Perhaps, she thought, she was pining for her youth. But it wasn't just her own personal story, her part in the tapestry that made her love this place. It was . . . what? What was it that she loved? She couldn't define it: it was one of those indescribable human feelings, as mysterious as honour, altruism, sentimentality.

When she'd been here as a student Laura had

written long letters to her friends in Illinois and South Carolina and to those at home in California about what she had learned. She had boasted about the place because she'd felt that she had become a part of it. To Laura, Oxford was a city of dreams, a super-real place that lavished unmatchable riches upon strangers and breathed fresh air into one's lungs. It was, she thought as she crossed St Giles on her way to the restaurant where she was expected at eight-thirty, quite simply a place that made life worthwhile.

Philip Bainbridge's image of Oxford at the same moment was altogether different. He had come into the city from his house in the village of Woodstock about fifteen miles beyond the old city walls to pick up his daughter Jo from her room at St John's College on St Giles. During the drive in he had seen only the worst aspects of the city. He had been cut up on the dual carriageway by a rusty Rover 216 containing three hyperactive youths from the local estate, Blackbird Leys, a sprawling ghetto only a few miles from the dreaming spires. Then, at a traffic light, he'd been verbally abused by the driver of a Mini Metro who had accused Philip of cutting *him* up on the slip road off the main route into the city. A few moments later, a drunk had stepped out onto Banbury Road directly in front of his car as he'd pulled away from another set of traffic lights – and it was not yet half past eight in the evening.

But Philip was used to it. He loved this city, warts and all, and had been in love with it since he had come up to read philosophy, politics and economics – PPE – at Balliol in 1980. Now, more than a quarter of a century later, he could never imagine living anywhere else in the world, claiming completely seriously that if Oxford had a Mediterranean climate, it would be a city called Complete Paradise and he could spend eternity there.

And this from a man who spent a great deal of his time contemplating – or rather, being forced to contemplate – the seamier side of the ancient city. He had been a freelance photographer for years, and now he earned most of his income with the Thames Valley police force working as a crime-scene police photographer. During his time in this job he had seen oceans of blood and had witnessed the outer limits of pain. Because of this, he knew that at its heart, in its human soul, Oxford was just the same as South Central LA or the East End of London. He still loved the place but he knew that, like all places in the mortal world, anything divine about Oxford was tainted with the blood and grey matter of many a corpse. That, he understood, was simply the way of the world, be it Venice Beach, Eighth Avenue or The High on an English summer's evening.

Parking on St Giles, he ran over to the porter's lodge of St John's where Jo was waiting for him. She looked incredibly beautiful, an Arthur Rackham painting in faded denim and a Ralph Lauren leather jacket. Her russet hair cascaded in tight natural curls to her shoulders. She had burned-wood eyes, pale skin, high cheekbones and full lips.

'Sorry I'm late.'

'Dad, I know you by now,' Jo replied, with a grin. Her voice was slightly husky – it could shatter the defences of any man who had managed to resist her looks.

Philip shrugged and offered her his arm. 'Good. So, are we ready for din-dins with mother?'

'Indeed we are,' she replied with a small laugh.

They headed down St Giles.

'So, tell me. You missing New York?' Philip asked.

'Not yet.'

'You never talk much about your old life.'

'Not much to say, I guess. And dad, "old life" sounds weird. I've only been here, what? Six months?'

'Feels like a lifetime.'

'Gee, thanks!' Jo turned to Philip with her mouth open.

'I'd close that if I were you.'

Jo shook her head and huffed. 'No, it's good here. It felt a little, I dunno, a little claustrophobic in

9

Greenwich Village. Cool place, but you know, apart-ment-too-small-for-suddenly-famous-author-mother-and-teenage-daughter syndrome.'

'Yes, quite a common social disease in one form or another. Glad I don't have to deal with it – one of the perks of being a committed bachelor, I suppose.'

Jo gave him a sceptical look. 'You reckon? Can't outweigh the disadvantages, though, can it? I've told you before, one of my missions before leaving these hallowed halls is to hitch you to a good woman. Someone who'll look after you.'

'Oh, please. You think I need fattening up?' Philip patted his slight paunch.

They crossed the road and walked past the old Quaker Meeting House. The pavement was narrow: rows of metal railings to the left, road to the right. Old bicycles lined the pavement, padlocked to the railings. Along the way, a ragged busker who had made this patch his own juggled oranges ineptly. 'Spareanychange?' he slurred hopefully as they passed.

Ahead of them, twenty yards off, they could see Laura waiting for them outside Brown's Restaurant.

Their plates had been cleared and the waitress had topped up their wineglasses. Laura considered the dessert menu sceptically and took a sip of her wine.

They were seated close to the kitchen doors and as staff charged in and out they caught glimpses of the controlled chaos that lay beyond. The smell of cigarette smoke wafted over from the smoking area, and the conversation of a hundred or so diners created a haze of human voices that interwove with barely audible acid jazz spilling from the sound system.

'We're going to miss you, Laura,' Philip said over the rim of his wineglass, and looked first at her then to their daughter.

Laura's time in Oxford had flashed past and she was due to fly back to New York the next morning. Although she was looking forward to seeing her neat and spacious apartment in Greenwich Village again, another part of her was drawing her in, grounding her here. She would miss Oxford too, and the two people who meant most to her in the world: Philip and Jo.

'Oh, I'm sure I'll be back again soon,' Laura replied, tucking some blonde strands of hair behind her right ear. 'I'll have to keep a check on this one for a start.' She glanced at Jo.

'Yeah, sure – like I need looking after.' Jo gave her mother a rueful look.

'Well, here's to a safe journey,' Philip said and raised his glass. Jo echoed the sentiment, but was easing out of her chair and looking at her watch.

'Hey, mom, I'm real sorry, but I have to split. I was supposed to meet Tom ten minutes ago.'

'That's cool,' Laura replied. 'You run along. Say "hi" to lover boy for me.'

Jo kissed Philip on the cheek. 'I'll see you in the morning, just to check you have your ticket and passport,' she said, turning back to Laura with a wry grin. Then she negotiated a twisting path between the closely packed tables.

At the exit Jo waved goodbye. Gazing across the restaurant, Laura recalled the many times she had sat here in Brown's. It had been a regular haunt during her student days, the venue for her first date with Philip and the place where she had broken the news that she was pregnant with Jo. She loved the never-changing decor – the cream walls and the old mirrors, polished oak floors and enormous palms. Looking across the room she could almost see her younger self at an adjacent table, and a fresh-faced Philip gazing back at her.

'So, has your trip been worth it?' Philip asked. 'Did you find what you were looking for?'

Laura took another sip of wine, placed the glass down and began to play with the stem. 'Yes and no,' she sighed. 'Well, actually, no, to be honest. I feel I've got stuck up a blind alley.'

'Oh?'

'Well, you know, it happens.'

'Does this mean you've wasted your time?'

'No,' she said emphatically. 'Just that I'll have to work harder.' Laura paused before going on. 'Well, in fact it's not been good. I think I'll ditch the idea.'

Philip looked startled. 'But it sounded so promising.'

'Yeah, but that's what writing is like. You think something's going to work and sometimes it does. Other times it definitely doesn't.'

After years as a struggling journalist in New York and writing half a dozen novels in her spare time, watching each of them flounder and sink, Laura had suddenly pushed all the right buttons a year earlier. *Restitution* was a historical crime thriller set in seventeenth-century New Amsterdam. The *New York Times* had called it 'scintillating'. It had garnered the White Rose Fiction Award and had sold enough to allow Laura to finally quit the day job. The media had taken to her immediately, promoting her on her looks and her career as a journalist who had specialised in covering the grisliest crimes in New York City. Seizing her chance, Laura had launched herself into the next project, a novel set in four-teenth-century Oxford in which the real-life theologian and mathematician Thomas Bradwardine was the central character in a complex plot to murder the king of the day, Edward II.

'So what about the mysterious monk, Brad-wardine?'

'Oh, I'm still interested in him. He was never a monk, by the way, Philip.' Laura smiled. 'It's just that I've come to realise that he could never have been involved in a plot to kill the king. He just wasn't the type. He was a deeply religious man who was the greatest mathematician of his time and went on to become Archbishop of Canterbury, but he was no Rambo. Anyway, it's OK, I hadn't gone that far with the idea. Besides, there are plenty of other stories; they're all out there in the ether ready to be grabbed. And I even think that Bradwardine may come back on the radar one day – I'm just storing it all away.'

'Sounds like something I would say,' Philip retorted.

'Yeah, well, perhaps I've been too harsh on your odd little personality traits all these years.' Laura leaned back in her chair and took a sip of her wine. As Philip looked away to attract the attention of a waiter, she caught a glimpse of his profile and was struck by the fact that more than twenty years had passed since they'd first met. In that time Philip had hardly changed. Of course, there were now quite a few grey hairs among the unruly mop of dark curls, and his face was podgier, his eyes more tired. But he still had the same confident, world-weary smile that she had found so attractive when he was twenty-two, the same devastating brown eyes.

She had throught so much about him when she was the other side of the world. She had been away so long it almost seemed impossible that they could be sitting here together in this crowded restaurant with the rain splashing against the windows and the massicot glow of the street lights outside.

Seeing Philip now, Laura knew why she had fallen for him in the first place, why she had given herself to him in a way she had never done before or since. For a second, she could not believe that she had walked away from it all.

'Coffee?'

She looked at him blankly.

'Hello! Coffee?'

The waiter was beside the table and Philip was waving a hand in front of her.

'Oh, yeah, ahem . . . sorry. I'll have a decaf latté . . . thanks.'

'You were miles away. In the land of Bradwardine and the Plantagenets?'

'I guess,' she lied.

'So, what're you going to do?' Philip asked as the waiter walked away.

'Don't really know right this minute. I'm sure I'll think of something.' Laura was being deliberately evasive and Philip knew it. He was about to move the conversation on when his mobile rang. 'Philip Bainbridge,' he said. 'Yes . . . Yes.' He sounded uncharacteristically curt on the phone, Laura thought. 'OK, I'm only a mile or two away. I could be there in – what? – fifteen minutes . . . yes? OK.' He flipped the phone shut.

'Problem?'

'No, just a nuisance. That was the station. They want me to take some pictures, an incident near The Perch. They wouldn't tell me anything more. Sorry, we'd better get the bill.'

Chapter 2

Philip didn't have time to drop Laura at his place first. It was freezing in his thirty-year-old MGB and Laura was relieved when she saw the blue lights ahead. They pulled off the road and across a stretch of muddy verge before stopping ten yards from a brightly lit white box-tent about fifteen feet square that marked the location of the crime scene.

Philip killed the engine and Laura looked through the dirty windscreen, as a figure in a white suit with FORENSICS stencilled on the back in green walked past the side of the car towards the tent.

'Laura, you'll have to stay here, I'm afraid. Police personnel only.' Philip got out, went around to the boot, pulled out a sturdy leather bag containing his camera equipment and slung it over his shoulder. He rummaged through the bag as he walked back to the door of the MGB. Fiddling with the lens of his Nikon digital he bent down to the window. 'You'll be OK?' he asked. 'I don't suppose it will be very pleasant in there, anyway.' And before she could answer, he had turned away.

Laura sat in the car for a few minutes but then curiosity got the better of her. She stepped out onto the mud and made for the flap of the tent. There was no one around to stop her. She would just take a peek, she told herself.

Pulling aside the plastic sheet just a crack she looked inside but all she could see were the backs of two police officers and the Forensics guy crouching down and placing something unidentifiable in a clear plastic wallet with a pair of tweezers. Behind him was a small red car, the doors open, mud splattered up the panels.

Closing the flap, Laura tiptoed around the edge of the tent. She crouched down and put her eye to a gap in the plastic. The car was only a few feet away and she had a clear view straight through the open offside door.

The body of a young woman was slumped on the back seat. Her arms and legs were splayed, her head pushed back, eyes open, staring, sightless, at the inside of the car roof. She was wearing a simple top and skirt, both blood-soaked. Her flesh was an intense white as though all the blood had been drained from her and her skin seemed to be bleached further by the powerful floodlights inside the tent. The interior of the car was smeared with blood; arterial spray had splashed across the windows and over the cream dash.

The girl looked very young, about Jo's age. She had once been very pretty: her long blonde hair cascaded across the back of the seat, but it was also matted with blood and had stuck to her shoulders in clumps. There was a deep red trough that stretched from ear to ear across her neck and another extending from her throat to her navel. Her ribcage had been opened up and the bones had been snapped back.

Laura stood up. For a long time now she'd believed that she had seen enough crime scenes for nothing ever to affect her, but suddenly she felt a wave of nausea sweep over her and thought she was going to throw up. She took great gulps of air and gradually the sensation ebbed away. She was about to make a dash for the MGB when she heard a voice beside her. 'Good evening.'

She whirled round and saw a young policeman staring at her. She must have looked a mess, she thought incongruously. Her skin felt cold and she knew that the blood had drained from her face. Beads of sweat had broken out on her forehead.

'I, er . . .'

'Come this way, please.' The policeman took her by the arm.

Just inside the tent, he called to a plain-clothes

officer standing close by. Laura was transfixed by the view she now had into the car a few yards away.

'Well, hello.' The officer looked her up and down. 'And what brings you out on a nasty cold night like this?'

She was about to respond when Philip looked over, lowered his camera and sighed heavily. 'Shit,' she heard him mutter.

'Inspector Monroe,' Philip made sure he did not catch Laura's eye. 'This is a friend of mine, Laura Niven.'

John Monroe was a tall, broad-shouldered beefy man wearing an ill-fitting brown suit and an off-mustard tie that had seen better days. In his early forties, he was bald except for patches of dark hair shaved to a mere stubble either side of his head. He had once been a promising sprinter but had let himself get out of shape. He had a large head sitting on a thick short neck. His most remarkable feature, and something that gave him the merest hint of phys-ical attractiveness, was a pair of large black eyes that suggested both intelligence and grit but no hint of softness or humour. 'Ah, a friend, Mr Bainbridge.' Monroe's voice was a classic baritone darkened with habitual sarcasm.

'Yes, and I apologise. I asked—'

'Oh, for God's sake, Philip,' Laura snapped suddenly. 'I *can* speak, you know, and I'm not a child.' She turned to Monroe who for a second looked a little startled. 'Officer . . .'

'Detective Chief Inspector . . .'

'Detective Chief Inspector . . . Monroe? I'm sorry. Philip told me to stay put. I was . . .'

'Curious?'

'Yes, I guess I was . . .'

'You realise now, of course, Ms Niven, that this is a murder scene, and a particularly nasty one at that. Members of the public—'

'Detective Chief Inspector, I can vouch for Laura,' Philip persisted. 'I think she knows she shouldn't have, but—'

He was cut short as a white-suited figure near the car called over. 'Chief Inspector? I think you should see this.'

Monroe spun round and took two paces towards the car. Philip glared at Laura and was about to say something when, to his disgust, she strode after Monroe.

'It was just inside the wound,' the Forensics officer said. Between his gloved thumb and index finger he held up a coin daubed with blood.

Monroe took it in his gloved hand and held it up to the light. Laura managed to get a good look at it before Monroe scowled at her and she took a step back. It was the size of a quarter, and the side facing them depicted a beautifully crafted scene with five naked female figures holding a bowl aloft.

'It looks to me like solid gold,' the Forensics officer said. 'But I'll have to confirm that back at the lab.' Monroe placed the coin gingerly into a plastic bag held open for him. Then, turning, he saw Laura only a few feet away. He gave Philip a sour look.

'Mr Bainbridge,' he said and ran a finger between his shirt collar and the skin of his neck. 'If you have finished here, would you be so kind as to escort your lady friend back to your car, and go home?'

'Well, good night to you too, Detective Chef Inspector,' Laura retorted as Monroe turned on his heel. 'Nice meeting you.'

Chapter 3

'What the bloody hell do you think you were doing?' Philip yelled. He was more angry than she could ever remember him being. 'This is my job, Laura. Stunts like that could get me fired.'

'Oh, for God's sake, Philip, calm down. I was just peeking through the tent flap. That cop made things far worse by bringing me inside, didn't he?'

Philip turned to look at her for a moment before glaring back at the road. 'You know, sometimes . . .'

'What?'

'A crime scene isn't open to the public unless the police say it is. You damn well know that, Laura.'

'OK, OK. I'm sorry. I would have apologised – I didn't get a chance.'

'You're lucky that Monroe was preoccupied.'

They fell silent for a moment.

'So, what do you make of it?'

'I'm not at liberty to talk about it, Laura.'

'Oh, come on, Philip – it's me, remember?'

He stared at the road and Laura could see the tension in his jawline.

'So that's it, ha? You're clamming up on me, just because I broke the rules?'

He continued to ignore her.

'Typical,' she huffed.

Suddenly Philip hit the brake and pulled the car off the road onto the verge. Leaving the engine to idle, he turned in his seat to face Laura.

'Look,' he said, unable to keep the anger from his voice. 'Laura, as much as I love you, sometimes you can be the most annoying, arrogant bitch.'

She made to protest.

'No, you listen to me for once.' Philip raised his voice a notch. 'This is my life here. You can swan off to New York tomorrow and get back to your books and your own private little world. I have to work with these people several days a week. It's my bread and butter. But you know, you never were big on respect, were you?'

'What?' Laura snapped.

'You've always done just what you pleased. You've come and gone as you liked.' He stopped, suddenly regretting that he had said so much and knowing that a part of his anger had nothing to do with Laura's performance this evening and a lot to do with the past. There was a long silence.

'I don't really think that's fair,' Laura said finally.

'You make it sound like a one-way street, Philip. If you're talking about Jo, about what we've chosen to do, you were every bit as involved in those decisions.'

'Was I?' Philip replied, his voice a little calmer. 'Was I really? Would you have stayed in England with her if I had asked you to? I don't think so.'

Laura didn't know how to respond. They had been kids, it was as simple as that. She had come from a broken home – her parents divorced, Jane, her B-movie actress mother, then living post-rehab in a commune in San Luis Obispo, her father a top-notch lawyer in LA. Laura had won a Rhodes Scholarship to Oxford to read history of art at Magdalen. She had been ambitious, a high-flyer.

Then she had fallen pregnant: morning sickness just before her Finals. While the others had been swigging champagne from the bottle after the last exam, she had gone back to her room to cry and vomit some more. Her parents had come over for Laura's graduation and she had managed to tell her mother. Jane Niven had taken it stoically and had never tried to push her daughter in any one direction. She had struggled with her own demons for years and a daughter pregnant at twenty-one was no big deal. Laura wondered now if it would have been better if she had been guided into a decision.

Philip had tried to be grown-up about it, but he had been little more than a child himself. He had graduated a year earlier, but he was living in digs, scratching a living photographing weddings and babies and dreaming of his own exhibitions that in reality lay more than a decade ahead. He was broke, immature and had no idea what to do. After the birth, Laura had contemplated staying in England and getting a job somewhere. Maybe she and Philip could have worked something out, shared their lives, but something had told her that it couldn't possibly succeed. Before their baby daughter was six months old Laura had taken the decision to move back to America with her.

Laura and Philip had remained friends, though, and Philip had come over to the States whenever he could. When Laura landed a job at the *New York Post* as a crime reporter she began to earn a little, and she was able to make a few trips over to England with Jo. Three years later she had married. Her husband, Rod Newcombe, had been a determined and ambitious documentary-maker and they had forged great plans to work together on a true-life crime series. Rod had been good for Jo, who had grown to adore him, and for a short time it was happy families. But then, in 1994, Rod had headed for Rwanda and had come home in a body bag. Jo had been seven and could not understand what had happened to her stepfather, and how all that remained of him now was an image on a videotape.

It had also come at a crucial time for Laura. She had just moved into crime reporting and hadn't yet learned to cope with the squalor and the agonies that she was forced to witness each day. After being sent to cover a murder in which a prostitute had bitten off a customer's penis before shooting herself in the face, Laura had resorted to antidepressants and weekly therapy sessions.

That phase had passed and Laura had become hardened to the grim realities of what she did to pay the bills. But so many times she regretted the choices she had made; and whenever she met up with Philip again she realised how things could have gone in other directions, how much she really loved him and how different her life might have been. But each time she did this she was also conscious that their lives were moving apart, that it was getting harder, not easier to ever consider an alternative reality in which the three of them – Jo, Philip, herself – could be together.

For an instant, what she had said and done tonight seemed strangely symptomatic. Laura felt overwhelmingly sad and it was all she could do to stop the tears. She didn't know the answer to Philip's question. Would she have done anything different?

Taking a deep breath, she said. 'I'm sorry, Philip. I was being unreasonable.'

Philip looked at her for a few seconds. She hadn't

been able to answer his question, but he could understand that. He had no answers either. He suspected that sometimes Laura wished that things had been different. He knew he did, more often than he cared to admit, even to himself. And when he did dwell on the subject, an insistent voice would end the internal conversation with the logical announcement that it was all too late now and what had happened had happened.

He smiled suddenly. 'Oh well, I'm sure Monroe will get over it. He's a good cop but a jumped-up bastard.'

Laura leaned over and kissed him on the cheek as he put the car into gear and pulled back onto the road.

'So, you going to tell me what you know?'

Philip let out a heavy sigh, but the anger had evaporated. 'God, woman, you don't give up, do you?'

'Nope,' Laura replied, with a smile. 'Not usually.'

'Well, to be honest, I don't know much more than you do. She was a young kid about twenty, driving back from a friend's house. Died sometime between seven and eight-thirty this evening. Discovered by a guy walking his dog. Nearest house a couple of hundred yards away. No one heard anything or saw anything.'

'But the wounds . . .' Laura began, her voice

trailing off. 'Nearly fifteen years of crime reporting back home and I never saw anything like that.'

'No, not nice.'

'I'm used to "not nice": tricks cutting the tongues out of hookers, heads blown apart by semi-automatics – that kind of thing. But that girl had her heart taken out, for Christ's sake. Surgically removed, carefully done.'

'I know, I photographed it.'

'Strikes me as way beyond the range of your average murder, Philip. More . . . I don't know . . . ritualistic, I guess.'

'Yes, maybe,' Philip replied, staring at the road ahead. 'I'm not a cop.'

They fell silent for a while, then Laura said. 'And that coin. What the hell was that about?'

'Why such interest?' Philip retorted impatiently.

'Search me. I guess I'm still an old crime hack at heart.'

Chapter 4

The wind rattled the windows in Laura's room in Philip's house and she drifted in and out of a disturbed sleep, dreaming the same thing she always dreamed on nights like this one: a dream that was not a dream, more a distorted memory.

It began with her flying over Los Angeles. It was night and she was going to visit her parents at their respective California homes soon after she had moved back to New York. They were over the outer suburbs before the pilot even announced that the plane was beginning its descent. Ten minutes later she was over the city proper and the plane was banking slowly to the north, moving up parallel to the coast. She could see the city now, all lit up, like a galaxy, like one of those incredible images from the Hubble telescope. And each car was a star, and each house a little solar system, a solar system of lights. The pollution in the air made them twinkle and fray.

Laura had taken this flight before of course,

maybe a dozen times, but never at night, and it was just amazing. And then she saw it. She was staring at the lights, this show of defiance, humankind sticking up a finger to the gods, pure chutzpah. It reared up, the I-405 with its million automobiles. But from three thousand feet up it looked nothing like a road. She could see no crash barriers, no tarmac, no borders, just a black strip between the lights. And the dots of sodium light – they could not be cars, could they? They had become disembodied, mere headlights moving by their own volition, just lights. It was then that it struck her, the whole view, the bigger picture, the long strips containing all those lights, all moving in strict columns, six lanes either way, dot after dot after dot, all moving together. For a moment back there they had been metal containers carrying Stan or Jim or Tabitha, taking them home to little Jimmy, to Dorothy and Delores: they had been just lights, they had been bubbles of humanity, cocoons with music spilling from the radio. They had been, in her mind at least, bundles of thought, packets of longings, desires and memories, worries and frailties. But then that moment had passed and now the dots had become something else. The freeway had become a blood vessel and the dots of light, the disembodied lights had become corpuscles, the red cells of the brake lights and the white of the headlights streaming up and down along an artery

31

of a darkened body that must be lying down there somewhere, invisible in the glare.

She jolted awake and sat up. Squinting at the clock, she could see that the time was 5.32 a.m. It was blowing a gale outside. Then she remembered that Jo had been out when they had returned home just before midnight. She hadn't heard her come in.

Laura was now wide awake and the images of the pale body she had seen in the car came rushing back. There had been blood and gore all over the inside of the car. Those things she was used to, but then she remembered the girl's chest splayed – the view she'd had when she'd stood close to the car, next to Monroe. The ribs looked like they had been cut through with a specialist's tool, something that a surgeon would use. The cut had been made with absolute precision, no effort wasted. Then she could see again the severed arteries and veins, the sliced edges of the heart's plumbing. They too had been snipped precisely, expertly.

She laid her head back on the pillow, refusing to give up on sleep, trying to rid herself of the images and to focus on her own life. Her suitcases were packed and stood at the foot of the bed. She was leaving for the airport at 10 a.m. By tomorrow night she would be back in Greenwich Village, back in her apartment trying to revive her dead plants and searching for a way into the new book. The new book, God, that was going nowhere, she recalled suddenly, and with this recollection sleep slipped further away.

Laura tried to grasp the plot that she had worked through, to disappear into a fantasy world. It was a trick she had used before and it often worked against insomnia, but tonight nothing seemed to take her away from the immediate moment.

Then she was back at the crime scene again . . . Monroe picking up that coin between latexed fingers. It had glistened in the illumination from the flood-lights, glistened except where the blood had caked and dried. She had never seen anything quite like it before. It looked extremely old. And to her untrained eye it certainly appeared to be gold, old gold. Why, she thought, would anyone leave such a thing behind? Apart from the fact that it was giving away clues, it must have been worth a fortune.

Philip had been quite right to be so furious with her, but Laura knew there was much more to it. There could be no coincidence in the fact that his outburst had happened the night before she was due to return home to New York. It was the old resentments rising again. He felt that she had deserted him all those years ago, even though they had both known – and now knew definitely – that they could never have coped. These past three weeks had been wonderful, and she could admit that sometimes she had found herself slipping into a fantasy in which they really were a family, that she lived here in this seventeenth-century house in a village close to Oxford, that Jo had grown up with them, together. The fantasy felt nice.

Laura had become so wrapped up in these thoughts that at first she did not hear the phone ring in the hall downstairs. Then came the sound of Philip's door opening and his heavy tread as he stumbled along the corridor and down the steep, winding staircase. She could hear him speaking, but couldn't make out what he was saying. Then the receiver was replaced and she heard him take the stairs back up. Now he was moving fast. A few moments later there came an urgent knock on her door and it swung inwards.

'It's Jo,' Philip said, his face looking pale and drained in the light from the hall. 'She's been in a car accident. She's at the John Radcliffe.'

Chapter 5

Cambridge: February 1689.

The previous night, Isaac Newton had been too tired even to unpack. His servant Elias Perrywinkle had dragged the heavy trunk filled with new purchases across the quad and up the winding stone stairs of Trinity College to the rooms that Newton shared with his oldest associate, John Wickins.

Dismissing the servant with a farthing and a mumbled word of thanks, Newton had barely found the energy to stow the unopened trunk in the laboratory adjoining his private chamber, remove his boots and throw his mud-splattered cloak over a chair, before he fell onto the mattress and slid immediately into a deep sleep.

He had awakened just before the seventh hour as the first rays of the weak winter sun spilled through the east-facing windows of his rooms. Perrywinkle was there a few minutes later with a pewter bowl of hot water and a fresh linen cloth. The water felt good.

Newton could feel it sink into his dry skin. Catching his reflection in the small mirror he had propped up on the windowsill he thought that he looked a sorry sight: a man to whom a healthy, dreamless sleep was a half-forgotten acquaintance.

Alone, after the greyed water had been removed, Newton changed his shirt, pulled on his boots and fished from his pocket the key to his laboratory. On his way he picked up a silver-plated dish and cup left by his servant. Upon the plate was an apple and a chunk of bread; in the cup, fresh, tepid water.

The laboratory was not a particularly large room: even though Newton had been the Lucasian Professor at Cambridge University for twenty years, the college authorities had not been over-generous with him. But it was enough. He lit a torch at either side of the door, creating dull puddles of light in the windowless room, and locked the door behind him. Wickins he knew was visiting his family in Manchester, but he could not risk any intrusion or suffer any prying into this his private domain. Pacing over to the fireplace, he stacked some wood, and using one of the flaming torches he soon had a good fire going which dispelled the shadows and allowed him to see through the heavy chemical haze that pervaded the room at all times.

The room was lined with shelves. Newton's library had grown to some three hundred volumes dealing almost exclusively with every aspect of alchemy and the Hermetic tradition. He had used the money earned annually from the family estate at Woolsthorpe in Lincolnshire as well as a good portion of his professor's income to acquire the collection; it was perhaps the finest in all Christendom. Here could be found Giordano Bruno's *Ash Wednesday Supper*, translations of Galileo's heretical works banned by the Vatican, transcriptions from *The Emerald Tablet*, the Rosicrucian Manifestos, Michael Maier's *Septimana Philosophica* and works by Ramon Lull, Robert Fludd and Jakob Böhme.

Not all the shelves were taken up with Newton's books. Some housed piles of papers, his notes and accounts of experiments; they spilled over onto a table placed to one side of the room. Taking up about a third of the shelf space were bottles and glass vessels. Some of the bottles contained coloured liquids and each container was corked and labelled. In one corner of the room stood an elaborate glass construction, a distillation apparatus, and in another was a telescope on a stand. Inside the large stone fireplace a metal cauldron was suspended on brackets driven into the sides.

To a stranger entering this room, the circus of smells would have been quite overpowering (even for those with the olfactory sensibilities of the seventeenth century). But to Newton the odours had become almost subliminal, and if a particular conglomeration of effluvia broke through the barrier of familiarity, he simply viewed them as somehow homely.

It was freezing cold, but the fire would soon turn the room into a veritable sauna. Years earlier, Newton had paid a pair of workmen to knock special ventilation holes in the outer wall of the laboratory, and this simple adaptation had probably saved him from asphyxiation on more than one occasion. Striding to the table, he cleared a space and deposited the plate and cup there before turning and crouching down beside the trunk that he had placed in the middle of the laboratory floor the previous night.

As he fumbled with the lock he began to think about his latest trip to London in pursuit of the missing clue that he was sure was there. For almost a quarter of a century now he had been searching, searching for the core secret of all existence, the *prisca sapentia*. Science had been his first mistress and he had bled her dry. His *Principia Mathematica* had been published two years earlier, making him a star in the academic world; but he had known all along that there was more to the universe than the nuts and bolts, the mechanical edifice he had observed and described in his acclaimed work.

Almost from the moment he had arrived here at

Cambridge University in 1661, he had been drawn into the world of alchemy and the occult. His old mentor and predecessor in the Lucasian Chair, Isaac Barrow, had struck the first spark, and it had been kindled into a raging fire by the writings of the great adepts of the past, men like Cornelius Agrippa and Elias Ashmole, John Dee and Giordano Bruno. Their search had been called the Great Work or *Magnum Opus*, and for long years these geniuses of occultism had conducted elaborate alchemical experiments in smoky laboratories. They had given their lives to the quest for the Philosopher's Stone, the legendary substance that would allow the alchemist to transmute any base metal into gold, the magical interface between the physical and the metaphysical that could also allow the adept to produce the *elixir vitae* and to find eternal youth.

Like every alchemist before him, Newton had based his ideas on that bible of the Hermetic experimenter, the doctrine of *The Emerald Tablet*. In his youth, Barrow had enlightened him about the existence of this wondrous text and had explained how it was the guide for all alchemists. It had been created in the time of the Ancients, Barrow had explained, a time when men knew far more about the workings of the universe than did all the intellectuals and philosophers of his own day. These Ancients had distilled their knowledge into the inscriptions to be found in *The Emerald Tablet*. No one knew where the original tablet now lay. It had vanished from the eyes of mortal men, but translations of the inscriptions had been handed down through the generations of alchemists, and each had followed what they believed to be the absolute truth as described by the Ancients. The tablet described for them the route to the Philosopher's Stone, how they must prepare both their own souls and the lumpen physical matter with which they worked. Newton believed that the reason why no alchemist had so far succeeded in producing the object of their dreams was no fault of the Ancients. Nor, of course, was it a failing of Nature; it was simply that no philosopher or alchemist had purified his soul sufficiently well, and no seeker of the Truth had committed himself to the task with sufficient vigour and single-mindedness.

Unlike almost every other alchemist from Hermes Trismegistus himself to his own inner circle, Newton had no desire to make gold simply for its own sake. He saw little value in unimaginable wealth. For him, the gold at the end of the rainbow was pure knowledge, the knowledge possessed by the gods, and he knew that he would do anything to find it. It was his reason for being. Over the many years he had stood at the furnace studying the microcosm, and relating it to the macrocosm seen through the lenses of his telescope, he had teased out connections and taken the notion of holism to new heights of reasoning. In that time he had grown to believe that he was himself semi-divine, that he had been placed here on Earth for one purpose – to find the Philosopher's Stone and to elucidate the Truth. God, he believed, had chosen him, marked him out as unique and empowered him with the greatest intellect of his generation, so that he, Isaac Newton, Lucasian Professor at Cambridge University, could do his Father's bidding and unravel for the rest of humankind the true meaning of existence, the innermost workings of Nature, the mechanism of the universe.

The hinges of the trunk creaked as Newton lifted the lid. Inside were carefully packed glass vessels swathed in wool to protect them on the potholed road from London. There were jars of chemicals. One contained sticks of grey-coated metal cylinders immersed in a yellowish oil. Beside this was a tube of powder, black as soot, and next to that another filled with a crimson talc. Placed on its side and nestled in a thick woollen wrap lay a large hourglass.

One third of the trunk was packed with neatly stacked leather-bound books. Newton lifted the top one and surveyed the spine. '*The Fame and Confessions of the Fraternity of the Rosicrucians*

41

by Thomas Vaughan,' he read aloud before placing it carefully on the floor beside the trunk. The book beneath it had its title embossed in gold on the cover: *The Sceptical Chemyst*. The name of the author, Robert Boyle, was written in large letters under the title. Newton leafed through the pages for a few moments and then placed it on top of the Vaughan.

He then lifted the remaining volumes from the trunk and took them to a table backed against the wall to the right of the fireplace, where he began to arrange them in piles before transferring them to the shelves above. As he lifted a particularly handsome tome, bound in green hide and carrying the title *The Compound of Alchymy: The Twelve Gates Leading to the Discovery of the Philosopher's Stone* and its author's name, George Ripley, a small piece of parchment slipped out from under the back cover. It dropped to the floor at Newton's feet.

He picked it up and unfolded it carefully. The parchment was dry and yellowed, but he could see writing in faded brown ink covering the surface. Pacing over to the fireplace, Newton held the parchment close to his face so that he could make out the tiny handwriting. It was written in Aramaic, an ancient Semitic language with which he was familiar. Translating it in his head, Newton whispered the words to himself:

Oh ye seeker, ye truth seeker, lose not heart.
For, whilst falling to our knees before the tablet
of green, there lies another and even deeper
Truth. My friends, I have seen it only as if in
a dream, but the gods proclaim it real. As the
fields are green, the blood of the Lord is red,
red as the ruby. And, as the tablet is of its given
shape, so the ruby is a sphere; for indeed, I
have seen it as if in a dream. And if the power
of the tablet is one, that of the ruby sphere is
a million-fold more. The glorious tablet leads
the way, the sphere opens the doors to the
world. If your soul be pure, seek the sphere
and with it ye shall possess the glory of the
Ancients. Seek the sphere under the earth, 'tis
cocooned in stone, great learning above and
earth below.

GR.

Beneath this was a picture of a sphere with a line
of minuscule writing following a close-packed spiral
from pole to pole. And at the foot of the page Newton
saw a single line of letters, numbers and alchemical
symbols that he knew to be a set of encrypted occult
instructions. Finally, in the lower right-hand corner,
there was a tiny illustration, an elaborate pattern of
criss-crossing lines like a tiny maze.

He could hardly believe what he had read. If this

was truly by Ripley (and he had seen the man's handwriting before and it matched) then this was a find of incomparable value. For him, as for all alchemists, *The Emerald Tablet* was the most important guide on the journey to the Philosopher's Stone. But according to Ripley, there was something more: this ruby sphere was immensely more significant. Perhaps, Newton concluded as he returned to the table under the bookshelves, this offered a hint about why the ultimate secrets had eluded him for so long. If that was so, then it had been God's will that he should have picked up this particular volume at the bookshop of William Copper in Little Britain, close to St Paul's where he had spent most of his afternoon the day before he set out for Cambridge. And, if it *was* God's will, he could not fail. The Lord, he knew, would guide him along this new stage on the journey. He would be led inexorably to the Truth.

Chapter 6

Later, Philip would say that he could remember almost nothing of the journey to the hospital that took them through the near-silent night. But his mind was racing, pumped-up with anxiety and spliced through with bad memories.

It had been over twenty years ago that his father Maurice had died in a car crash, and that had been the most profound, life-changing event of Philip's life, an event that had altered radically the direction in which he was heading. He was twenty-two and had learned two weeks earlier that he had won a First. On the day of the graduation ceremony he was having breakfast with his housemates in their ramshackle house off Cowley Road when the phone rang. It was his Uncle Greg, his father's brother. His father's car had collided with a truck that had jumped across the central reservation. It had hit Maurice head-on, killing him instantly.

Philip had believed that he did not really love his father, that he would not miss him whenever the time came for him to die. He had too many sour memories of the man. He couldn't forget his father's bullying ways, the fact that he had made his mother's life a misery and then turned in upon himself, pulling down a veil of silence the moment she walked out on him.

Philip had done everything he could to please his father. Before going to university he had been a keen photographer and had won awards for his work – he had even started to sell a few pictures. But it was an aspect of his life that his father had constantly belittled, telling him that he could never make a fortune from photography. So Philip had put away his cameras and gone up to Oxford to study PPE, suppressing his own hopes and ambitions to follow a path that his father had laid out before him.

And as Philip had stood over his father's open coffin in the funeral home on the day of the burial, all he could think about was the irony of it all. All his life he had sought this man's approval; then, on the day of Philip's greatest triumph, the bastard went and got himself killed. It was almost, he thought in his most irrational moment, as though his father had done it deliberately to spite him.

But later, when he could think straight, Philip began to understand that there was more to it than this simple emotional judgement. The man had been a bully but he had also been an obsessive with an exaggerated need for privacy. He had harboured a paranoid belief that the world was prying into his life. As Philip had stared down at the husk of a human being, he couldn't shake the thought that here lay the man who had trusted no one, who had shredded his correspondence before putting it in the trash, the man who had triple-bolted his house each night. Yet now here he lay, on show, all dignity stripped away.

It was this more than anything that had convinced Philip to begin afresh. All his life he had been in thrall to his father, but deep beneath the surface he knew that in character he was far closer to his mother, Joan. Joan Bainbridge had once been Joan Ghanmora, one of the most successful artists to come out of the Caribbean. Her black father had disappeared when she was young and she had been raised by her Scottish mother, Elizabeth, and encouraged from the age of six to be a painter. She had met Philip's father when he had been invited by his boss to Joan's first exhibition in New York in 1957. Philip never understood what his mother had seen in Maurice. He had been a businessman with no real understanding of art – or of anything cultural, come to that. His entire life had been dedicated to numbers on a ledger sheet, whereas Joan was the very opposite, a free spirit who had no interest in money, or even in fame.

Philip had kept in touch with his mother and visited her occasionally in Venice where she had lived for twenty-five years with her second husband, an opera singer. But he had refused to be drawn into Joan's world even though he found it immensely seductive. With Maurice's death a series of doors in Philip's mind had suddenly become unlocked. Within a few months of gaining his First in PPE he had discarded all the plans his father had set in train for him. Eschewing the City and a promised six-figure salary, he picked up his camera again and vowed to make photography his life.

But the changes went deeper still. Philip had never shown the slightest interest in anything to do with the paranormal, but by the end of the year he had became fascinated with the concept of the aura and Kirlian photography. He read every book on the subject that he could find and attended workshops and courses. But then, after two years of submersing himself in this world, he stopped abruptly. He had never consciously thought about why he had left this all behind to concentrate on photographing crime scenes and corpses. To Philip it was merely a way to pay the bills while he continued with his creative work, exhibited and dreamed of international recognition. For many years those close to him had understood his motives, but they had chosen to keep their theories to themselves. By photographing corpses, they realised, Philip was somehow trying to find something he had been unable to see in the body of his dead father. Some semblance of a soul.

It began to rain again as they neared the hospital and this snapped Philip out of his reverie, bringing into focus the cold moment. They pulled into the hospital grounds and after parking in the first available space they ran to the brightly lit reception area, neither of them noticing the gorgeous red splash of the sunrise ahead of them.

The call had come from one of Jo's friends, Samantha, who had been in the car with Jo and Jo's boyfriend Tom. Samantha had only received cuts and bruises herself but had no idea what condition the couple were in. They met her at reception; she was talking to a young doctor who led them along a corridor to a small room containing four beds. Jo was in the end one, curtained off from the rest.

Laura and Philip were relieved to see her sitting up. She had a nasty cut above her right eye and her arm, lying over the top sheet, was bandaged to the elbow.

'She's suffered concussion,' the doctor said, looking at Jo's chart. 'But a CT scan was clear. She needed a few stitches, but I think she'll live.'

Laura hugged her daughter gently and Jo smiled up at Philip who was standing beside the bed.

'My God, Jo,' Laura said. 'I thought . . .'

'No, mom, I'm still here,' Jo whispered and touched Laura's cheek.

'Is your friend Tom OK?' Philip asked and turned to the doctor.

'He was very lucky too. A couple of cracked ribs, two broken fingers and more cuts and bruises. He's along the corridor, getting patched up.'

'So what the hell happened, Jo? Tom wasn't drinking, was he?'

'No, mother, he doesn't drink,' Jo replied and flashed her mother an irritated look. 'Actually, *I* was driving.'

Laura looked surprised for a moment, then gave her daughter a wan smile and held her hand.

'We were just going along St Aldate's, heading back to Carfax, when a car pulled out of a side road. I guess I overcompensated, swerved and skidded across the wet road. The car hit a lamp-post.'

'A lucky escape.' Philip sat down with a sigh on the other side of the bed from Laura.

'But mom, aren't you supposed to be on your way to Heathrow?'

Laura looked at her daughter as if she had recalled something lost in the mists of time. She rubbed her tired eyes. 'Well, that plan's shot. I certainly won't be leaving England until you're fully recovered.'

Jo made to protest, but she was interrupted by the ring tone of Philip's mobile.

Philip looked quickly at the doctor. 'God, sorry. I should have turned this off. Won't be a second.' He walked over to the window, speaking quietly into his phone.

The doctor looked irritated. Turning to Jo, he said, 'You're free to go as soon as you feel well enough.'

'What about Tom?'

'I think he may be in for a couple of hours. We need to run a few more tests, but you can see him if you like.' And he headed towards the door. Catching Philip's eye, the doctor made a cut-throat sign. Philip nodded sheepishly and quickly wound up the call. Walking back to the bed, he said. 'I'm afraid I've got to go. There's been another murder.'

Chapter 7

The scene of the killing was little more than a mile and a half from the hospital. But the traffic into Oxford from the M40 through Headington was starting to build up, so it took Philip almost twenty minutes to get there.

Laura had stayed at the hospital with Jo, which was an arrangement that suited him just fine; he was in no mood for a repeat of last night's performance with Monroe. Still shell-shocked from the fright that his daughter had given him, he knew he had to focus on the task ahead. He parked his car in a residents-only zone at the bottom of Cave Street close to the river, put his police pass on the dashboard, retrieved his bag from the boot and walked towards the towpath that ran parallel to a tributary of the River Cherwell.

The path down to the river was slippery and Philip took the steps slowly. The rain started up again, and ahead of him he could see the murky grey river. About ten yards away stood a bedraggled-looking group – two uniforms, Monroe with his back to the path, and a sergeant holding an umbrella over the head of the DCI. Further off, two CSI guys were walking away towards a house that extended out on stilts into the river. The rain grew heavier and Philip was tempted to run back to the car for his umbrella. But just at that moment Monroe spotted him.

'Mr Bainbridge. Alone today, are we?'

Philip sighed, put his hands in his pockets and risked a brief smile.

'Well, we have a real doozy for you this morning. Better prepare yourself.'

'What? Worse than last night?'

'Depends how squeamish you are. Woman out jogging found her about seven o'clock. Forensics tell me she's been dead between four and six hours. Follow me. You're going to have to work to find a suitable angle – and watch yourself.'

Monroe picked his way carefully along the path. Some plastic sheeting had been draped over the branches of a tree on the bank and a single flood-light was shining onto the lapping river under the lowest bough. Just behind Monroe, Philip could see the red stern of a punt. As he took in the full horror of the scene, he felt his stomach lurch.

A young woman was half-sitting, half-lying at one end of the boat. She was dressed in jeans and a T-shirt and was staring at the bank with sightless eyes.

She looked completely drained of blood. Her arms were spread wide and her left hand hung over the side of the punt. Streaks of blood could be seen on the inside of her arms and across her shoulders. Her eyes were open, but what had been their whites were almost completely red: the blood vessels had burst. Over her eyes lay a slimy film that dulled the colour of her blood. Her throat had been cut and the top of her head had been removed cleanly, expertly, a hemisphere of bone and scalp sliced away. Where her brain had once sat there remained nothing but a red and black bowl. In a few places the dead tissue had been scratched away to reveal startlingly clean white bone.

Inside the woman's head, a highly polished silver coin caught the light: a silver twin to the gold coin that Philip had seen in Detective Chief Inspector Monroe's gloved hand the night before.

Philip turned away and took a couple of deep breaths.

'I'll give you a few minutes,' Monroe muttered, climbing back to the path. 'But I'll need the pictures at the station within the hour.'

Philip wasted no time in setting up his shots. He knew from long experience that this was the only way he could deal with these situations. The more horrible the images that lay before him, the more intently he had to disconnect, to go into a robotic state where he simply did his job and forced himself to become blind to what lay beyond the camera's lens.

He took a series of shots from the prow of the punt: some close-ups using the telephoto attachment and a couple of wide-angle pictures. Then he walked along the bank, and took some shots side-on before crouching close to the stern where the boat had lodged against the bank, and where the most horrific images could be captured, digitised and stored on a chip in his camera – a human life reduced to pixels.

It wasn't until Philip had clambered up the bank, given the two uniforms left at the scene a careless wave and turned the corner into Cave Street that he realised how much his hands were shaking. Reaching the car, he was about to open the boot when a wave of nausea hit him. He vomited into the gutter and watched the bile wash away in the speeding rainwater flowing down the street.

Chapter 8

London: October 1689

Gresham College in the heart of the City was an oasis amidst the squalor and filth of London. Although the buildings were old and crumbling and there had been increasingly vociferous calls to redevelop the site, it possessed a tranquillity and a mesmerising charm that belied its sorry physical state. Its appearance was also remarkably understated for the regular meeting place of some of the greatest minds of this or any other age.

The Royal Society had been founded almost thirty years earlier by Christopher Wren and a few close associates. It had quickly grown, gaining royal approval and with it a name. But in recent years that name had diminished in stature. Part of the problem for this illustrious gathering of men was that they could never settle anywhere for long. Their original home had been here within the faded grandeur of Gresham College, but after the twin tragedies of the

56

terrible plague of 1665 and the Great Fire the following year the college had been requisitioned by the City merchants whose own premises had been destroyed. Then it was transformed into a temporary Exchange while a new financial centre was under construction. The Royal Society, with its books and its experimental apparatus, its sextants and charts, its telescopes and microscopes, had been offered the library of Arundel House by the owner, the Duke of Norfolk. This was located a couple of miles to the west, in a street just off the Strand. Here the Society had continued to meet for a while to discuss the latest scientific ideas and to conduct scientific investigations organised by its Curator of Experiments, Robert Hooke.

While it was ensconced in Arundel House, the society started to publish books, including Hooke's own *Micrographia* and John Evelyn's *Sylva*, and, keeping up a tradition begun by the earliest scientific societies in Galileo's Italy, it also published a journal, the *Philosophical Transactions*, in which there were descriptions of discoveries and reports of lectures and the works of the Society's members. But then, after a few years in Arundel House, they had been obliged to start meeting again at Gresham College, in rooms put aside for the purpose by the influential Hooke, a Fellow of the college.

Although Isaac Newton knew all this, as he

entered the main quad of Gresham College at two minutes before six, the darkening western sky drenched in orange, he felt almost no affinity with the Society that he had joined as a young man of twenty-nine, seventeen years earlier. In spite of the fact that the illustrious Fellows had published his *Principia Mathematica*, a book that had made him the most important scientific figure in the world, during the past decade he had attended the Royal Society no more than a handful of times. He could consider no other member his friend, and he was barely able to extend a degree of trust to just three other figures within the scientific community. The elderly Robert Boyle was one, the young genius Edmund Halley was another, and the third was the man who had persuaded him to leave his cloistered world of Trinity College, Cambridge to visit London this evening: Christopher Wren.

However, the main reason for Newton's conspicuous absence from Society meetings had been the even more conspicuous presence of Robert Hooke. The man had become a bitter enemy almost as soon as they had met and when, in 1676, the Society members had elected Hooke to succeed Henry Oldenburg as Secretary, Newton had offered to resign his own Fellowship. Persuaded to continue by those who saw him as a man too valuable to lose, he had finally capitulated. But he had vowed to attend meetings only when it suited him to do so.

Newton understood that people considered him to be a difficult man. He was undeniably someone who shunned the company of others and he cared nothing for the effect this had on the sensibilities of those around him. He was completely self-contained and proud of it. He needed no one, but people needed him and they would grow to rely upon him increasingly in the future, of that he was sure. It was sentiments such as these that had kept him in his laboratory in Cambridge. The only man in whom he had confided a little was John Wickins, a scholar of theology and his room-mate for more than twenty-five years. But, Newton ruminated as he crossed the quad and passed under an archway to turn left into a stone passageway, even Wickins understood only a fraction of what was going on in Newton's mind and almost nothing about what actually happened in the laboratory so close to his own bedchamber.

As he thought about this, Newton cast his mind back some six months to the morning when he had been forced to change the direction of his investigations. It was the morning when he had learned of the ruby sphere. It was his greatest secret and he could discuss it with no one. For days and nights he had done little else but ponder the meaning of the message left by George Ripley. He had scoured every text in his possession. He had returned to London to search through the damp cave of Cooper's book-shop in Little Britain, and he had bribed the book-seller to allow him to sift through his mildewed storerooms.

Ripley clearly had been writing about an ancient and crucially important artefact. The ruby sphere undoubtedly was the missing link, the key to the universe. The text describing this wonder had been written in his hand, and Ripley, who had died two centuries earlier, had been a man of huge talent and integrity. But, even with these clues, Newton could do little without actually possessing the sphere. He needed to discover where it was hidden.

A week earlier he had received the invitation from Christopher Wren to attend a special meeting of the Royal Society at Gresham College. The occasion was a celebration of the building of the Sheldonian Theatre in Oxford, completed twenty years earlier. It had been Wren's first commission and was a bril-liant start to the man's career.

At first Newton had been tempted to toss the beau-tifully embossed invitation onto a pile of papers on his desk where it would be ignored, like almost all other invitations, requests and correspondence with his peers was ignored. But apart from Wickins, Wren was the closest person he had to a friend, a man he respected more than he did any other mortal.

At the double doors to the lecture hall, Newton

took a deep breath and pushed on the handles. The room was no more than a dozen yards square, and Wren, a former president of the Society and one of the most famous men in England, could pull a crowd – so the room was packed. Newton was obliged to stand just a few feet inside the door.

He surveyed the room. It was a rectangle lined on three sides with shelves extending from floor to ceiling, every inch taken up with books, their leather spines unreadable in the dim light that flickered from a pair of chandeliers. The fourth wall was painted duck-egg blue, but in places the plaster had cracked and a great jagged line ran along it and across the ceiling like a vine.

There were perhaps a hundred members here this evening. Newton knew almost all of them by sight, but was acquainted with only a few. There, near the front, was Halley and next to him stood Samuel Pepys, dressed in a vibrant orange jacket. John Evelyn was in the row behind, dipping into a worn leather pouch of snuff. Beside him sat the society painter Godfrey Kneller, whom Newton had met in Cambridge only a few months earlier when the artist had visited in preparation for his latest commission, a painting of the Lucasian Professor. Across the room sat Robert Boyle, an exceptionally tall man and stick-thin; his white wig looked almost supernaturally bright in the candlelit gloom. A few rows back,

Newton could see the two Italians who were currently guests of the Society. Giuseppe Riccini and Marco Bertolini had arrived from Verona three months earlier and they had generated considerable gossip because of their penchant for 'mollies' – boys who dressed as girls and provided specialist erotic services. To the left of them, he spotted the enchanting profile of Nicolas Fatio du Duillier, an exceedingly interesting young man to whom he had been introduced just a few weeks earlier. The boy turned and, seeing him, produced a brief, warm smile.

On a raised platform at the far end of the room sat Robert Hooke and the President of the Society, John Vaughan, third Earl of Carbery, resplendent in a purple and gold brocade tunic and a luxuriously powdered wig. As much as the earl appeared to Newton to embody the finest virtues and attributes of the English nobility, he considered the nasty little ferret of a man beside him to represent the very worst that the world could offer. Hunched and misshapen, standing only four feet ten inches even in heels, Hooke appeared to have shrunk into his chair. Newton loathed the man with every fibre of his being and he knew that Hooke felt the same way about him. The Secretary, he understood, would do anything he could to discredit or defame him, and Newton could not help remembering with amusement a particularly Janus-faced letter that he had written to this dwarf, in which he had made the comment that if he, Isaac Newton, had ever achieved anything great as a scientist it had been by standing upon the shoulders of giants.

Suddenly Christopher Wren strode to the platform. The members rose as one and applauded before settling back into their seats.

Wren, Newton was irritated to concede, did look magnificent and carried himself with regal dignity. He was a man who deserved his acclaim. He was a polymath, a professor of astronomy, an internationally renowned architect, a medical experimenter and a writer of genius. Yet he was also extremely modest. Years earlier, when Newton had been a boy, Wren had been the first to observe the rings around the planet Saturn. Yet, when the Dutch astronomer Christiaan Huygens had published his own observations first and had accepted the laurels for the discovery, Wren had been unruffled and entirely magnanimous. This was a stance that Newton found almost impossible to understand, but in a hidden part of his soul he knew that Wren was a better man than he because he could show such grace.

For the next thirty minutes, Wren kept his audience spellbound. His voice, low and melodious yet never soporific, drew in the listener and made the most specialised aspects of what he was describing interesting and easy to visualise. Illustrating his talk with sketches he had made, he first told the audience how he had designed the Sheldonian Theatre, and then went on to describe the engineering challenges that it had presented for him as a young architect who was both nervous and keen to impress his masters. He had produced immaculate drawings at every stage of the theatre's construction, from the floor plans that had secured his commission through the many stages of the building process to the grand unveiling of the completed project in 1669, five years after it had begun.

Newton enjoyed the talk but, after a while, he had found himself drawn back to the problem that had occupied his mind so completely since February: the meaning of Ripley's cryptic message. The room melted away. The sound of Wren's voice faded. Newton could see Ripley's words, the encrypted message and the strange drawing, as though he were holding the document in his hand. His eidetic memory could reproduce what he had seen down to the last wrinkle in the parchment but, frustratingly, such prodigious mental powers had been of almost no help in his efforts to understand what the message meant.

'It was a most startling moment . . .' Wren was saying. 'The foundations were almost complete and I was most assuredly loath to see further delay, but my curiosity was piqued. I permitted the exposing of the odd construction to the limit of one day of work, as I felt it worthy. By the end of the day it had become clear. There was a natural and quite possibly an extensive cave system under this part of Oxford. I duly noted it in my diary and, with the permission of the Master of Hertford College, I ran a narrow corridor from this subterranean void to the cellars beneath the nearby college, with the thought that one day I might go back to learn more. That, sadly, was twenty-five years ago, and commitments to His Majesty have, alas, kept my enthusiasm in check.'

The audience laughed and Wren took a deep breath. 'So, forgive my digression. Now, as to the construction of the roof . . .'

A tingling that had begun at the base of Newton's spine slowly rippled up through his body. As he stood transfixed, staring intently at the great architect, he could feel rather than hear the words of Ripley resonating inside his head: *Seek the sphere under the earth, 'tis cocooned in stone, great learning above and earth below.*

When Newton tapped on the door and peered in, Wren was alone in an ante-room off the main lecture hall, removing his wig and trying to untangle his straggly grey hair. 'Well, what an excellent surprise,' he said with a smile.

'May I bother you for a moment, Sir Christopher?'

'Naturally, sir. Come in. Take a seat. Did you enjoy my lecture?'

'Yes, I did – very much,' Newton replied gravely. He was trying to control his excitement.

'I'm most honoured by your presence, sir. Indeed, we had a fine audience tonight, did we not? So, how may I help you?' Wren left his hair alone and began to remove his jacket. Newton noticed that it was stained with sweat.

'I found your description of the construction of the Sheldonian Theatre most beguiling. But . . .' He hesitated briefly. 'I was particularly taken with your mention of the subterranean cave system.'

'Oh, really? I am crestfallen, sir,' Wren dead-panned. 'I thought you would have favoured talk of the engineering feat, the genius of the design, the extraordinary accommodation of Nature's forces.'

'Please forgive me.' Newton looked lost for a moment. 'I did not mean . . .'

'I'm jesting, Isaac. Ye gods, it must be true what they say about you – that you never laugh and have been known to smile but once.'

Newton, po-faced, said nothing. Sensing that he had offended the scientist, Wren placed a hand on the younger man's shoulder. 'Forgive me. I meant no insult, my friend.'

Newton took a step back and bowed. 'No offence taken, I'm sure. Sir, I was enamoured with your entire talk, but the cave fascinated me. Perhaps this interest comes as a result of some inexplicable primeval connection in my mind. Whatever it may be, I would like to know more about it.'

'Sadly, I can add almost nothing to what I said earlier tonight. It was a quarter of a century ago. I was young and idealistic and I believed I could go back to explore at my leisure.'

'But there *are* caves under the Sheldonian?'

'Oh, indeed there are. But they remain unexplored.'

'Did you record the layout on paper?'

'I did not.'

'So what exactly did you see?' Newton found it hard to keep the rising excitement out of his voice.

Wren frowned. 'There were two openings, I recall. I had the workmen dig around them for a day, as I said. They uncovered a flat roof, a winding corridor, tunnels. I sent two men down with a lantern. Yes, it's coming back to me now. They were gone an inordinately long time. And we were about to dispatch a search party after them when they re-emerged, a little shabby and feeling somewhat sorry for themselves.'

Newton raised an eyebrow. 'What had befallen them?'

'I managed to obtain from them only a few facts. Apparently, there was some sort of maze beyond the opening. But they were confused about even this.

One of the men said it was a natural convolution of the tunnels, the other thought it was a demonic creation. They were superstitious and ignorant workmen, of course, but I could not have spared anyone with more intelligence at that time. It was perhaps a little foolish of me to digress from the work to which I was committed. It appeared that there were natural corridors leading off towards Hertford College to the south-east and to a point beneath the Bodleian Library almost directly south. I knew from experience that at Hertford College the cellars extend far underground with tunnels leading outward in the direction of my theatre. It was a trivial matter to join them up, and in that way I thought I was satisfying the calling of my curiosity and respecting my muse. You understand?'

Newton seemed far away, staring at Wren without speaking. Then he pulled himself together.

'Apologies, sir,' he mumbled. 'I was totally absorbed by your words. I do understand. We must satisfy our muse lest we shrivel up and die.'

'Quite.'

Newton appeared to have nothing more to add and an uncomfortable silence fell between the two men.

'Well, if that is all you seek, Isaac . . .' Wren said.

'I'm most grateful to you,' Newton responded abruptly. 'Most grateful. Farewell, Sir Christopher.' He bowed and made for the door.

Chapter 9

Laura was sitting in Philip's house with the Aga on full and a fire blazing in the grate, wondering for perhaps the sixth time that evening how anyone could live in a house without central heating, when Philip's car pulled up outside.

In the hall he hung up his sodden coat and walked into the living room.

'God, you look awful,' she said.

'I feel awful,' he replied without looking at her. 'How's Jo?'

'She's upstairs, asleep. Battered and bruised but basically in one piece.'

'And is she cold?' Philip asked sarcastically. 'I can't believe the bloody temperature in this house.'

'Hah!' Laura said. I can't believe you enjoy living in the Stone Age. Have you not heard of that great new invention, the radiator?'

Philip sighed and slumped into a chair, put his elbows on the table and cupped his head in his palms. 'Yeah, OK . . . whatever.'

'Bad day?'

He looked up at her. His eyes were bloodshot. 'I could do with a drink.'

A few moments later Laura handed him a huge malt whisky and settled into the chair next to him. 'You look like you need to get something off your chest.'

Philip took a gulp of his drink. 'Yes, and you won't give up until I tell you about it, will you?' he replied lightly.

'Absolutely not. So, what's been happening?'

He glanced over her shoulder at the TV. The local news programme had just started and Detective Chief Inspector Monroe was about to give an interview to a journalist. 'Let's watch this,' Philip said and turned up the volume with the remote.

'So, Detective Chief Inspector,' the journalist was saying. 'You can confirm a second incident?'

'Yes, the body of a young woman was found this morning on a tributary of the Cherwell close to the city centre.'

'And was this murder similar to the first, the one that was discovered last night?'

'It does share certain characteristics,' Monroe replied guardedly.

'I see. Some people are suggesting that we have a serial killer at large. Can you deny or confirm this?'

'It is far too early to jump to conclusions. You'll appreciate that we are doing everything we can—'

'But,' the interviewer interrupted, 'is it true that there is some ritualistic element to the murders?'

Monroe looked weary. 'All we can say at the moment is that there are some common characteristics.'

The journalist quickly changed tack. 'So, Chief Inspector, what happens now? Can you offer the public any advice?'

'Yes, indeed I can. I would like to reiterate that every effort is being made to find the person or persons responsible for these murders. We simply ask that members of the public remain calm, support us in our investigation in any way they can, and if anybody has any information that they come forward.'

Philip turned off the TV.

'Very cagey,' Laura said.

'Well, he has to be. Standard police procedure: never give details away. If someone comes forward with evidence to support the facts that have been deliberately kept from the public, you know they are leads worth following. It also lowers the risk of nutters trying to copycat.'

'Yeah, I know that, Philip. Remember what I used to do in New York?'

Philip smiled. 'Sorry.'

'So, you're going to be more forthcoming than Monroe, I hope.'

'Naturally, Laura,' he replied. Leaning back in his chair, Philip stretched out his legs and took a deep breath before telling her about the woman in the punt. After describing the pictures that he had taken he fell silent and drained his glass.

'My God,' Laura said slowly. 'I thought New York was a brutal place. You were told the body had been there for – what? Four hours?'

'She was partially concealed by the branches of a tree. Spotted by a woman out this morning.'

'Nice thing to stumble upon.'

Philip raised his eyebrows.

'So, that would place the murder in the early hours of the morning – 3, 4 a.m.'

'I guess so,' Philip replied and stared at Laura wearily. 'She lived in a house along the river. It's an out-of-the-way stretch of the Cherwell, no tourist punts there. Besides, it's out of season. It was the family boat. The parents are in Europe. Thing is, though, she wasn't murdered in there. Monroe went straight to the house. The girl's bedroom looks like the inside of an abattoir. She was placed in the punt later, which was guided to a spot under the trees and tethered to the bank.'

'Carefully planned. Like the murder at The Perch. You say a silver coin was left in the girl's skull?'

'That's right.'

'Did you notice where the gold coin was at the scene of the first murder? Did you see it before Monroe had it?'

'No.'

'Surely they would have left the scene untouched until you took your pictures?'

'Yes, you're right. But the wound was a total mess. I got the feeling from Forensics that the coin was embedded in the chest cavity and they only found it when they inspected the wound.'

'Well, there you are: another ritualistic element.'

'So, what're you suggesting?'

'The murders took place within a few hours of each other. Two young girls, mutilations performed with expert precision.'

'And?'

'Well, I've heard of something similar – and so have you. Whitechapel, 1880s? Young women murdered and torn apart?'

'Oh, great.' Philip offered his glass for a refill. 'Just what Oxford needs: a twenty-first-century Jack the Ripper.'

Chapter 10

'What's brought this on?' Philip asked as Laura, sitting on the edge of his bed, shook him awake.

'Oh, just felt like it,' Laura replied lightly, laying a breakfast tray on the quilt between them

'You're after something.' Philip sat up and rubbed his eyes.

'Philip . . .'

'You want to get involved in the investigation. Am I right?'

Laura could not pretend for long. 'I've been thinking about it all night. Hardly slept a wink.'

'But, Laura, this is a *police* investigation. You have no authority . . . *I* don't have any authority, for God's sake!'

'I'm not suggesting I enrol in the police force, Philip. I'm just saying I want to conduct, well, a parallel line of inquiry.'

'"A parallel line of enquiry"?' Philip scoffed. 'This isn't *Kojak*, you know.'

'I think I can help.'

Philip said nothing. 'Could I at least have some tea first?'

Laura poured milk into his cup.

'Agh . . . bloody Americans and tea! Let me do this. And you tell me what you've been mulling over all night.'

She placed a couple of pillows at the far end of the bed and settled herself against the ironwork of the bedstead. 'I kept thinking about what I said last night – you know, about Jack the Ripper? But I soon realised that there are actually very few similarities between our murders and the Whitechapel killings. Sure, the Ripper's victims had organs removed and there were ritualistic aspects to the murders. The police at the time discovered some weird Freemason connection, but they never really got it figured. Even today we still don't know for certain who the murderer was.'

'So, what're you saying?'

'For a start, all the victims in Whitechapel were prostitutes, as were most of the more recent murders of the Yorkshire Ripper back in the 1980s. Also, the way the organs were removed from the current victims is very different to the historical cases. Sure, all the Whitechapel victims had their throats cut, left to right, but each murder was more brutal than the last. The Ripper's final victim, Mary Kelly, was practically ripped apart. There was also a clear sexual aspect to the murders. The two MOs are quite different.'

'You've certainly been doing your homework,' Philip said half-mocking.

Laura shrugged. 'I've read a few books about Jack the Ripper. Always fascinated me.' She took a breath. 'There's a very specific ritualistic aspect to these two cases. Gold coin, silver coin, heart removed, brain removed. Maybe there's something significant in the fact that the second murdered girl was placed on water while the first victim, the one near The Perch, was on land. But it's not a whole lot to go on, is it? Did you find out anything more yesterday?'

'Not really, Laura. I'm a police photographer. I spent most of the day producing prints and backing up the digital files, sending material to Scotland Yard and looking up pictures on the police database.'

'But surely you've got buddies at the station? You must have found out something. Jesus! Surely you're curious?'

Philip poured himself a second cup of tea. Picking up a piece of toast, he said, 'Well, of course I've done some prying. But why should I tell you about it?'

Laura looked shocked.

'You're going back to New York, aren't you? What's the point?'

'I've decided to stay a while.'

'Oh, you have, have you?'

'You don't have to put up with me here if . . .'

'Oh, Laura. Of course you can stay, stay as long as you like . . . If you can put up with the plumbing.'

She smiled suddenly. 'It was Jo's accident . . .'

'I realise that, but now?'

'Well, now I'm intrigued. I'm ditching Thomas Bradwardine and thinking more in terms of a modern mystery.'

'Ah-ha. Well, that's honest, I suppose.'

'I wasn't . . .'

'OK,' Philip said softly. 'What do you want to know?'

'Well, the whole shebang, Philip.'

He laughed out loud and sat back against the pillows. 'You're amazing.'

'So?'

'Well, I don't know all that much . . . *they* don't know that much. Both girls were university students. The first victim, the girl in the car, was Rachel Southgate. Eighteen, a Fresher, daughter of a bishop – Leonard Southgate, a widower living in Surrey. Rachel had three older sisters. The girl in the punt was Jessica Fullerton. Nineteen, just starting her second year. Oxford family, live in a house about a hundred yards from where her body was discovered. An only child – both parents were immensely proud of their academic daughter. As I told you last night, she had the house to herself, parents in Europe. Mum and dad were contacted yesterday. Should be back in Oxford by now.'

'Was there anything about the victims that linked them? Apart from the fact that they were both students? Which college were they at?'

'No link. Jessica was at Balliol reading law, Rachel was at Merton studying English.'

'What about physical characteristics? Families? Friends? Did they know each other?'

'Rachel was blonde, tall, slender, Jessica was brunette, shorter, heavier. Both came from vaguely middle-class families. No idea if they knew each other. I guess Monroe's boys are covering that, it's routine stuff.'

Laura nodded and looked out of the bedroom window. It was a fresh, crisp spring morning – yesterday's rain was far away now. 'Doesn't tell us much, does it?'

'I called one of the guys at the station for an update last night,' Philip said after a while. 'Forensics have found that the two coins are solid precious metals, but not ancient. They were minted recently and made to look old.'

'The originals must be incredibly rare. But just leaving replicas has to mean something very special to the killer.' Laura paused for a moment. 'Could you sketch them? Didn't they have some figures on them?'

'God, let me think.'

She walked over to a chest of drawers and found a piece of paper and a pencil.

'Actually, we don't need those. I can do better, if you can stomach it.'

'Your camera.'

'If you're feeling athletic, it's in the hall.'

A couple of minutes later Philip had found the close-ups stored on the memory chip in his Nikon, picked one, zoomed in on the coin and turned the camera round so that Laura could see the screen on the back. 'That's about the best one. I could print it out for you.'

Laura did her best to ignore the exposed raw flesh in various shades of red encircling the coin and to focus on the object at the centre of the image. It showed the profile of a head, a thin angular androgynous face with a long noble nose. The person depicted on the silver coin left inside Jessica Fullerton's cranium was wearing some sort of rectangular headpiece. 'I'm sure there were some female figures on the first coin.'

'Yes, I think there were,' Philip replied.

Laura grabbed the notebook. 'Something like this, wasn't it?' She showed Philip her drawing of robed figures holding up a bowl.

'Well, it's no Rembrandt. But yes, it was something along those lines.'

'So what do you think it represents?'

'Search me.'

'And this figure. Looks vaguely familiar,' she said, pointing to the digital image. 'He, she looks like an ancient Egyptian, a Pharaoh, don't you think?'

Philip shrugged. 'Maybe. The other side could be some religious imagery. The Egyptians were sun-worshippers, weren't they? Maybe this bowl,' and Philip pointed to Laura's sketch, 'represents the sun.'

Laura stared at the photographic image and then at the rough sketch she had made. 'I'd really like a print of this.' She tapped the screen. 'And I have to do a little more digging.'

Chapter 11

'Old Fotheringay at St John's told me about Jo's accident,' said James Lightman, turning to Laura as they walked along the corridor leading to his office. The walls, the floor and the ceiling were all limestone and the sound of their shoes echoed around them. Laura followed Lightman up a wide marble staircase, and through a doorway she caught a glimpse of book stacks lining a vast room into which broad shafts of sunlight fell.

'Sorry I didn't call you, James. Things have been, well, a little crazy.'

'Good Lord, Laura, I understand. The good news is that it's kept you with us a little longer. It was only a couple of days ago that you were bidding me farewell.'

'It's given me more research time, a week at least.'

They had reached the Chief Librarian's office and Lightman held the heavy oak door open for Laura. She stepped in and looked around, struck by the familiar old rush of the senses that she had first experienced when she was eighteen. The office was a room with a vaulted ceiling and it was stacked with ancient books, antiquities and curios – a stuffed owl in a glass case, a brass pyramid, strange stringed musical instruments and marquetry boxes from North Africa. She could hear Bach playing faintly in the background.

Little more than a week after going up to Oxford Laura had spent her first morning at the Bodleian revelling in the fact that she had a pass into the most exclusive library in the world. It was a particularly memorable experience. She was in the newly refurbished history of art section when a shelf had collapsed immediately above her head, sending a collection of heavy books down on top of her.

She had been very lucky and was left only with a few bruises along her right arm, but James Lightman had been at her side almost instantly. Taking control in that gentle but firm way of his, he had insisted that she sit down and he had checked that she really was all right. In this same office he had offered her a cup of strong tea and a biscuit and had asked her about herself. It was the start of what was to become a close relationship that had been sustained throughout Laura's time in Oxford. It had survived her move back to America and infrequent visits to England. During her time at the university Lightman had been a kind of a surrogate uncle, a father figure far closer to hand than her real parents six thousand miles to the west. Although they worked in very different areas, they chimed intellectually. Something of a polymath and an eminent scholar, James Lightman was world-renowned as the foremost authority on ancient languages, with a particular interest in Hellenistic-Roman Literature. Laura's favourite era was the Renaissance with its revival of Classical influence in art, and she had heard of James Lightman from a book about Classical painting that she had read when she'd still been a precocious fifteen-year-old high-school kid in Santa Barbara.

Laura had only learned after knowing the man for several months that Lightman had once been married to an heiress, Lady Susanna Gatting of Brill. But she and their daughter Emily had been killed in a car crash in 1981, less than a year before Laura had arrived in Oxford. Emily would have been almost exactly Laura's age if she had lived.

Lightman was easing himself into a worn leather chesterfield in front of his desk and gesturing for Laura to do the same, when suddenly she became aware of someone else in the room. Sitting in an armchair near the wall furthest from Lightman's desk was a young man. He was wearing a neat black suit and a white shirt. His hair was long and greased back over his ears. He had a long birdlike nose and very prominent cheekbones.

'You've not met Malcolm, have you, Laura? Malcolm Bridges, my personal assistant. Malcolm, this is Laura Niven.'

Bridges stood up and extended a bony hand. 'I've heard a lot about you,' he said, his face expressionless. His voice was surprisingly deep, and a slight Welsh twang lent it something of an Anthony Hopkins intonation. It was a voice that seemed quite ill-matched to his appearance.

'At least some of it good, I hope?' Laura studied Bridges's face. There was something about him she disliked instantly, but she could not put her finger on it. Then she turned to Lightman. 'I hope I haven't caught you at a bad time.'

'No, no, don't be silly,' the old man replied. 'Malcolm, we're finished with the details for the drinks evening, aren't we?'

'Yes, I think we're done. I'll get things organised.' Bridges picked up some papers from a nearby coffee table. 'Well, I hope to see you again soon,' he said to Laura before he left.

Lightman sat back on the chesterfield. 'So, what can I help you with, my dear?' he asked. 'You sounded very excited on the phone this morning.'

Laura examined his familiar face. The dark brown eyes were heavily lidded and the white hair was long and unruly. At times he had the appearance of an elderly W.H. Auden, at others the look of a biblical patriarch without the beard. He was not yet seventy, she knew, but he looked older. His skin had a leathery texture to it, while his forehead was so covered in wrinkles and lines that up close it looked like a NASA image of the Martian surface.

'It's the book I'm working on,' she said.

'The Thomas Bradwardine novel?'

'Well, no, actually.' She was a little embarrassed. 'I've decided to put that on the back burner. I'm going to write something with a contemporary setting: a murder mystery.'

'Oh?'

'I'm thinking of setting it here in Oxford, or maybe in Cambridge. Not sure yet.'

'Oh, good God, Laura, don't go with "the other place", for heaven's sake. Unholy dump!'

She smiled. 'I want to link the murders with something ritualistic. The killer leaves something significant at the scene of each murder. At first I was thinking of maybe a ceremonial knife, but last night I started to wonder about using coins. The police find them near the bodies of the victims.'

'Coins?'

'Yes, ancient coins. Trouble is, I know precisely nothing about the subject.'

Lightman leaned over to pick up a strange V-shaped contraption that lay on an occasional table beside the chesterfield. It consisted of a tightly coiled spring with two handles. Laura looked puzzled.

'Arthritis,' Lightman said. 'Doctor's told me I have to squeeze this thing for five minutes every hour or my wrist will seize up completely.' He rolled his eyes. 'I'm not convinced.' After a couple of squeezes he stopped and looked at Laura. 'But how can I help? Coins are not really my thing.'

'I . . . well. I thought there would be some great stuff here at the Bodleian. Problem is, I'm no longer a member. Um . . . are American tourists allowed to join?'

Lightman laughed. 'Only very special ones. I imagine you're in a hurry – you usually are.'

Laura tilted her head to one side. 'Can't help it, I'm afraid.'

'Well, we do have a very good numismatics section. I could take you downstairs and get you started. I think we can forget about form-filling for today.'

As Lightman stood up, he seemed to notice for the first time what she was wearing around her neck. 'Good gracious, Laura. That's the pendant I gave you . . . when was that, now?'

It was an opal on a delicate silver chain. Laura had put it on this morning without consciously real-ising that it was the one Lightman had given her. 'When I was a student,' Laura said. 'Must have been

1983. Long time ago. I wear it almost every day, though.'

'Did I ever tell you that was my daughter's birthstone?'

'No, you didn't.'

'Right, well. Let's go.'

Downstairs in the main hall of the library Laura followed Lightman along the parquet-floored walkways that transected the room between rows of vast oak bookcases. They crossed the hall and, at the far end, Lightman led the way through a tall doorway. Turning left, they walked along a corridor, through an archway to the right and into another room, a smaller version of the main hall. Halfway along this room's walkway Lightman turned right again and stopped at a set of bookcases against the wall. In front of them stood a large table with a computer on top of it. They were alone in this part of the library.

'This is the section,' Lightman said and scanned the shelves. 'I think you'll find everything you're after here, Laura. If you need anything, Mrs Sitwell is just around the corner.' He pointed to the far end of the room. 'She knows this section like the back of her hand. But if you want any more information from me, don't hesitate. I have some bureaucratic nonsense to sort out upstairs.' Leaning forward, he pecked her on the cheek. 'Come and see me before you go.'

Laura sat down and looked up at the great array of books. She suddenly felt a pang of guilt over spinning a yarn for the old man. But, she reasoned, she couldn't have done much else.

She had no clear idea exactly what she was looking for and plucked out a book entitled *Ancient Coins,* published by Oxford University Press. Then she pulled out the print that Philip had run off for her and the notebook containing her rough sketch of the other side of the coin.

Within a few moments Laura had learned that although early coinage is known as a Greek phenomenon, the earliest known coins were actually from the Lycian region of Asia Minor, found beneath a sixth-century BC temple of Artemis. The coins left at the murder scenes looked like they might have come out of Egypt, but this book mentioned nothing about early coins from that part of the world. She took down another volume. *Coins of Antiquity* by Luther Neumann.

Close to the start it offered a couple of speculative paragraphs on Egyptian coins and currency from the period after Egypt had been absorbed into the Roman Empire. It didn't seem that important, though, and the author offered little more than a brief account of how some of the earliest coins in Egypt may have been designed by alchemists and occultists who were obsessed with gold and other precious metals. These men had been court magicians for some of the Pharaohs.

Laura was about to return the book to the shelf when an odd thought struck her. It was something that James had said. 'The opal was my daughter's birthstone,' she repeated Lightman's words out loud, and she opened the book again. Turning to the page she had just read, the word 'alchemist' jumped out at her.

Feeling her pulse quicken, she pulled the notebook over, flipped the page and wrote down: 'Alchemist, Magician, Ancient Egyptians, Birthstones, Gold and Silver' – followed by four large question marks.

Returning *Coins of Antiquity* and *Ancient Coins* to the shelves, Laura ran a check through the computerised catalogue, looking for anything that might deal with the very earliest coins. She found just one title, a Victorian book called *Lost Numismatics* by a Professor Samuel Cohen. Then she ran another search for 'Egyptian Alchemists'. Apart from a clutch of modern sensationalist titles that she decided she couldn't trust, this again offered only one book of original scholarship, another ridiculously obscure Victorian tome: *The Black Arts of the Pharaohs*, written by one Erasmus Fairbrook-Dale.

Laura was starting to enjoy herself. It reminded her of college days: fond memories of afternoons spent in rooms just like this one following leads that took her from one concept to another, a winding path through an intellectual maze. Maybe, she thought as she opened *Lost Numismatics* and turned the huge pages with exaggerated care, this was what had first inspired her to work in crime journalism, the thrill of sniffing out the clues to a mystery. If that was true, it had also led her inexorably onward to become a thriller writer.

Then she saw it: in the centre of page nine, a picture of two discs, the dual aspects of a coin. The first disc showed an image of five women in long flowing robes holding a large deep bowl aloft at arm's length. Next to that, the other side of the same coin, was the head of a young Pharaoh. The face was slightly different to the one in Philip's photograph, but everything else about the coin was identical. With growing excitement she read the text printed beneath the pair of pictures:

Known as the Arkhanon coins (c. 400 BC, Napata region), these were handmade by the court magicians of King Alara. Each contains images reflecting the Ancient Egyptian concern with the unity of all things, the holistic pairing of complimentary elements. This example is a gold coin and it carries the image of a quintet of women holding a representation of the sun. Two other very similar Arkhanon coins have been found at the same site: a silver coin bearing the image of five women holding a bowl containing an image of the moon, and a third made from iron with another sphere (supposed by some authorities to be the planet Mars) held aloft by another quintet of robed female figures.

'Christ,' Laura said aloud. 'Well, clever me.' Then turning to the second Victorian book, *The Black Arts of the Pharaohs*, she flicked through the pages, reading random sections until she reached a chapter entitled: 'The Birth of Holism'.

Three hours later, Laura emerged into bright afternoon sunshine that burst through low black clouds. The road outside the library was glistening from very recent rain and a faint rainbow shimmered over the Radcliffe Camera, but Laura was almost completely oblivious to the sight. She was lost in an ancient world of magic and occultism, thrilled that she might just have stumbled on a crucial clue.

Chapter 12

The Acolyte was proud of the work that he had done. It came as the fulfilment of a long-cherished dream. He was working for one of the greatest men alive, doing work that made a difference, work that had meaning, purpose. And he was part of the great plan, the Great Work as it had once been called hundreds of years before his time.

He had trained for many years so that he might complete the tasks for which he was now responsible. That training had been gruelling. He had studied at the best medical schools, practised in the operating theatres of three internationally respected hospitals, roved through disciplines and acquired many skills while honing his considerable natural talents. He had studied cryogenics, psychology and mathematics as well as pursuing occult studies that included numerology, astrology and alchemy.

He pulled his inconspicuous black Toyota into a vacant visitors' space in the car park of Somerville College, Oxford and stepped out onto the gravel. The soles of his handmade black brogues crunched on the stones. He brushed imaginary flecks of dust from the front of his immaculate Cerruti suit, smoothed back a few strands of hair above his ears, straightened his already perfectly aligned silk Hermes tie and studied his reflection in the rear nearside car window before walking towards the main quad of the college.

The Acolyte glanced at his Patek Philippe. It was almost three o'clock. Samantha Thurow, a third-year history and politics undergraduate, would, he knew, be emerging from Staircase 7 at any moment. From the second she appeared here until 9.08 p.m. precisely he would keep close track of her movements. In a broad sense, he already knew what those movements should be: he had wired her room in a student house in Summertown just north of the city centre and he had tapped her phone.

As he recalled these facts and began to feel the first tingle of sweet anticipation, he saw Samantha walk from the darkness of the entrance of Staircase 7. She was talking to another student, a short Asian girl. Samantha was a tall and exceptionally pretty brunette with sensual almond eyes and full, brightly coloured lips. Her hair was arranged with care to look a mess. She was wearing a short tartan skirt over black woollen tights, a pair of black Doc Martens, a tight red sweater and a black cardigan.

She was carrying an armful of books and had a small leather bag slung over her left shoulder. The Acolyte considered Samantha Thurow's sartorial choices with some distaste as he walked slowly around the quad, watching the two girls go past the Porters' Lodge into the street beyond.

He had committed to memory almost every detail of the file he had constructed on Samantha Thurow. Born 19 May 1986 in Godalming, Surrey. Father an arms contractor; mother a teacher; two older brothers and a younger sister. A scholarship student in her third year at Somerville. Samantha was on the fast track, a high-flyer. Medical: perfect health, usual childhood illnesses, broken arm at the age of nine; kidneys in A1 condition. Love life: current boyfriend Simon Welding, a trainee teacher, twenty-four. He shared a rented house in East Oxford with two other students, and Samantha stayed there at least twice a week during term time.

Samantha unlocked her bike and pulled it away from the wall, waved goodbye to her friend and turned right, crossing St Giles and heading towards the city centre. The Acolyte knew where she was going and felt no need to hurry back to his car. Reaching the Toyota, he pulled on his gloves, removed a wipe from the packet he always kept with him and cleaned the driver's seat before lowering himself into the car. He cleaned the dash and the wheel and put the wipe into a small plastic bag that lay on the passenger seat. Then he smoothed his trousers and jacket and arranged himself so that he would suffer only the minimum of creasing to his suit. Turning the key in the ignition, he drove off.

He passed Samantha along St Giles; she was cycling among a cluster of other bikes. Taking his time on the route around the city centre and along Cowley Road, he reached Princes Street and parked opposite number 268. Ten minutes later, Samantha appeared at the Cowley Road end of the street and cycled down the narrow road lined with gentrified terraced houses before drawing to a halt outside the one that the Acolyte was watching. There she wheeled her bike onto the path, secured it against the wall of the house and used her own key to open the front door.

According to the schedule, her boyfriend Simon Welding would not be there for at least four hours, and Samantha was planning to study all afternoon. During most of the evening the two of them would be alone. The others who lived at number 268 were expected at a party in a nearby street. At just before 9 p.m. he would enter the premises with his equipment, and he would be out by nine-fifteen. A quarter of an hour after that he would be with the Master – and they would be one step closer to completing the Great Work.

Chapter 13

'So you're really going ahead with this?' Jo asked incredulously.

'Don't be so dismissive. I'm hardly new to crime, now am I? Remember how I put food on the table before I became an illustrious author?' Laura retorted.

Jo was up for the first time since the accident, reclining on Philip's sofa with a rug around her and a cup of soup in her hand. She was wearing cow-patterned pyjamas that were at least three sizes too big for her. The grandfather clock in the hall had just struck six o'clock, and Laura and Philip had finished explaining all that had happened during the past two days up to the point when Laura had gone to visit James Lightman earlier that afternoon.

'Besides,' Laura added breezily, 'I think I've made a breakthrough.'

Philip sat up in his armchair. 'What sort of break-through?'

'The results of four hours' intensive research at

the Bodleian, that's what. Turns out the coins are replicas of something called an Arkhanon. It's just about the oldest known Egyptian coin, dating from about 400 BC. Before that the Egyptians simply bartered. What's most important is that the Arkhanons were designed by alchemists who worked for the Pharaohs. According to one source, the image of the women and the bowl is linked with the alchemists' obsession with holism – links between seemingly unconnected things.'

'Yes, of course, there were alchemists in ancient Egypt, weren't there? Philip said. 'I seem to remember reading that's when the whole obsession with making gold and the elixir of eternal life began.'

'Mom . . . I mean . . .' Jo frowned. 'Isn't all that alchemy stuff simply a load of baloney?'

'Just hear me out, OK?' Laura said.

Philip and Jo looked at each other and fell silent.

'Good. Well, this is the deal. Turns out that one of the connections alchemists cared about was the link between humanity and the universe. Most alchemists tried to draw parallels between the human body, the planets, the stars and the movement of the heavens. They believed that the human form was a reflection of the celestial sphere. That God created these patterns – these repeat images, if you like – and that it was their job to unravel the links. Almost a sacred duty.'

'And you think this has something to do with the murders?' Philip looked completely confused.

'Alchemists believed they could only make gold if they discovered the legendary Philosopher's Stone, a magical substance that when united with any base metal could turn that metal into pure, solid gold. The Philosopher's Stone could only be discovered by the noble of spirit, by an alchemist who truly understood the holistic aspect of the universe and who could free his mind to flow with the Universal Spirit. Crucially, the alchemist drew links between metals and parts of the body.'

'Don't tell me,' Philip interrupted. 'They connected gold with the heart and silver with the brain?'

'Ten bonus points to Mr Bainbridge. But there's a whole heap more. Alchemists believed that the body and the celestial sphere mirror each other. So the planets may also be associated with the organs of the body . . .'

'Mom? So let me get this straight,' Jo said. 'You've spent all afternoon finding alchemical links between – God, what was it? Gold, the sun and the freakin' heart? Where does Santa come into all this?'

'The point is,' Laura said, 'there is quite possibly a connection between all this hocus-pocus and the murders. Simply because the murderer believes in it. It doesn't matter if it's all complete bullshit.'

Jo looked rather shamefaced. 'OK, mom . . .'

'There's more.' Laura replied. 'If you want to hear it, of course.'

'Oh please!' Jo rolled her eyes.

Laura grinned. 'If you thought what I just told you was weird, here comes the really kooky bit. Some alchemists devoted their entire lives to the thankless task of trying to produce the Philosopher's Stone: blending chemicals together to make a magical substance that they believed could transmute base metals into gold. It has consumed and spat out centuries of hope, from ancient times to . . . well, some say there are still alchemists out there today. But the point is, the effort expended to make the Stone was incredible. The adept had to follow a set of instructions that came from many different sources and they spent literally months, sometimes years on a single experiment.'

'Anyway, as I was reading this stuff I started to wonder what it was that guided them. Then I thought about the most important connections the alchemists made and it struck me that most of them must have also been astrologers. I was quite into astrology when I was a student. I snapped out of it pretty quick, though.' Laura stole a glance at Jo who was shaking her head. 'Alchemists did everything by the stars. Each stage of the process was undertaken on partic-ular dates and at significant astrological alignments.'

Laura's audience was silent.

'For the alchemists, one particular day of the year stands out as the most important. The vernal equinox.'

'The what?' Jo asked.

'The vernal equinox, the first day of spring, when the days start to get longer than the nights,' Philip said.

'Correct. Alchemists viewed it as the most auspicious day for starting new plans. It was the time when most of them would begin a fresh set of experiments to produce the Philosopher's Stone. It falls on 20 March, two days ago – the day of the first murder.'

'So what are you thinking, Laura?' Philip asked after a few moments. 'It's, well . . . creepy, I suppose, but how does it help us catch whoever is killing these women?'

'I've not stopped thinking about that since I left the library today. I don't know whether it can help right away, but it could prevent more murders.'

'How?'

'Well, think about it. Monroe told you that Forensics believed Rachel Southgate was killed on the evening of the twentieth. That was when the sun entered Aries and the Earth passed through the vernal equinox. For the murderer it was a new beginning, the start of a project.'

'Nice,' Jo exclaimed. 'Good project.'

'The point I'm making,' Laura went on, 'is that the timing of the second murder probably has an astrological connection as well. God knows what. But if it does, and if there's a planned third or fourth murder, they could be linked with precise dates and times too.'

'Makes some sort of sense, I suppose,' Philip muttered.

'Of course it does,' Laura snapped. 'Trouble is, I don't know the half of it.'

'Well, don't look at me,' Jo exclaimed. 'I'm a mathematician.'

'Beg your pardon,' Laura laughed.

'But . . . I was about to say, you may be in luck.'

'Oh?'

'Tom is depressingly into the whole thing. I don't get it, such a bright young chap in all other ways,' Jo concluded, putting on a plummy British accent. 'And he's supposed to be coming over. Any moment now.'

'He is?' Philip asked.

'Hope you don't mind, dad. He wanted to see how I was.'

Philip threw up his hands. 'No problem at all.'

'We'll get him to sing for his supper,' Laura said.

Tom arrived twenty minutes later. He looked surprisingly healthy apart from the aluminium cast encasing two fingers of his left hand which had hairline fractures from the car accident. A rugby Blue at Oriel, studying medicine, he was six feet three inches tall and weighed more than two hundred pounds without an ounce of fat on him. Square-jawed and with large blue eyes and well-cut wavy brown hair, he was strikingly handsome. Tom sat next to Jo on the sofa and Laura explained what was going on as Philip went off to the kitchen to get a drink.

'Wow,' Tom said after Laura's monologue. 'Wow. And this is for real?'

'Afraid so,' Philip said as he came back into the room and handed Tom a glass of cranberry juice. 'Laura's spared none of the gruesome details, I imagine.'

'I hope not!' Tom laughed. 'So, you think the murderer is planning his moves according to an astrological timetable?'

'I'm not sure yet.'

'But you know for sure the killer committed the first murder around the time of the vernal equinox and left a gold coin and . . .' He paused. 'Removed the girl's heart. The second murder was less than twelve hours later: that time the killer left a silver coin and he took the victim's brain.'

'Correct.'

'Well, you're right about the connections. The brain is linked with silver and with the moon. So I would think it's obvious that the moon entered Aries at the time of the second murder.'

'What do you mean?' Jo asked.

'Of course,' Laura exclaimed. 'Why didn't I think of that?'

'Think of what?' said Philip.

'Well, it's obvious now. The sun, the moon and the planets all move across the sky, don't they?' Laura explained. 'The movement of the sun through the zodiac over the year gives meaning to the twelve star signs. Is that right, Tom?' He nodded. 'So,' she went on, 'during the first month of the year, the sun is seen in Capricorn, then in Aquarius, Pisces and so on. The sun enters Aries sometime late on – what? The twentieth or early on the twenty-first of March. Which is also around the date of the vernal equinox. After that it goes on to Taurus and all the others. But the planets and the moon can also enter and leave the star sign during the month.'

'But that doesn't happen all that often,' Tom added. 'The moon and the planets might be the other side of the sky all through the month, but sometimes they succeed each other into the star sign.'

'Yeah, b—' Jo began. Tom was there before her. 'I know what you're going to say, Jo. We've had this discussion before. You think it's all nonsense, but you have to differentiate between real astrology and the rubbish printed in women's magazines and

Sunday supplements. That stuff is based on nothing but the imagination of the hack who writes it. A properly trained astrologer deals with a far more complex set of ideas – a consideration of the effect of all the heavenly bodies, not just the sun.'

'The implication being,' Philip remarked, 'that these other heavenly bodies sometimes follow the sun into the sign of the zodiac and contribute to the astrological influence?'

'Exactly.'

'So it might well be that the moon went into Aries soon after Aries became the current sign and that's the link with the date and time of the second murder.'

'I would put money on it.'

'Yeah, but hold on . . . You'll probably shoot me down in flames, but isn't there an elemental error here? These star signs were worked out – what? Ten thousand years ago?'

'Well, not quite that long,' Tom replied. 'Astrology began in Mesopotamia about 4,000 BC, I think.'

'OK, whatever! Six thousand years ago. The thing is, the constellations can't be the same as they were then because, relative to the Earth, the stars move quite a bit during a few thousand years. The constellations are not the same shape they were during ancient times and they are certainly not in the same places they were in then.'

'Well, actually, Jo, it's irrelevant,' Laura said.

'Why?'

'Because it only matters to tabloid astrologers.'

Jo looked bewildered.

'Well, think about it. If everything has shuffled along one sign or more, it doesn't matter except to those who try to attach characteristics to people born under a particular sign. You know . . . if you're an Aquarius you're unconventional and have weak ankles. All that crap.'

'The celestial shift is something that real astrologers take into account. Laura's right,' Tom interjected.

'But then the vernal equinox is no longer in Aries.' Philip said.

'It doesn't matter unless you subscribe to Sunday-supplement astrology.'

Jo sighed. 'I guess.'

Laura grinned. 'It's OK, doll, you're just a mathematician.'

Jo laughed resignedly and took a sip of her soup.

'Anyway,' Philip added, 'our murderer appears to be inspired by astrology. We only need to concentrate on what *he* believes, not what *we* think of it all.'

'All right,' Laura said, putting her hands up. 'Let's get back to the real issue. Tom? You reckon it's likely the moon moved into Aries at the time of the second murder?'

'Well, it's easy to find out.'

'It is?'

'Just look it up at almanac.com. I'm a subscriber.'

'Oh my God!' Jo said.

Tom was already walking over to a computer on the desk close to the sofa. 'Is this on-line?' he asked.

'Yeah. I've got ADSL,' Philip said and joined him at the terminal.

They brought up Google and Tom typed in almanac.com. It appeared a second later and he put in his personal ID. Then a new menu appeared. Along the left-hand column was a list of questions with empty answer boxes.

Laura had followed them over, but Jo remained on the sofa.

'I just need to put in a few figures,' Tom said. 'It's a cool site, software that calculates the location of any planet and the moon at any time between now and the year 3000.' He hit the keyboard. 'OK, so, the moon, date: 21 March 2006.' He followed this with a few more numbers and answered a succession of questions before clicking on SEARCH.

The response came back with surprising speed.

'Cool,' Tom said.

'What is?' Laura asked, unable to make head or tail of the data.

'The moon entered Aries at 3.47 a.m. on 21 March.'

'That could be exactly the time of the second murder.' Philip was clearly impressed.

'Monroe was sure of the time?' Laura asked Philip.

'He said his forensic team believed that the murder had taken place between four and six hours before I got there. That was just before 8.30, so the murder must have been sometime between 2.30 and 4.30 a.m.'

'Tom, with this software you can track any of the planets as well as the moon?' Laura asked.

'Yes.'

'We need to find out if any of the planets are going to enter Aries, and when. Can we go through each one?'

'I can do better than that,' Tom replied. 'I can tell you the movements of all the planets as far into the future as you want.'

'Don't exaggerate, Thomas,' Jo said lightly. 'Only until the year AD 3000.'

Philip gave a snort of laughter, but Tom ignored her and tapped the keys, answering a succession of questions at the prompt. After a few moments he hit the SEARCH prompt again and pushed his chair back from the terminal. 'OK, do your stuff,' he said.

It took longer this time, but after perhaps twenty seconds a new screen filled with diagrams and lists of numbers appeared.

'What does it tell us?' Laura asked impatiently.

'I'm getting there,' Tom replied. He scrolled down, peering at the screen, then closed his eyes, lost in concentration. 'Jesus!'

'What?' Philip said.

'This is really something.'

'Will you please . . .' Laura hissed.

'Sorry. Every so often you get a conjunction of planets—'

'When the planets line up?' Philip interrupted.

'Yeah, when two or more heavenly bodies – the moon and the planets – appear to line up as seen from the Earth. Getting a conjunction of two planets or a planet and the moon, say, happens quite often – that's called a three-body conjunction. Getting a four-body conjunction is rarer – it only happens every few years. A week from today, early on 31 March, at a few minutes after midnight to be precise, the moon and three planets will be almost perfectly arranged to form a five-body conjunction with the sun. That is so rare it's only happened maybe ten times during the past thousand years or so.'

Laura was the first to react. 'So that means three planets are going to enter Aries during the course of the next few days?'

'Yep.'

'You can find out which?'

'I already have,' Tom replied and pointed to the screen.

'Venus, Mars and Jupiter, in that order.'

'When?'

'Jupiter, just after midnight on 31 March; Mars, a few hours earlier, the evening of 30 March; and Venus . . . let me see,' he muttered, scrolling down. 'Venus passes into Aries tonight, at eight minutes past nine.'

Chapter 14

Cambridge: the evening of 10 August 1690

John Wickins had come up to Cambridge in 1663 and now it was as familiar to him as his mother's face. He knew every turn of every lane, every plant and every weed that sprang forth from the paving stones on his regular walks. He knew every college Fellow and each townsman who crossed his path. He had enjoyed many of the same routines for almost three decades: he bought his books at the same shop, filled his inkwell from the same stationer's, had his clothes tailored in precisely the same way by the same, now elderly tailor, and he purchased his snuff from the same dealer who had first procured it for him twenty or more years earlier. But now he was leaving, and the place no longer seemed the same.

Wickins had been in great haste, and had hired a horse to make the journey back from Oxford that day. Arriving at dusk, he had handed the reins to the stable boy and the horse had been fed and watered in the college stables. It was an unusual luxury to allow himself, but he had big plans and he could not waste time on overcrowded snail-like coaches. There was no denying that he was excited by the prospect of the new position offered him, the rectorship of St Mary's, Oxford. It was an opportunity he could not let pass. Now was the time to make the break from Cambridge and all that his life there entailed.

Of course, that meant leaving Isaac Newton. Wickins and Newton had had a very odd relationship. They had met during their first term, each of them miserable and less than enamoured with the majority of the other students. Each had arrived expecting to fall into a challenging whirlpool of learning, but instead they had found that very few students cared for anything but drinking, gambling and whoring. He and Newton had similar backgrounds: each had been raised within the lower gentry. Wickins's father had been a schoolmaster, Newton's father had died before Newton was born and his mother had married a local vicar. Neither of them had the slightest thing in common with most of the young men who had gone up in their year. Many of these had been the sons of wealthy landowners and successful merchants; but even those clots had been better than the laziest and stupidest of all students – the vile offspring of the nobility whose families paid for the academic success of their sons.

Wickins crossed the quad of Trinity College and entered under the archway leading to his staircase. He was walking slowly, almost as though he was trying to put off the inevitable. He had experienced some good times here in this great city. He could admit that most of his life had been a mundane routine comprised of study, then his theological researches. But these had been interspersed with times helping Newton with his scientific work, copying texts for him, assisting whenever he could. During those periods, he could tell himself with confidence that he had come closer to the great Isaac Newton than any other man had ever come. Then there had been times when physical need had brought them a unique intimacy, actions about which they never spoke and kept locked away from the world. And, of course, there was always the real purpose to his living in such close proximity to the man, the reason he had first been encouraged to meet Newton and befriend him. Newton, he had grown to understand, was the most dangerous man alive.

Wickins reached the door to their rooms, fished his key from the pocket of his tunic and turned it in the lock. The hallway and the rooms leading off to left and right were cast in gloom. Warm air blew through an opened window at the end of the hall. The door to his bedchamber was closed, but the one to the right, leading into Newton's room and beyond that to his laboratory, stood ajar. It was unusually quiet. The only sound came from a pair of thrushes nesting in an elm tree just beyond the opened window.

Now that he was there, Wickins suddenly experienced a great swell of uncertainty about his plans. This was his home. He felt secure here. Was he doing the right thing by throwing it all away and chasing after a new life in Oxford?

He felt sure that his mission in Cambridge was now over. The work had been of great importance and he could not have left any sooner. So, about this at least, he felt no guilt. The conjunction of the planets was due the following night, 11 August, and it was clear that no one was about to try the experiment. If Newton was not preparing for it, then nobody else would have the ability, the knowledge or the ambition to do so. Wickins's friends in Oxford had been watching for tell-tale signs, but there appeared to have been nothing suspicious going on there. They had learned of one murder the previous week, but it was clear to them that the girl had died at the hands of her lover who had then killed himself. Or, at least, that was all they had managed to ascertain. But even his friends had to admit that many crimes could be easily covered up and that they could never know for sure. Most crucially, though, Wickins thought as he removed his shoulder bag, jacket and hat and placed them on the hooks in the hall, the ruby sphere was almost certainly safe in its repository. And no alchemical genius had emerged with the ancient codes and Hermetic knowledge to acquire the precious thing.

Wickins was surprised to see that the door leading into Newton's laboratory was open. The bedlinen lay in a crumbled heap. Plates of food had been left ignored on the floor. The window was open and on the wide windowsill stood a bowl of water. It was clean, untouched. Wickins edged his way over to the laboratory. His heart was pounding. A sudden irrational fear had shot through him. Newton was always so careful to maintain his privacy.

His friend had not heard him. Newton was standing with his back to the laboratory door, the glow from the fire lighting up one side of his face. He was cradling something in his palms. It was a thing that Wickins had never before seen in the waking world, a thing of mythology, but something he also knew to be real, sacred beyond words, the nexus of all meaning: the ruby sphere.

Wickins thought he was going to scream, but thankfully no sound came. Yet still the horror would not dissipate. With an almost supernatural effort he managed to raise his hand to his face and grip the skin of his cheeks with his fingernails. It was an almost involuntary act, as though he was trying to convince himself that he was still alive, that what he was witnessing was wholly real.

One of the thrushes landed on the windowsill and tapped at the water bowl. Newton spun round.

During the two seconds that followed, a million clashing thoughts ran through Wickins's mind, but he was really only aware of two. One told him to flee, to race to Oxford and to warn his friends. The other impulse screamed at him to rush into the room to grab the sphere.

In the time it took him to cover the distance to where Newton sat, the scientist had raised himself out of his chair and braced himself for the onslaught.

For a man of almost fifty who had spent his entire life in study, Newton was surprisingly agile. Wickins made a grab for him, but Newton shifted to one side; he lost his balance but managed to break his fall by gripping the table by the fireplace. He spun round and saw Newton grasping at a sheaf of papers that lay on a table close by.

'Isaac, you cannot do this thing,' Wickins screamed. 'Please . . . you know not . . .'

But Newton seemed oblivious to him. A sudden fury seized Wickins when he realised in an instant that he was wasting his breath. He sprang forward and grabbed Newton by the shoulder. The scientist twisted. Wickins lost his grip and whirled around. He could see the sphere cupped in his room-mate's right hand, and then Newton's fist encasing the sphere came rushing towards his face. He just managed to sidestep the blow, and as he swerved to one side he brought his hand across Newton's face, scratching his cheek. Newton yelped and with blind fury lashed out at Wickins, catching him squarely on the jaw. ''Tis mine,' he yelled, his eyes ablaze.

Wickins fell backwards and landed heavily against the shelves, his head smashing against the wood and causing several jars and bottles to wobble and fall. They crashed to the floor except for a bottle of yellowish liquid labelled 'Oil of Vitriol' which landed squarely on Wickins's shoulder, popped its cork and spilled its contents across his arm. He screamed but, almost before the sound had left his mouth, Newton, a look of manic fury etched into his features, took one step forward and kicked him squarely in the face. Wickins slammed back against the floor, unconscious.

When Wickins awoke, it was completely dark. The fire had dwindled to nothing, it was chilly and the smells that reached him were almost overwhelming.

Most disturbing was the unmistakable odour of corroded flesh.

Wickins pulled himself to his feet. The pain in his head almost made him fall to his knees, and his arm throbbed. Stumbling into the next room he saw that there was a little more light. The moon had risen and a silver haze hung over everything. He looked at his arm. The fabric of his shirt had burned away and his flesh was red and blistered. He strode over to the bowl of water on the sill and, soaking a shirt that lay nearby, he dabbed the wet cloth on his arm.

So Newton had the ruby sphere. This was Wickins's worst nightmare come true. He tried to think through the pain. The cool water on his arm helped, but the burn was agonising and his head felt like a dozen workmen with mallets were slamming into his skull as though attacking a resistant mound of rock.

Wickins remembered the timepiece that Newton kept in his room and went to check it. The fourth hour after midnight had passed. He must have been unconscious for a long time. He cursed under his breath. Cupping his hands in the water bowl again he swilled some water around his mouth before spitting it out, red, into the bowl.

Once again he tried to think, but the pain continued to stifle his thoughts. Newton had gone. He could be close to Oxford now, or perhaps he had gone elsewhere to prepare. The conjunction was less than twenty-four hours away. What was Wickins to do? He could send a message to Oxford, but he could not trust a courier with such a grave matter. And besides, what would he say?

A few moments later he was heading out the door, making for the stables, his jacket and hat on, bag over his shoulder.

The stable boy was not best pleased to see Wickins but a shilling brightened him up and he led the way to the stalls. Newton had been there earlier in the evening, the boy told him, but he had said nothing and had seemed even more distracted and unfriendly than usual.

Wickins chose a chestnut mare, one of the best horses in the stable, and gave the payment to the lad in a sealed envelope to be passed on to the bursar. He would, he told him, explain everything to the stable master upon his return a few days hence. He had urgent business to attend to and he simply could not waste a moment. Then, feeling half-dead, Wickins snapped the reins, pulled the mare round and headed for the gates and the main road beyond.

He made Ickwell village, sixty miles west of Cambridge, in two hours, and as the sun rose full above the hedgerows, a fresh horse, a grey gelding, took him through Brill, Horton-cum-Studley and then Islip before he joined the road that would take

118

him to the Eastgate of Oxford. He reached the city walls an hour and a half later. At a trot, he turned along Merton Street before dismounting and allowing a boy to lead the horse away. Then he headed straight for University College.

'Great shit!' Robert Hooke exclaimed as John Wickins finished recounting his story. 'A pox on the man.' And he took a huge snort of snuff up his nostril.

They were sitting in a commodious apartment in University College overlooking The High, a set of rooms that Robert Boyle occupied each August as part of his honorarium. Wickins felt utterly drained and his arm and head throbbed. He had been received by Boyle who, in spite of the fact that he looked frail and tired himself, had insisted that he inspect and treat the other man's wounds immediately. With practised delicacy, he had probed at the blistered skin on Wickins's forearm before bandaging it tightly. To his sore head Boyle had applied a paste of cat urine and mouse droppings that he found particularly efficacious for headaches. As the old man tended him, Wickins described the recent events in Cambridge. Boyle was calm and he absorbed the information with a sigh here, a mild grunt there. Occasionally pausing for a moment in the task of tending the wounds, he would search Wickins's face, his piercing green eyes searching for something indefinable. Then Hooke had arrived, responding to the urgent message taken to him by a footman. The very opposite of Boyle, he had blustered and fumed, sworn and cursed before throwing himself into a chair by the empty fireplace.

'That abominable creature, that . . . that . . . clyster-pipe,' he growled, reaching for his pouch of snuff.

Wickins, in spite of his agonies, was shocked. 'Sir, please, refrain . . .'

'Why should I refrain?' Hooke snapped back. 'There is no better way to describe your esteemed Lucasian Professor. Indeed, 'tis perhaps too mild a description. And I might add that you, sir, are little better than he.'

At that moment Wickins could see precisely why Newton so loathed the man. Hooke's twisted, stunted frame was almost as ugly as his personality.

'Come now, gentlemen,' Boyle interjected. 'I think John would be entirely happy to concede before us here that he has made errors over the matter of his room-mate. But what is now essential is to forge solutions, not recriminations.'

'But it was I who warned you both,' Hooke insisted. Turning from Wickins to Boyle, he added. 'There is no limit to the man's ambition. I told you, sir, in London, after Wren's talk, that Newton had discerned something of value.'

'I do not even recall his presence there,' Boyle replied.

'He stood to the rear of the hall, close to the door. I glimpsed him from the stage. I was not mistaken. He was gone almost as Wren reached his conclusion.'

'And you claimed that you confronted Wren on the matter.'

'I did,' Hooke said almost as a whisper. 'But he would tell me nothing. The man has never liked me.'

Wickins failed to stifle a snort. 'Master,' Wickins said looking across to Boyle. 'I am devastated by my stupidity over this. But if I may be allowed a single expression of self-mitigation, it would be simply to say that even if we had held genuine suspicions about Newton's awareness of the ruby sphere, I would have found it almost impossible to believe that he had the knowledge to snatch the precious thing from under our very noses. Nor could I have brought myself to believe that he might know what to do with it if he had.'

'It was you, dullard, who was assigned the task of watching over the demon!' Hooke exclaimed.

'Gentlemen,' Boyle said, 'I have neither the energy nor the will to repeat myself this sorry morning. You must drop this malice, or else all may be lost. If you do not start to assume the mantle of intelligence and dignity, our friend Isaac Newton will have the better of us. And, make no mistake, he is a most formidable opponent.'

They fell silent for a moment. Wickins was suddenly aware of the sounds of the city coming through an opened window. It was almost nine o'clock and, although Oxford was virtually empty of students, the city remained alive with the noises of traders and street hawkers, of carts ambling along The High. Far off, the clatter of hammers and the crisp rush of saw against wood could be heard as builders worked on repairs to a college roof.

'What are your thoughts, Master?' Hooke refrained from looking in Wickins's direction. 'You know my feelings about Newton. He is piss-proud. Others know this to be true – some from bitter experience. But only a fool would deny his brilliance.'

'Your words are typically plain, Robert, but of course they are true. It pains me to say such a thing, but I fear we must assume the worst. Newton will be working with others. That is a necessity even he cannot avoid, however much he would naturally hate the fact. We must also assume that these men have been in this city a while and that, in spite of our failure to learn of such things, they have bloodied their hands. We all know what the ritual entails.' Boyle looked at each of the other men gravely.

'Gentlemen, through inaction we now face terrible danger. We must, each of us' – he fixed Hooke with a stare that would have made stronger men wither – 'do all that is within our power to thwart the Lucasian Professor tonight. Time is against us, my friends. We must begin our preparations immediately.'

Chapter 15

Detective Chief Inspector Monroe's office was as austere as the man himself. His desk filled a third of the room and it was empty except for a top-notch computer, a pair of phones and a tray of pens. There were no pictures on the walls and a single, almost dead spider plant dangled its leaves down the side of a filing cabinet. Two worn chairs were positioned at the corners of the desk facing Monroe's own low-backed PVC swivel chair. But it was none of these things that made the first impression: it was the smell, an unpleasant medley of fast-food odours. Evidently, Laura mused as she took the chair offered her by the DCI, Monroe was a man who thought proper lunches were a waste of time and resources.

A glass wall ran along one side of the room. It offered a view onto the open-plan area filled with workstations, its walls covered with charts. Monitors were flickering and computers were manned by uniformed policemen and plain-clothes officers who were drinking coffee, scrutinising screens, talking with great intensity and leaning back in their chairs, feet on their desks. Others were surveying papers, running hands through their hair, scribbling on notepads, tapping on keyboards, talking and listening on the phone. It was 7.45 p.m. but it could have been any time of the day or night. The place was over-lit, noisy and abuzz with activity. Whatever the city, police stations, Laura knew from long experience, never slept.

It was almost with a start that she became aware that Monroe and Philip were staring at her.

'So, Ms Niven,' Monroe fixed her with his intense black eyes, 'you have some information that you think may help my investigation.' His voice betrayed only a hint of the scepticism and impatience she was sure he felt. Laura had met his type before – many times, in fact. Monroe was a stereotype, a Brit equivalent of the hardened career cops she had known during her time as a crime reporter. Guys like the detective chief inspector were impervious to most of the weapons she knew she could use to hold her own in male company, immune to the talent for persuasion and ability to get her own way that she could usually employ so effectively. At the same time, she was well aware that the Monroes of the world made the best cops. They were all men who appeared, on the surface at least, to have no home life, no emotional baggage, nothing to weaken or deflect them from the task in hand.

'Yes, I do,' she replied. 'And I think it's important.'

'Well, that is a relief.'

Glancing again at Philip to check his approval that she should tell the full story, Laura began to explain what she had discovered, about the search on almanac.com and the expected conjunction. The DCI maintained an almost expressionless mask with merely an occasional frown to indicate that he was listening to her at all. When Laura had finished, he leaned back in his chair and folded his arms across his chest. The sleeves of his jacket had ridden up and they looked so tight it seemed as though the fabric might split at any moment.

'Astrology.' The single word emerged rounded and pure Home Counties, the 'ol' like an echo in a hollowed-out oak. Monroe gazed up at the ceiling.

'I know what you're thinking. Sure, it does sound, well . . . odd, I guess . . .'

'You believe our killer is working to an agenda written in the stars, a crank who is murdering to a carefully designed plan.'

'Yes.'

'All because of these coincidences you've found?'

Laura bristled.

'I know.' Monroe raised a hand to silence her. 'I know, Ms Niven – you don't think they *are* coincidences.'

'Chief Inspector, I think these facts are more than

coincidence,' Philip interjected. 'I don't have any faith in astrology, in case you're wondering. And I know that Laura is very sceptical too.'

'Look, Mr Bainbridge, Ms Niven. I understand what you're driving at. I realise that you don't need to be an astrology nut to decide that a killer is operating by the rules of the so-called art. But don't you think you're pinning rather too much on a set of facts that could be explained in any number of different ways?'

On the drive into Oxford, Philip had warned Laura that Monroe was not an easy man to convince of anything. In fact, he had added, he wasn't an easy man, period.

'Like what?' Laura challenged.

'The murderer might be laying a false trail. He might be making us think he is working to some cranky agenda just to piss us off. Or, simplest of all, as I said, it could just be a coincidence.'

'I don't buy either of those,' Laura said impatiently. 'I don't buy the idea that someone could plan a pair of murders that fit the data we've unearthed, only then to do something totally different. And I buy even less the idea that this data is nothing more than a set of coincidences.'

Through years of experience, Monroe had learned how to read people and how to get them to read in him what he wanted them to read. He couldn't help admiring this American woman. She had guts, but that did nothing to stop him resisting her theories.

'I understand the physics, Ms Niven. I realise that the astronomical facts, as opposed to the astrological interpretation, are quite irrefutable. But how accurate is the computer programme?'

Laura was thrown for a moment.

Monroe drove home his sudden advantage. 'Your entire theory hinges on accurate timings, linking the murders with the planets entering . . . what was it? Aries, yes?'

'I have no reason to believe the website is anything but accurate,' Laura said.

'And what of the times of the murders?'

'Rachel Southgate was murdered between 7 p.m. and 8.30 p.m. on 20 March,' Philip replied. 'Jessica Fullerton the next morning, some time between 2.30 and 4.30.'

'Yes, but you know Forensics can't pinpoint the moment of death with the accuracy you need. Astrology appears to be a far more precise science.' Monroe gave a humourless smile.

'That's a crock, and you know it, Chief Inspector,' Laura retorted. 'There's more than a coincidence in all this. Besides, for God's sake, two young people have died. Do you have any better theories?'

She knew she had made a mistake as soon as the words left her mouth. Philip flashed her an irritated glare.

Monroe remained icy cool. 'I am of course well aware of the seriousness of the situation. And we do have our own theories. I am grateful for you sparing the time. Now, if you'll excuse me . . .'

'What . . . !' Laura exclaimed. 'You're going to ignore everything I've said, and the next murder is scheduled for just after nine? In . . .' She quickly checked her watch. 'Just over an hour?'

'I'm afraid I am, Ms Niven. My resources are limited. I have a team of twenty officers following up what I think are more, let us say, orthodox lines of inquiry. Besides, what exactly do you expect me to do?'

It was a good question, of course. Both Laura and Philip had each thought about it in the car without ever broaching the subject. Even if their ideas were right, and the Chief Inspector had bought into them, what good did this information do right now?

'Look,' Monroe said, his voice uncharacteristically soft. 'Ms Niven, I appreciate your concern. I'm sure you have only the best intentions, but . . .'

'It's OK.' Laura grabbed her bag and got to her feet. 'Sorry to have troubled you. We'll let you follow your own leads. I just hope you're right.'

As a scowling Detective Chief Inspector Monroe pushed open the swing-doors to the CSI lab, Head of Forensics Mark Langham turned to his chief technician with an 'Oh shit, he's in one of those moods' expression.

'This had better be good,' Monroe snapped.

Langham said nothing but led the way to a white plastic and glass table in the centre of the room. The top of the table formed a light-box, and lying flat on the glass was a sheet of plastic about a foot square that looked like an X-ray photograph. In the centre of the image was a black-and-white shape about three inches long, a quarter-oval with tiny dots and dashes around the edge.

'What is it?' Monroe asked.

Langham placed a lens over the image. 'Take a closer look.'

Monroe put his eye to the lens and moved it around the plastic sheet.

'A partial print,' Langham remarked matter-of-factly. 'The marks around the edge . . . stitching. Expensive shoes.'

Monroe straightened. 'Handmade?'

'Quite possibly.'

'Anything else about them?'

'From this partial it looks like a size ten, standard width.'

'Where was this?' Monroe asked. He sounded considerably happier suddenly.

'Near the house, close to where the punt had been moored.' Langham handed Monroe some black-and-white prints of the impression just discernible in the mud. As Monroe studied them, Langham walked around the table to a workbench. The pressed-steel top was spotless. On the surface and against the wall stood a row of machines, all digital displays and clean plastic lines. In front of these were two Petri dishes.

'We found these inside the print.' Langham plucked a fragment from the dish with a pair of tweezers. 'Leather, high-quality, new.'

'And what's this?'

Langham picked up a similar-sized piece of green material from the other dish. 'Plastic. A variant on polypropylene, to be precise. But this is top-end stuff too, an expensive cross-polymer, extremely light-weight but very strong.'

'And it was in the print?'

Langham nodded. 'And in microscopic quantities along a trail leading from the first-floor bedroom in the house to the mooring at the back of the ground floor.'

'Can you get anything more on this plastic? How special is it?' Monroe asked.

'Unfortunately, it's not that unusual, and there're no markings on the fragments we've found so far. A nice piece an inch square with a manufacturer's mark on it would be good.'

'Yeah, and your wife's going to beg you for sex tonight.'

Langham laughed and took a step back to the first Petri dish. 'We may have more luck with this. You won't find too many handmade shoes using this type of leather in Woolworths.'

Monroe took the tweezers and lifted the scrap of leather up to the light. It looked completely unremarkable, a brown sliver no more than a couple of millimetres long.

'I'll check out the database and send someone round the cobblers in town. You reckon these shoes are new?'

'This leather is and the print is remarkably clean. It's possible that the shoes were recently resoled, I suppose.'

Monroe handed the tweezers back to Langham. 'Let's not get our hopes up about this. And . . . keep it quiet for the moment, OK?' He strode past him back to the door. 'Good work, Mark,' he said without turning round.

Chapter 16

The Acolyte had waited patiently in the car for almost six hours, rarely taking his gaze from the terraced house at 268 Princes Street. He had watched as those who lived there and their friends came and went. At 6.04 p.m. the two students who shared the house with Samantha's boyfriend, Simon Welding, arrived. They were followed twenty-seven minutes later by two girls, third-year Oxford Brookes University students Kim Rivedon and Claudia Meacher. They all stayed in the house for a further twenty-one minutes and all four left together at 6.52. The Acolyte knew from his surveillance and from his contacts that the two students who lived with Simon Welding at number 268, Dan Smith and Evelyn Rose, and the two girls were not expected home until at least eleven. Simon Welding pulled up outside the house in his battered ten-year-old Mazda at 7.32 p.m. He would not leave the house alive.

At two minutes before nine, the Acolyte stepped out of the car. He was wearing plastic covers over his shoes and in his left hand he carried a feature-less metal box. It had sturdy latches at the front and it was twelve inches long, ten wide and ten deep, a temperature-controlled organ-carrier, one of five that he had commissioned, each made to his personal specifications by a specialist in Austria. In his right hand he carried a small black plastic bag, its zip fastened and locked. He looked each way along the street. At the far end of the street stood a noisy pub, and running perpendicular to Princes Street was the busy Cowley Road, a main artery into the city from the east and London. These features were hidden from view by a bend in the road, making this end quieter and darker. He entered the garden through the wooden gate and moved quickly to the side entrance that led to a passage running along the side of the house and on to the rear garden.

It was very dark in the narrow passage; clouds were obscuring the moon and the steely glow from the nearest street lights made little impact here. Two-thirds of the way along, the Acolyte stopped. He was hidden from the street. He put the box and the bag on the ground, unlocked and opened the zipper of the bag and carefully removed a clear plastic over-suit, gloves, a perspex visor and a hood from inside. With great care he pulled on the suit and pressed together Velcro fasteners around his neck, wrists, ankles and waist so that every inch of his body was covered. He checked his watch through the plastic. It was 9.04.

At the back of the house the garden was unkempt and overgrown. The Acolyte stepped carefully, silently towards the door of the kitchen that led directly from the garden. He stopped there to listen for any sounds from inside the house. He could hear nothing except distant strains of music that seemed to be coming from upstairs.

He moved through the kitchen and into the hall and took the stairs with slow, deliberate steps. All his senses were heightened – he was ready for anything. After reaching the landing he checked each of the rooms to make sure he was alone with his prey and then he moved towards the front bedroom. He could make out the music now – the Allegro of Schubert's String Quartet in D minor, one of his favourites. At the door he stood listening for any human sounds over the music. He could just detect heavy breathing, the occasional moan. Easing the door open, he could see into the room.

Samantha was on top, her back arched, face to the ceiling. Simon, his hands at her small firm breasts, was gazing at her expression of ecstasy. The Acolyte shivered almost imperceptibly, feeling a wash of emotions – jealousy, disgust, fascination. Together they produced a rush of sexual energy that shivered down his spine. He felt himself stiffen. Then, knowing he could not wait a moment longer, he lowered the metal case to the floor, removed a scalpel from his pocket, unsheathed it and took three rapid steps forward, reaching the end of the bed before either Simon or Samantha were aware of his existence.

In one deft movement, he pulled Samantha's head back and slit her throat with a single slash of his scalpel. He cut through her jugular, sending blood spouting across the room, before pushing the blade down further, slicing her larynx muscles. The emerging scream was silenced immediately and the girl fell to the floor clutching her throat, blood gushing between her fingers. She looked up at the Acolyte, her eyes huge, trying unsuccessfully to understand.

Simon was paralysed by shock and the Acolyte took advantage of the second or two this gave him. He slashed at the young man's throat with such force that he almost decapitated him, cutting through his neck from ear to ear. Blood hit the Acolyte's visor and he wiped it away. Simon Welding's body convulsed and dark blood spewed from his mouth, covering his face in a red liquid mask.

Leaving him to writhe on the soaked sheets, the Acolyte leaped from the bed and crouched down beside Samantha. She was still alive. The Acolyte could not spare a second. He placed a hand on her forehead and another under her neck, and with a single twist he snapped her spine between her top two vertebrae, C-1 and C-2. She went limp instantly.

He retrieved the metal carrier and placed it at his side. Then he rolled Samantha onto her front. In two simple movements he opened her body, making nine-inch incisions either side of her spine. Pulling apart the flesh, he could see her ribcage. Removing a battery-powered surgical saw from a zippered pouch in his plastic suit, he cut through the bones in seconds. Prising apart the ribs, he then used his scalpel to carefully sever the vessels and tubes leading to the left and right kidneys.

Opening the organ transporter, the Acolyte felt the cold on his hands. He could see the freezing air spill over the sides of the box. He heard a loud gurgling sound from the bed and then silence as Simon Welding shuddered and died.

The Acolyte placed his gloved hands inside Samantha Thurow's warm body. Slowly removing each kidney, he placed them in individual clear plastic bags, sealed them and placed them delicately inside the transporter. From a pocket at the side of the box he removed a metal coin. Carefully, he placed the coin in the right-hand opening in Samantha's back. He then closed the lid of the organ box and set the combination on the lock. Removing a detergent-infused wipe from a pocket in the oversuit, he cleaned his gloved hands and removed the blood from the handle and the top of the metal box before returning the wipe to his pocket. Placing a protective shield over the blade of his scalpel, he put this in the same pocket.

At precisely 9.13, nine minutes after entering the house, he was once more in the dark narrow passageway alongside the house. He removed his visor, gloves, one-piece oversuit and shoe covers, taking great care not to allow a trace of blood or a particle of tissue to reach his skin or his clothes. Putting on a second pair of clean plastic gloves and replacing the shoe covers with fresh ones, he removed a small bag from his trouser pocket and placed inside it the oversuit, visor, gloves, the first pair of shoe covers, the scalpel and the wipes. He then removed the second pair of gloves, slipped them into the top of the bag and sealed it. Picking up the organ transporter, he moved quickly to the front of the house. Crouching low, he checked the street. A young couple were walking towards him just two houses closer to Cowley Road. He ducked down. They passed by, the girl giggling.

As the couple reached the end of the street and turned out of sight, the Acolyte checked to left and right again. It was clear. He moved quickly but calmly over the low wall of the garden. Opening the boot of the Toyota with a key rather than the remote, he placed the organ transporter inside and used two leather straps to secure it in place. Then he laid the plastic bag next to it, closed the lid of the boot and walked around to the driver's door. Once inside, he removed his shoe covers and placed those in a plastic bag which he put on the seat. He cleaned his hands with a wipe and added this to the bag. Thirty seconds later he was driving towards the centre of Oxford humming along to a Beethoven piano sonata, feeling very pleased with his night's work.

Chapter 17

Oxford: the evening of 11 August 1690

It was six o'clock as the coach descended Headington Hill a mile beyond the city walls, and the weather was still unbearably hot. At the Bear Inn, a manservant carried Newton's case up the winding staircase and asked if he wanted a meal brought to his room. After he left, Newton could rest, enjoy the isolation and reflect on the past twenty-four hours.

He had ridden wildly out of Cambridge, thrashing his poor horse. But after changing mounts twice, first at Standon Puckeridge and again at Great Hadham, he had completed the journey in little over four hours, reaching the capital not long after midnight. As usual, he had travelled using the name Mr William Petty, and as such he had spent the next few hours at the Swan Tavern in Gray's Inn Lane in the City of London.

All through the journey and in the quiet hours in

London Newton had contemplated the task ahead of him, and had recalled time and again the horror that he had left behind in Cambridge. He still could not fully understand what had possessed Wickins. Maybe, he speculated, it was some power within the sphere that had this effect on some people. One thing he knew for certain was that the strange incident in his laboratory had exaggerated his already highly tuned sense of danger. Enemies could be waiting for him at every turn, he realised. He could trust no one. So, to help confuse any potential rival, any others who thought that they could steal the priceless orb, he determined to do everything he could to throw them off his scent. Having first ridden to the capital, he had decided that from there he would take the coach so that he would arrive in Oxford in the same fashion as most other travellers. The scratch on his face caused by Wickins still stung but there was little he could do to hide the welts. By wearing a subtle disguise, he would do all he could to keep himself to himself. Roused from a restless doze by a servant at 4 a.m., he had resumed his onward journey to Oxford, arriving in the city some thirteen hours later.

Now, here at the Bear Inn, Newton suddenly felt exhausted and needed to sleep, but excitement kept him awake and active. He swallowed some broth and read by the evening light, watching dispassionately as a rat scurried across the wooden floor. As arranged, at ten o'clock sharp he heard his friend approach along the corridor outside and tap quietly on the bedroom door. Walking to the door and opening it, he saw Nicolas Fatio du Duillier. With his black cascading curls du Duillier looked younger and more handsome than he had been in Newton's memory; and they had only been apart for three weeks. Newton beckoned him to enter and the younger man stepped forward, with a broad smile. The two embraced.

'Your face,' Fatio said, full of concern.

''Tis nothing,' Newton replied impatiently and turned away.

'You look distressed, my friend. Something has happened?'

'Some minor incident in Cambridge. Nothing with which to concern yourself, my good Fatio. Now, have you made ready?'

'I have done my best, sir. It is not an easy thing you ask. The standard works bear little fruit, but I believe I have done as much as any man could. Landsdown and I have been here two weeks now, and we have harvested all that is required. I check the caskets daily and, although we cannot waste a second, I have faith that all will be well.'

Newton studied du Duillier's pretty young face. 'That is good news.'

'The treasure is safe?'

'Of course it is. Now, let us go through the procedure once more.'

Thirty minutes later they left the inn together.

It was a short walk to the college and they completed the journey in silence. There they were met by a third man whom they always referred to as Mr Landsdown. He was even taller than Fatio du Duillier, but muscular rather than slight. His hair was greying at the temples. They each gave a slight bow. 'It is good to see you,' said Landsdown. 'You have everything?'

Newton tapped his overshirt just below his left shoulder. 'All is well.'

'Then we should proceed. Follow me.'

Landsdown led them across the quad and through a doorway that took them to a long narrow passageway with many doors to left and right. At the fourth door on the left the three men stopped. Landsdown removed a key from his breeches and turned it in the lock. Taking hold of the door handle, he eased it round and pushed gently.

Directly ahead of them stood another door. This was open and through it they could see a steep, narrow stone staircase leading down into darkness. At the top of the stairs a torch was positioned in a wall bracket. Landsdown lifted it and stepped forward into the opening.

They went down a short flight of steps and found

themselves in a room filled with racks and shelves containing many hundreds of bottles of wine, port and brandy: the college wine cellar. Landsdown took them to the far end of the vault and stopped at the wall. It was cold and wet to the touch. Landsdown ran his palm slowly across the wall. He held the torch close to the stone but seemed to be guided more by touch than by sight. After a moment his hand stopped moving and his finger looped around a small dark metal ring, its circumference no greater than that of a guinea coin. He pulled it firmly and they all heard a sound like a heavy weight falling. Very slowly, a panel opened in the wall to reveal an opening no broader than a man's shoulders.

Landsdown turned to his companions. 'Well, gentlemen, our evening's work is about to begin. Are you ready to proceed?'

Chapter 18

At five a.m. Philip's house possessed a particular charm that had been largely absent from Laura's life for at least two decades. In Greenwich Village, five a.m. was not so very different from any other hour. From her apartment she could hear traffic noise, including sirens and the blare of car horns, throughout the day and the night. It was background mush and she only really noticed it when it was no longer there. Here, in this sleepy Oxfordshire village, in the pre-dawn, the cars of New York were as real to her as Pinocchio.

Laura had a woollen wrap around her shoulders and tried to warm herself up by the Aga as the kettle boiled. Then, with a hot cup of strong coffee in her hand, she walked through the hall into the main sitting room with its low-beamed ceiling and bowed leadlight windows. The floorboards creaked and, conscious of Philip and Jo asleep upstairs, she closed the door behind her. She turned on a couple of lamps and walked over to the fireplace. There was some residual heat there from the night before when Tom had been over and they had worked out so much about the dates of the murders – the ones that had already been committed and the ones she felt sure would come. Indeed, if her ideas were correct then another young woman somewhere not far from here would now be lying dead, her body probably still undiscovered.

Sipping her coffee, Laura paced around the room, gazing abstractedly at the pictures Philip had on his walls. There were three of his mother's paintings, fantastic bold blocks of colour with tiny spindly figures standing in the foreground: figures that seemed to be on the verge of being overwhelmed by some nameless horrible thing. These paintings would not have looked out of place in a Manhattan duplex or a Milan studio, and perhaps, she mused, a few could be found there too.

When it came to art, Philip had eclectic tastes. Close to his mother's modern paintings he had hung Victorian oils and even a couple of early 1940s land-scapes. On the same wall beside these could be found a few of his favourite photographs, mainly abstracts taken in the mid-1980s. And to cap it off he had hung with them some ancient-looking family portraits, figures from the nineteenth century, great-great-grandparents in bonnets and wing collars.

Tom had said something in passing last night that

Laura had taken little notice of at the time, but now it was clamouring for her attention. She sat down and stared at the grey ash and embers in the fireplace. Then she had it. Tom had described the five-body conjunction. 'That is so rare,' he had said. 'It's only happened maybe ten times during the past thousand years or so.'

'Of course,' she said aloud. 'Of course. Ten times during the past thousand years or so. Which means it must have happened a few times in the not-too-distant past.'

Jumping up, Laura walked over to the computer. Finding Netscape, she pulled up 'History' and scrolled down to open the home page for almanac.com. Tom had left her his password in case she needed it and, recalling what he had worked through the previous evening, she typed in information at the prompts and pressed 'enter'. Taking a sip of coffee, she watched the screen changing until a new page appeared. In a box near the bottom of the screen entitled 'Five-body conjunctions AD 1500–2000' she could see a list of three dates: 1564, 1690, 1851.

Laura smiled to herself and drummed her fingertips on the desktop. Then, returning to the keyboard, she exited the website, called up Google and typed in: '1851 + Oxford + murders'.

The results were disappointing. In its inimitable

way the search engine had dredged up a medley of what seemed like spurious links to the three words. Top of the list was material on the Great Exhibition of 1851. Lower down came references to the murder that year of a policeman in South London. Other pages offered insights into the *Oxford Dictionary* definition of murder, books published in 1851 with the word 'murders' in the title, and a left-field entry offering a gateway to the work of an American acoustic pop duo called Murder In Oxford.

Google had turned up more than two thousand links to the three words, and Laura was determined not to give up. The two pages that followed were filled with ephemera, more *Oxford Dictionary* links and plenty more about the Great Exhibition. On the verge of trying some other combination of words, Laura scrolled down to links 60–80 and something caught her eye. Halfway down the screen was a link that read: 'Victorian Psycho? Brother Norman thinks so.' She hovered the cursor over the link and clicked.

It was a garish amateur site and a lot of the material appeared to be bordering on the delusional. Called *Brother Norman's Conspiracy Archive*, its creator – Norman, Laura presumed – seemed obsessed with the usual topics: Roswell, the Kennedy assassination, Princess Diana's death in Paris, the CIA plot to blame an innocent Bin Laden for September 11. She had seen it all before and ignored the blaring titles along the left-hand margin that promised 'New Revelations that will Rock your World'. Scrolling down impatiently, she found a title that held some promise. 'Oxford Slaughter: A Victorian Charles Manson?'

Disappointingly, it consisted of no more than three paragraphs. In breathless prose, Brother Norman described the scant facts known to conspiracy theorists. Three murders in Oxford, England during the summer of 1851. Three women killed and mutilated. Could it have been a young Jack the Ripper almost four decades before he turned up again in East London? Was it a conspiracy propagated by the British Parliament? Or were there Satanist overtones?

Feeling tired suddenly, Laura rubbed her eyes and drank the last of her coffee. If there had been a series of murders in Oxford in 1851 wouldn't she have heard of them? She looked at the screen without really seeing it, letting the thoughts meander through her mind.

Maybe the murders had been forgotten. How thorough were police investigations in those days? Would the killings have been reported methodically? Was there a local newspaper in Oxford over a century and a half ago?

There were so many questions and so few answers. Worse, every time Laura thought she was peeling back a tiny corner of the mystery more puzzles would fall into her lap. All she had were pieces of the jigsaw, oddities that did not fit together. Indeed, they were pieces that seemed to have come from completely different jigsaws, and all she kept turning up were new chunks of these puzzles that appeared to have no link to any of the others. She considered delving further into other conspiracy websites but felt little inclination.

But she was convinced now that some contemporary murderer was working to some weird astrological agenda, and, if Brother Norman was to be believed, something not too dissimilar had happened at the time of the last conjunction and perhaps the time before and the time before that. And the link was astrology, the occult, some crazy alchemical connection. Laura's years of experience following New York City homicides and corruption could offer no help. But as she stared at the blue screen and Brother Norman's words drifted out of focus, she knew exactly what her next move should be.

Two hours later Laura was on the London train, peering through a grimy window onto dew-covered fields as they sped along. She hadn't woken Philip but had left him a note which said simply that she was going to London for the day to follow a lead, and that if there was any news he must call her on her mobile right away.

The idea of visiting Charlie Tucker now seemed obvious. He had been one of her best friends during her student days, and they had stayed in touch for a while after college. He was one of the most exciting and dynamic people she had ever met. His working-class Essex family had provided him with a colourful background. His father was a stallholder in a fruit market in Southend, and his mother, a former stripper, had died from cancer at thirty-nine. He had entered Oxford with the highest grades in the country that year, but had loathed almost everything about the city and the university. A socialist activist, on at least three separate occasions he had just escaped being sent down, and before he was twenty-one he had been investigated by M16 for his involvement in an extreme left-wing group. In his third year he had spent so much time on hunt sabs, demonstrations and covert anarchist activities that he almost missed a crucial final. Most astonishing of all was the fact that he still ended up with a First in mathematics.

Laura had never shown the slightest interest in politics, and that had probably been at the root of their closeness. Being an American, she hadn't cared much about modern British politics even though the politics of previous centuries fascinated her and had informed her studies in Renaissance art. She liked Charlie for his energy, his wit and his razor-sharp intelligence. He liked her, she supposed, because she didn't care about his views: she was a blank sheet upon which he could write any political slogan he wanted.

Just as Laura was leaving Oxford, Charlie had started a PhD on the Group Theory of Encryption, a topic, he claimed in letters to her, that was as far removed from human trivia as one could get. This seemed to satisfy him until, for no apparent reason, he dropped out and disappeared. In the last letter that Charlie had sent her from Oxford, he'd said simply that he was leaving – no explanations, no details.

And that had been that until, a year earlier, a post-card had arrived at Laura's apartment in Greenwich Village. It had been from Charlie and was post-marked London. He was going to be visiting the States, he'd written – would she like to meet up with him in New York?

He had of course despised the place, even though Laura could see in his eyes an irrepressible admiration for the undeniable glamour of it all. They had gone to a bistro on West 34th Street and she had listened to him mock the vanity of Manhattan, but he could not disguise from her entirely what she interpreted as a deeply buried acknowledgement that this city really was something amazing.

Charlie had turned forty a few years earlier, and

he was, he could now admit, tired: tired of radicalism, tired of seeing so little coming from his efforts, tired of life. He had all but given up, he had told her. About ten years earlier he had started to write a book about the circle of thirteenth-century mathematicians who became known as the Oxford Calculators: William Heytesbury, Richard Swineshead, John Dumbleton and, most prominently, Thomas Bradwardine. But he had never completed it. Instead, his research had drawn him into a line of investigation that took him to the heretical philosopher Roger Bacon, and from there to the entire world of medieval occultism.

The upshot, he told her, was that a few years earlier he had exchanged his political cap for a fascination with alternative lifestyles. He had gone deep into mysticism, the occult and what he referred to as 'the rich underbelly of the intellect'. He had even opened a little shop – near the British Museum in Bloomsbury – called White Stag, which specialised in arcane and alternative literature. He made a living of sorts from the place and it gave him the time and resources to pursue his own researches.

Laura had been a little surprised by these twists in Charlie's life. She herself had never been at all interested in the occult. But after a while, as she listened to him speak, it seemed to make sense that Charlie would have become absorbed with such ideas. And, indirectly, it was Charlie's visit that had given her the idea of a thriller about Thomas Bradwardine and a plot to kill King Edward II. Now, as she headed towards London hoping to find Charlie sitting quietly in his little shop, she felt a pang of guilt that she had failed to make contact with him during the entire three weeks she had been in England. Nor had she even told him that she was going to be coming over.

Arriving at Paddington Station a few minutes after eight-thirty, Laura caught the Underground to Warren Street. Emerging into heavy morning traffic, she realised she would be too early for Charlie. To kill time, she stopped for a coffee and a croissant at a Starbucks and then walked south down Tottenham Court Road. At an Internet café she stopped to check her e-mail, bought a newspaper and nursed a second cup of coffee, before heading east past Centre Point and along New Oxford Street to find the lane off Museum Street where she knew White Stag was situated. On the way she called Philip's mobile but all she got was an answer service.

As Laura turned along a street no more than four yards wide and within sight of the British Museum, she spotted the tiny shopfront, whose window was piled high with books. Above the door was an old-fashioned painted sign of a magnificent white stag.

From the outside the shop looked dark, silent and closed, but the door opened gently as she pushed. She smelled old paper and the fug of cigarette smoke. A single light bulb dangled from the cracked ceiling; the bare floorboards were scuffed and scratched. Every inch of wall space was covered with shelves packed with books of all shapes, colours and sizes. It was dingy but oddly comforting.

At the far end of the room stood an old desk. It had ugly, carved ash legs and the top was strewn with papers. An ancient-looking computer stood to one side, an overflowing ashtray the other. A waste-paper bin beside the desk was also over-brimming with scrunched-up paper and other detritus. Behind the desk a door leading to a pantry in the back of the shop stood open. Dull orange light emanated from inside and Laura could hear a kettle whistling. A few moments later a man emerged from the doorway and walked over to the desk. He seemed completely unaware of her. From his mouth dangled a cigarette and in his hand was a large grimy-looking mug. Laura gave a little cough.

'My God!' Charlie exclaimed, and put the mug down on the desk so carelessly that milky tea spilled over a pile of papers next to it. Stubbing out his cigarette in the ashtray, he bounded around the desk, his arms outstretched in welcome. 'Laura, baby,' he said as he embraced her.

She giggled and hugged him.

He held her at arm's length. 'You've lost weight, girl, and your 'air's too short.' His accent was pure Essex, untainted by Oxford, arcane literature or half a decade in Bloomsbury. 'Fancy a cuppa?'

'No, thanks, Charlie, just had enough caffeine to last me a year. But, boy, it's good to see you.'

He pulled over an old and battered chair and wiped the seat with his hand. Then he strode over to the door, locked it and flipped over the 'open' sign. 'You never know – the 'ordes we get in 'ere.' He laughed as he threw himself into the chair behind the desk.

Charlie had never been precisely the model of health and had always been underweight and pasty, but now he looked positively haggard and far older than his forty-four years. Laura had last seen him just a year ago but since then he had lost hair, lost weight, lost even more colour from his skin. He looked very unwell, as though he was suffering from a terminal illness, she concluded.

'Charlie, I hate to say this but you look dreadful.'

He shrugged. 'Been working 'ard, Laura. I feel great, though. Just me 'air falling out,' and he tugged at the thin greasy brown strands that hung down over his ears. 'Anyway, don't worry about me.' He grabbed a packet of cigarettes from beside a pile of papers on the desk, fished one out and lit it with an old-fashioned lighter. 'What brings you to this neck of the woods, then?'

'Actually, it was you . . .'

'Pull the other one!'

'I was starting a new novel, a book about Thomas Bradwardine. Remember we talked about him that night in New York? After you left I began to weave a little web.'

'You said you started – past tense. You hit writer's block?'

Laura looked around at the thousands of books lining the walls from floor to ceiling. Suddenly she felt very small. 'No, just a better idea.'

'Go on.'

'You've seen the news about the Oxford murders?'

'Yes,' he said quizzically.

'Well, can I trust you? As an old friend?'

'Of course.' He looked both surprised and a little hurt. 'You know that . . .'

'Yeah, I'm sorry. It's just . . . Well, the police haven't told the public everything they know. But then, they're actually in denial anyway – at least they were when I last spoke to them.'

'You're speaking in riddles, Laura.'

'The thing is, these murders have a ritualistic aspect to them. No, more than that – the murderer is following a schedule, an astrological schedule.'

Charlie's eyes narrowed. He took a long drag on

his cigarette. 'You say the murderer is working to a schedule, which implies you think he hasn't finished yet.'

'That's exactly what I think. I'm afraid he's only just begun.'

'OK.' Charlie leaned back in his chair, scrutinising Laura through the smoke that billowed in the air between them. 'Could you start from the beginning? I need to get a handle on this.'

Laura told him as much as she dared. When she had finished, she was alarmed to see that he had turned even paler than usual.

'You know something about this, don't you, Charlie?'

He took a final drag from his cigarette and pulled another from the packet, lighting it with the fading red tip of the first. 'Why do you say that?'

'I know you. Remember?' Laura noticed how dirty his fingernails were. She also saw that the index and middle fingers of his right hand, through which the cigarette protruded, were stained orange.

'Look, all I've 'eard are rumours. That's how the occult works these days. It's all Internet chat rooms, but we have to be discreet. If you know the language you can talk the talk, as they say.'

'And what does the talk tell you, Charlie?'

As he dragged deeply on the cigarette, his face became a skeletal mask. 'Something big is going down, something very big and very nasty.'

'What do you mean?'

'A group, a small group – completely anonymous, you understand – are playing dangerous games.'

'In Oxford?'

'In Oxford.'

'What sort of games?'

'That, darlin', I can't say, 'cos I dunno.'

'You don't know . . . ? Can't you hazard a guess?'

'People are too nervous to talk too much about this one.'

'OK.' Laura could not conceal her exasperation. 'I understand it's delicate, but forget the details – give me the broad strokes.'

Charlie was sucking on his cigarette again, filling the air with more grey smoke. Finally, he said: 'The word is that some very old hands are involved. I don't know what they're doing, nor do I wish to know, to be honest. But I've 'eard . . .' He paused for a full ten seconds. 'I've 'eard that there's a manuscript.'

'A manuscript?'

Charlie stubbed out the cigarette, took a gulp of his tea and picked up the lighter. He flicked it on, then closed the lid. Laura tried her best to ignore him but after he had repeated the action four times she suddenly sprang forward and grabbed the lighter from him.

'Charlie . . . *what* manuscript?'

'Laura, doll, I'd tell you if I knew, but you see, that's it. You know all I know. Whoever's behind this, it's someone big, and not just big within the community, either. Someone with great power.'

Chapter 19

After leaving the White Stag bookshop Laura tried Philip again, but still all she got was his answer service. Frustrated, she snapped her mobile shut. Part of her was almost ready to believe that Monroe was right after all and that the astrology stuff was just so much nonsense.

Five minutes later her phone rang. It was Philip.

'No news,' he said immediately. 'I have two missed calls from you. Sorry, my battery was flat. When are you getting back?'

She looked at her watch. 'As I'm here I might as well make a day of it. I'll probably catch a train about five-ish. Any chance of a pick-up?'

'No problem. Call me from Paddington.'

Laura caught the 5.29, which turned out to be a bad choice as it was stuffed with commuters. Fortunately, she had arrived at Paddington early and had found a seat; even so, she was jammed in for most of the journey and almost everyone on the train was getting off at Oxford. She allowed the rush of passengers to flow past her as they pulled into the station and she was one of the last to emerge from the carriage. She passed through the barrier, handed her ticket to the collector and saw Philip waiting for her at the door to the street.

'Something's happened, hasn't it?' Laura said, thrusting her hands into her pockets. She gazed down at her feet and took a deep breath before meeting his gaze. He put an arm around her shoulders and walked with her to his car, parked a few yards away. Their breath produced puffs of white in the chill air. It was a clear, starry evening and the temperature had dropped suddenly.

She folded herself into the passenger seat of the tiny old MGB and Philip turned the rather feeble heater to max.

'So tell me,' she said finally and sighed. 'And don't spare the grisly details.'

Philip started the engine and put the car into gear. Reversing out of the parking space, they joined the queue for the Botley Road. 'I would have phoned you,' he began. 'But I was only called in just over an hour ago, while you were on the train, and I thought it would be better if I . . .'

'Sure, Philip, that's OK.' Laura gave him a weak smile. 'I'm not angry with you. I'm just . . . fucking angry, period. So what happened?'

'According to Forensics, the murder occurred

between eight and ten last night. A couple this time, otherwise exactly the same MO.'

'A couple?'

'Young lovers. Caught in flagrante.'

'And – don't tell me – the girl's kidneys were taken?'

'Yes.' He looked at her, a little surprised.

'I did some reading on the train: *Ancient Astrology* by Evaline Tarintara. Garbage, of course, but it contains some useful hints for following the thoughts of a believer. Venus, the planet that entered Aries last night, is linked with the kidneys. I imagine the killer left another coin – copper this time?'

Philip nodded. 'You're right. So how do the planets, dates and metals match up?'

'From what Tom found out, it looks like there are two more planets due to join the conjunction, Mars and Jupiter, and two more murders planned. According to Ms Tarintara's book, Mars is linked with iron and the gall bladder; Jupiter is associated with tin and the liver.'

Philip nodded again but said nothing.

'So, this latest murder?' Laura asked matter-of-factly.

'Two students, house in East Oxford. They were having sex when the killer struck. Both victims had their throats slashed. The guy . . .' He paused for a moment. 'Simon . . . Simon Welding, untouched after

163

he was dispatched. The girl, Samantha Thurow, a beautiful . . .' As they pulled out onto the main road, Laura could see the muscles in Philip's jaw tense.

'Her kidneys were removed with surgical precision. According to the lab guys there is not a single fingerprint or any DNA from the perp left at the scene – just like the first two.' He hit the steering wheel with the flat of his hand suddenly, making Laura jump.

She looked out the passenger window, watching the buildings flash past. Ahead, a set of traffic lights had changed to red and Philip slowed to a halt.

'The bodies weren't discovered until early this evening. The couple were in a shared house. Two other students came back with their partners at about midnight. They went straight to bed and left for college this morning. It wasn't until after they got back from lectures that someone noticed bloody footprints on the landing carpet and leading from the couple's room. They hadn't heard anything from Simon and Samantha, and at about quarter to five they knocked down the bedroom door. The police arrived there just after five and I got the call about five-thirty.'

'Did the kids say when they last saw the victims?'

'They went out about seven.'

'Well, that doesn't help to narrow down the precise time of the murder, but surely Monroe believes me now?'

'I guess maybe he does,' Philip said. 'He wants us to go see him . . . at his house.'

Monroe's one-bedroomed apartment was in a massive house in North Oxford. It was the very opposite of his grubby little office at the police station. Furnished tastefully and decorated with style, it showed a completely different side to the man.

The sitting room was a high-ceilinged space with a fireplace, and there were real logs burning in the grate. Over the fireplace hung a huge modern abstract painting. The walls were painted a gentle green and a pair of cream suede sofas added warmth. The lighting was subdued and from a pair of expensive-looking speakers came the mellow strains of a Brian Eno album.

'Sit down,' Monroe said, gesturing towards one of the sofas.

'I know you think I owe you some sort of apology, Ms Niven,' he began. 'But I don't feel I do. However, I did want to thank you for the information you've given us.'

'You want to thank me? Is that it?'

'Well, what . . . ?'

'It strikes me that you had nothing much to go on in this case, Detective Chief Inspector. What Philip and I have told you may not have led to the killer – yet – but it deserves more than a mere thank-you.'

Now it was Monroe's turn to be confused. 'I'm sorry, I don't quite . . .'

'You don't quite understand? Well, first, stop calling me "Ms Niven". My name is Laura. And second, I think I have earned a place in this investigation.'

Monroe stared at her, his black eyes even more intense than usual. 'Why should I do that?' he asked.

'I think that what Laura is saying,' Philip chimed in, 'in her typically charming way, is that she can help us. And, for the record, I agree with her.'

'And I have some more information which may be of use,' Laura said coldly.

'What sort of information?' Monroe could not disguise his growing irritation.

'Why should I tell you?' Laura replied.

'Because, Ms Niven, if you don't, I will charge you with withholding information pertinent to a murder investigation, that's why.'

'Look, for Christ's sake,' Philip snapped. 'This is ridiculous. You're both behaving like children.'

Monroe stood up slowly. 'Forgive me,' he said. 'I've been rude. Would either of you like a drink?'

Laura shook her head.

'No, thanks,' Philip said.

Monroe walked over to a walnut cabinet, removed

a bottle of Scotch and a crystal tumbler and poured a small measure.

'I have every confidence in my men,' he said, 'and in my methods. Now, I would like you to apprise me of this new information, and of everything else you have found out about the case. And I will be happy to forget you ever threatened to withhold anything.'

Laura took a deep breath and met Monroe's gaze. 'Fine, Detective Chief Inspector. I have to cooperate, but at the same time you can't stop me conducting my own investigation into these crimes.'

'You're right, I can't. But equally, I can throw the book at you if you refuse to impart valuable information or in any way hinder the work of my team.'

'Of course you can. But that won't happen.'

'And you say this friend of yours claims he has no idea about the contents of the manuscript?' Monroe said when Laura had finished.

'Apparently not.'

'And that is all you know?'

'It is.'

For a fleeting moment, Laura could see suspicion flicker across Monroe's face, but then it was gone. 'Well, thank you for this,' he said and drained his glass. 'If you'll excuse me, I have a massive amount of paperwork to get through.'

Philip gripped Laura's arm and shook his head

almost imperceptibly, warning her not to argue. It was time to go.

Philip stepped into the car and unlocked the passenger door from the inside. Laura lowered herself into the bucket seat. He slipped the key into the ignition, but didn't start the engine. 'You didn't tell Monroe everything, did you?' he said.

Laura grinned and raised her eyebrows. 'You know me too well, honey.'

'What is it?'

She told him about the conspiracy theories and the murders of 1851.

'Just as well you didn't mention any of that. He'd probably think you'd finally flipped.'

'Yeah, you're probably right.'

'So what you going to do now, Holmes?'

'What do you mean?'

'After getting the bum's rush from Monroe.'

'Oh, that?' Laura snorted. 'People like Monroe just make me more determined than ever.'

From the window of his living room, John Monroe watched Philip's car pull out of the driveway. Then he refilled his glass and sat down in one of the sofas.

It was just his luck, he mused, that he should be landed with this pushy American who was opening up a whole can of writhing worms. But then, he had to admit, what she had unearthed *was* compelling. It was just that there were areas he had cordoned off in his mind.

How many years had it been now since that last incident? He cast his mind back. It must have been 1989. He had only been a police officer for two years by then. Yes, it was late in '89, the year when he and Janey had married. Cecilia Moore was the woman who had nearly destroyed his career before it had even started properly. She had been a clairvoyant, or at least that was what she and her followers claimed. She had been called in to help find an eighteen-year-old girl, Caroline Marsden, who had been missing for three weeks. He had been young, naive and optimistic, and he had also quite fancied Cecilia. He had put too much trust in the woman and her powers, and he had wasted valuable police time and resources after convincing his superiors that this medium could lead them to the missing girl.

Cecilia had made a big show of 'sourcing' Caroline Marsden, using what she had called 'remote viewing' to give clues to the police about where the girl would be found.

Monroe had been given too free a rein, he knew that now, but it was still no excuse. Believing Cecilia Moore's descriptions of where Caroline was being kept alive in a basement in Ealing, he had charged in only to find that the place was home to a retired couple from Bangalore. Caroline was found two weeks later – or, at least, enough of her had been found on a waste dump under the Hammersmith flyover for Forensics to flag a positive ID.

Promotion had come painfully slowly for the first five years after that, and Monroe had only survived through sheer stubbornness and determination. That struggle had ruined his relationship with Janey; they had split in 1993, childless after just four years of marriage.

He sipped his Famous Grouse and contemplated the fire. Could he let himself be drawn back into the occult again? Almost all the CID guys and uniforms who had mocked him behind his back last time round were either retired or working in other forces in other cities; the one or two who could remember Cecilia Moore wouldn't dare say anything this time. But it wasn't that: it was the principle of the thing. Monroe realised that he had no need to believe in this astrology junk himself for it to be the genuine motivation for the murderer, and he knew that Laura Niven and Philip Bainbridge were not cranks. In fact, he had to concede, they were both intelligent and well-meaning people whom he would probably have rather liked if he had met them under different circumstances.

And, of course, there was another factor, something he had not yet shared even with his team. He knew his local police history inside out: it had been one of his hobbies when he'd been a teenager. These murders bore a remarkable similarity to a long-forgotten case, the slaying of three young women and a male Oxford University student more than one hundred and fifty years earlier, in 1851.

Monroe put his glass down and paced over to the new Mac that he had bought only the previous week. He gave the mouse a nudge and the computer snapped out of hibernation mode. Going to a search engine, he paused for a second or two, thinking back to his meeting with Laura and Philip at the police station the night before. What had Laura called that website? Then he remembered and, in two-finger style, he tapped in almanac.com.

Chapter 20

They were sitting in a room adjoining the Inner Chamber. It was a small room, a pocket of air encased in stone sixty feet beneath the Bodleian Library. The walls were smooth, the floor polished and with a large Khotan rug covering the centre of the space. On this stood a mahogany table bare except for a silk runner stretching the length of the table and spilling over the ends. The room was lit by two dozen candles in a metal chandelier suspended from the centre of the curved ceiling. Two men sat opposite each other.

'I'm extremely disappointed in you,' said the Master, his voice devoid of emotion.

The Acolyte, dressed in a cream linen Armani suit, wide-collared white shirt and a green-and-red-striped Louis Vuitton silk tie arranged in a Windsor knot and nestled close to his Adam's apple, was seated in an identical chair. He stared across the table separating him from the Master and felt the colour drain from his face. 'I was going to explain.'

'I'm glad.'

'I was disturbed at the house. Someone was there.'

The Master raised an eyebrow.

'It was not an easy procedure, Master. I did not want to make an error and time was pressing.'

'You have been trained well, no?'

'I heard a sound from downstairs. I thought the girl's parents were returning early. I was obviously wrong.'

'Yes, you were.'

'I had not completed the removal. I took the body into the garden, but that was not suitable. Then I noticed the mooring for the family's punt. It seemed appropriate.'

'But why did you then move the punt along the bank?'

The Acolyte took a deep breath. 'I had the woman arranged in the punt. I had removed her brain when the tether came loose and the punt started to move away from its mooring. I tried to stop it, but I realised that if I was to scramble along the bank or fall in I would disturb the scene too much. I could do nothing but let it go. It must have become stuck in the bank a short way from the house.' The Acolyte looked down at his perfectly manicured nails.

The Master considered the other man's handsome face. He thought how much younger than his years he looked. He had been lucky with his genes – high cheekbones, a well-shaped mouth and eyes so blue that he could have been wearing coloured contract lenses. 'You haven't heard, have you?'

'Heard what, Master?'

'Your mistake may yet have very serious consequences. Thames Valley CSI have found physical evidence close to the house on the river.'

'That's impossible. I . . .'

'They have a partial print, as well as traces of leather and plastic.'

The Acolyte shook his head. His eyes were ablaze with indignation.

'Did you check your protective suit before disposing of it?'

The Acolyte closed his eyes and let out a small sigh.

'Well?'

'No.'

'So, it is not impossible, then.'

Chapter 21

James Lightman's house was one of the finest in Oxford. Although he had come from a relatively ordinary background – his lawyer father and teacher mother had been intellectually solid but never wealthy – his deceased wife, Susanna Gatting, had been the only child of one of the most powerful and influential men in England, Lord Gatting. Once a Chancellor of the Exchequer, Neville Gatting had been able to trace his family and their vast fortune back to the time of George I.

Lightman's father-in-law had died almost twenty years earlier. Susanna's mother had succumbed to cancer two years before her daughter was killed; and, as a result, Lightman had inherited the Gatting billions. His four-storey Georgian house in North Oxford served as a city home while a staff of a dozen maintained the Gatting estate in Brill on the Oxfordshire-Buckinghamshire border.

'Three visits in one week, Laura? People will start to talk,' Lightman said.

Laura laughed and walked over to peck him on the cheek. 'Strictly business, I'm afraid, James.'

'How disappointing. Anyway, come into the study, dear girl.'

Laura sat down in one of a pair of old leather chairs close to a homely blaze burning in the fireplace. She had been disappointed at first when the front door was opened by Malcolm Bridges, the assistant whom she had first met a few days earlier at the library. He had asked her in politely enough but had seemed to resent the intrusion. Then James had emerged from his room, full of welcoming smiles and banter. Bridges had taken her coat and headed off quickly to the kitchen to make some tea.

'I thought your assistant worked just at the library,' Laura said.

'You don't like him, do you, Laura?'

'I didn't say that. I was just surprised to see him here.'

'There's nothing sinister about it, dear girl. He helps out here to earn some extra money. Malcolm's a post-doc research assistant in the Psychology Department. He has a girlfriend and a potholing passion to support, apparently.' Lightman jabbed the burning logs with an ornate antique poker before settling back into the other chair a few feet from Laura. 'Anyway, I have a bone to pick with you.'

'Oh?'

'You weren't entirely honest with me the other day, were you?'

'What do you mean?'

'About the plot of your novel.'

'Yes, I'm sorry,' Laura said. 'I wasn't really telling a lie. I *am* planning a contemporary novel, but these recent murders were the inspiration. I should have been straight with you. I knew you would find out sooner or later.'

'To be honest, I don't usually take much notice of the news. I only heard about this because Malcolm happened to mention it this morning.'

'Well, that's good – because I need your help again.'

'Hah!' Lightman laughed. 'I always admired your cheek.'

'I thought that if the Chief Librarian at the Bodleian, and a world authority on ancient literature, couldn't help, who could?'

'You say all the right things, Laura. Cheek and charm – a deadly combination. So, what is it?'

'In the novel I want to build part of the plot around a mysterious document, an ancient manuscript, perhaps a Greek or Latin text that has something to do with the murders.'

'And you're basing this on something real?'

Laura paused for a moment and looked into the fire, watching the flames lap around the glowing logs. 'Well, that's really what I wanted to ask you. What is the likelihood of something like that turning up?'

Lightman was about to reply when Malcolm Bridges appeared with a tray and walked over to the fireplace.

'I hope tea is all right,' he said to Laura.

'Perfect,' she replied. Bridges laid the tray on the table. Pouring tea and milk into two cups, he handed one to Laura.

'Sugar?'

'No, thanks.'

Bridges was about to go when Lightman said. 'Malcolm, ancient manuscripts surfacing in the modern world? What are the chances?'

Laura turned towards Lightman, feeling surprised and irritated, but he was not looking her way. She realised immediately that her old mentor had done this just to be annoying, so she said nothing.

'Manuscript? What sort of manuscript?' Bridges looked a little startled by the question.

'I don't know.' A brief sardonic smile played across Lightman's lips. 'Laura was about to explain. Do sit down, dear boy.'

Bridges took a seat by the desk.

'Laura's plotting a new novel and wants to introduce the idea of an ancient document or text appearing in the twenty-first century.' Lightman turned back to Laura. 'Have you thought about what sort of ancient manuscript is discovered?'

'Well, I was hoping *you* would have some idea, James. But if . . .'

'There have been some amazing finds in recent decades,' Lightman declared. 'The most famous of all, of course, was the discovery of the Dead Sea Scrolls over fifty years ago in Wadi Qumran. So it does happen. However, that said, I haven't heard of anything new appearing for quite some time. Have you, Malcolm?'

'Nothing very recent,' Bridges replied. 'There was the Elias Ashmole material found at Keble College, of course, but that was almost thirty years ago.'

'And don't forget the *Codex Madrid*, the Leonardo notebooks. They were found in some discarded boxes in a Spanish library in the 1960s. Oh, and Wainwright's unearthing of that manuscript attributed to Herodotus, but that was found, when? 1954, 1955?'

'OK,' Laura said, distractedly. 'So at least it's not silly fantasy.'

'No, no, not at all,' Lightman replied. 'Just, well, extremely rare . . . sadly.' He took a sip of tea and was about to add something when the front doorbell rang.

'That will be Professor Turner,' Bridges said. 'He was due here at 9.45.'

'Oh hell,' Lightman said. 'I'd completely forgotten about him. Look, I'm sorry, Laura, but I have to see Turner now – I've put him off twice already. Wants to talk about a new annexe to the library – frightfully boring, but essential, I'm afraid.'

Although she had hoped to delve deeper, Laura hid her disappointment. 'No problem, James,' she said. 'I feel very reassured.'

They walked towards the door of the study. 'There was one other quick question I had for you, though. Can you spare just a second?'

Lightman nodded.

'Have you ever heard of a serial killer in Oxford in 1851?'

Lightman hesitated for a second. Then he said: 'You know, I *do* recall hearing of something along those lines. It was the year of the Great Exhibition. Two young women. But that hardly constitutes a serial killing, does it? I'm sorry, Laura. Goodness, I haven't been of such great service today, have I?'

Chapter 22

After two unsuccessful attempts to telephone Philip, Laura remembered that he had told her that he was going to London to see about a possible commission to do the photographs for a book about Tasmania. He would be staying in London overnight.

Back in Woodstock, she went through the books in Philip's library to see if she could find anything on the murders of 1851. But there was absolutely nothing and an Internet search proved equally fruitless. That evening she stayed on the sofa with Jo, watching TV and eating chocolates.

Next morning Laura was returning from a long walk in the woods near the house when she saw a car pull into Philip's driveway. She had hired a new vehicle the previous evening and was vaguely surprised that the company was delivering when they'd said they would. Half an hour later she was on the road to Oxford and keying in the number of Philip's mobile.

'Where are you?' she asked excitedly.

'Just coming into Oxford on the M40 – why?'

'I need to see you a.s.a.p.'

'Well, I've got to drop off a couple of discs at the station. I'm late with them already. I was going to go straight home, but do you want to meet for a coffee?'

'Sounds good. Where?'

'How about Isabella's on Ship Street off Cornmarket?'

'OK. How soon can you get there?'

'Look, give me half an hour – no, forty-five minutes.'

Laura glanced at her watch. It was approaching quarter to nine. 'OK, see you at 9.30.' And she snapped the phone shut.

Isabella's was a tiny, seriously understated coffee shop on one of the quieter roads off the pedestrian thoroughfare of Cornmarket Street in the centre of Oxford. It consisted of fewer than a dozen little tables and the decor was drab and faded, but Philip liked the owner, Isabella Frascante, a middle-aged Italian widow who was always friendly and welcoming and made, he believed, the best espresso in the Home Counties.

Laura was there ten minutes early and saw Philip pass the window and walk in. They had the place to themselves and as Philip sat down the owner saw him and beamed.

'The usual, please, Isabella,' he said and leaned back in the chair.

'How was it?' Laura asked.

'What?'

'You got the job?'

'Oh, maybe. I hope so. They're supposed to be e-mailing me about it this afternoon. So, what's new with you?'

'I went to see James Lightman, but he wasn't much help, unfortunately. I think we have to get hold of some more information on the 1851 murders. But where would you begin to find out about a series of murders in this city over a hundred and fifty years ago? The newspapers of the day?'

'I guess,' Philip replied. Isabella arrived with the coffee and Philip took a sip. 'Bloody excellent. I've got to get her to tell me her secret some day,' he whispered as she walked away.

'Hah! The secret is that she's Italian, Philip. A pasty Brit with no culinary skills like you is hardly going to match up, now, are you?'

Philip laughed off the insult. Taking another mouthful, he smacked his lips.

'So,' Laura said. 'Newspapers?'

'Not sure there was a local paper in Oxford in 1851.'

'There must have been, Philip. This place is built on paper.'

'Yeah, books, Laura, books. Newspapers would have been considered vulgar.'

'By the university, maybe. But other people lived here then, remember, just like they do now.' She rolled her eyes.

'OK,' Philip replied. 'We can find out at the library. Local history section. If there was a contemporary report on the murders it will be there, probably on microfiche.'

'Cool. Let's go, then.' Laura was out of her chair and ignoring Philip's protests. 'Goddamn it, man, put it in a take-out cup. It can't be *that* special. And for Christ's sake wipe your mouth!'

It turned out that there had been three local newspapers in Oxford in 1851. *Jackson's Oxford Journal* was the most popular and the oldest, having been published since 1753. The other two, the *Oxford University Herald* and the *Oxford Chronicle and Berks and Bucks Gazette* were relative newcomers.

'Looks like you were wrong, Philip. Not one but three vulgar newspapers,' Laura noted.

'I stand corrected.'

'How do we access the archives?'

'Look in the library catalogue,' Philip replied. He moved the mouse to flick back to the file manager.

'The library has everything catalogued by decade. Then we'll have to search by newspapers and journals.'

A few more clicks and they had opened the file for 1850–1860. A couple more and they had the newspaper catalogue on the screen. 'Now we do a search by keywords. You don't have names, I suppose?'

Laura shook her head.

'OK. Well, that makes it harder. But we could try putting in 'murder', I guess, see what happens.'

There were 1819 entries.

Laura groaned.

'Don't be so impatient. Refine the search,' Philip said.

'Try "serial killer".'

'The expression didn't exist then.'

Laura was trying to recall what she had read two mornings earlier. 'The website I mentioned talked of three women being killed and mutilated during the summer of 1851'

'OK, let's refine the search with "young woman".'

Philip pressed 'enter' and a new screen appeared. 'Three hundred and forty-two entries containing the words "murder" and "young woman". Better, but not good.'

'OK, refine the search again with "mutilation". That should definitely narrow things down,' Laura pulled her chair closer to the screen.

Philip tapped the keys and the list changed. This time there were seventeen entries that included the words 'murder', 'young woman' and 'mutilation'.

'Now we're getting somewhere,' Laura said.

The records were on microfiche. Philip noted the catalogue numbers and they joined the queue for the harassed librarian at the main desk. It took twenty minutes for them to find the films, learn how to use the machine and to feed the first roll of microfiche into the viewer.

The first reference was from *Jackson's Oxford Journal* and was dated 16 June 1851. It gave few details.

The next reference came from the *Oxford Chronicle* of 18 June. This reported the same story but with a little elaboration. In this article the woman had reportedly been found in a 'state of undress' in a barn in Headington, and she had died from unspecified knife wounds, her body 'horribly mutilated.'

The next three were reports from the trio of Oxford papers and all from the same day, 24 June. A second murder had been committed, and the killer had followed a slightly different MO. A young couple had been found dead in a field north of the city. They had been left naked, and the woman's body had, according to the *Oxford University Herald*, been 'cruelly disfigured'.

By the day after the third incident on 9 July, it had become the biggest story in Oxford for years; the reporting was now extensive and the innate gentlemanly restraint of the journalism had become tinged with what was, for the time, an unseemly overexcitement. An editorial in the *Oxford Chronicle* of 10 July read:

With the latest report yesterday of a further abhorrent murder, in this instance a young woman in the neighbourhood of Forest Hill on the road to London, considerable fears are growing that the Police Force are facing unprecedented difficulties in elucidating the factors behind the succession of vile murders that have plagued our city and its environs since the death of a young woman on 16th June. Whilst commending the skill and dedication of the officers leading the investigation, we feel that it is our duty to highlight the natural anxieties of all the people of Oxford. The police have of course noted that all those murdered have been young people, the eldest being just twenty-one; and in one case the obscenity involved an unchaperoned couple meeting illicitly. It is also a matter of public knowledge that with this second incident the young man was a university student, that the man's body was unmolested after the murderer had dispatched him, but that the unfortunate young ladies, were, in each case, killed by knife, before being mutilated in the most foul manner.

Sources, which it is our duty and obligation to withhold, have divulged the fact that a suspect was apprehended at the scene of the latest atrocity and subsequently questioned. So there remains hope, and we all pray that this latest development may speed the police to an early resolution to this most horrendous series of crimes, thus removing inordinate fear from all who live within these city walls. In this cause, the *Chronicle*, and, I feel confident in believing, the great majority of our readers, will support the officers of the Police Force with whole-hearted enthusiasm.

'Positively tabloid,' Philip said as he and Laura finished reading the piece.

For the next hour they ploughed through every report they had found from the catalogue.

Either through fear of offending their readership or because details were never revealed by the police, all three newspapers were short on explicit detail. Phrases like 'horrible mutilation', 'devilish disfigurement' and 'cruel abuse' littered the accounts. But what interested Laura and Philip most was the story of the suspect picked up at the scene of the Forest Hill murder.

Nathaniel Milliner was what the politically incorrect journalists of the time referred to as an 'imbecile'. He was fifteen but could speak only with a severe slur, he walked with a limp and his back was deformed. He was the son of a professor of medicine, John Milliner, who had steadfastly refused to put his son into an institution. After hours of interrogation the police had finally accepted the boy's claim that he had merely stumbled upon the dead bodies while he had been out near Forest Hill flying a kite. They had no evidence with which to convict Nathaniel and it seemed clear that Professor Milliner, who was one of the most important figures within the academic community, had protected his son during the investigation in the same way that he had for fifteen years protected him from the prejudices of Victorian society.

Two of the three Oxford papers had remained sceptical and it was clear from almost all the reports in the *Chronicle* and the *Herald* that the editors had wanted to see Nathaniel swing. Only *Jackson's Oxford Journal* reported the events in a balanced fashion and refused to come out against the boy. Then, suddenly, the whole pace of the story changed. A week after the Forest Hill murder, the police arrested a man named Patrick Fitzgerald, an Irish labourer who was working on the construction of a new canal in Oxford. Two witnesses came forward to say they had seen him at the first two murder scenes just before the bodies were found. Another, an anonymous workmate, told police that Fitzgerald had been 'stinking drunk' in a pub called the Ferret and Fox close to the canal excavation site, and that late on the night of the double murder he had, according to a report in the *Chronicle*, confessed to him: 'I have blood on my hands, so much blood.'

Fitzgerald's trial began on 9 August. After just two court appearances the jury was unanimous in finding him guilty. He was hanged on 12 August.

'Frustrating,' Laura said. 'The murders sound identical to the recent killings, but there are no details; without those it could all just be a coincidence.'

'But it must be significant that the murders stopped after the police caught this Fitzgerald character.'

'Yeah, but what evidence were they working on? What do you think about Nathaniel Milliner?' Laura asked.

'He could have been a complete innocent. The police obviously concluded he was and they hanged the labourer. But it all seems a bit too neat to me.'

'Why?'

'The witnesses suddenly coming out of the woodwork and claiming to have seen Fitzgerald near the scenes of the murders just before the bodies were found. The victims had probably been dead for hours before they were discovered; it proves nothing.'

'Yeah, but the guy had been at both the first two murder scenes, hadn't he?'

'So they claim.'

'And this workmate. People can say some pretty wild things when they're drunk. Means nothing.'

'We would certainly need a little more precise evidence to bring a conviction today,' Philip said.

'And have you noticed?' Laura asked. 'These reports say almost nothing about the killings. There're no details here. It smells bad, you know?'

Philip nodded.

'God, it really is frustrating. There must be more on these murders.'

'Maybe, but I doubt you'll unearth any more detail than you have here.'

They fell silent for a moment and Laura looked at the screen where the last report was still on display. Then, suddenly, she said: 'What about police records? Surely there must be an official report on the murders?'

'From 1851?'

'Well, why not?'

'I suppose it's possible. It wouldn't be here in Oxford, though. The police station was rebuilt in the 1950s, and with the amount of paper that place gets through each year I can't imagine they keep records more than ten years, at most.'

'But the records must go somewhere.'

'Yes, they do,' Philip replied. 'The Public Records Office in Kew.'

'Would they be computerised?'

'I doubt it.'

Laura was about to reply when her phone bleeped. Looking at the screen she saw that she had an SMS. 'It's from Charlie,' she said. 'He says he has some new information on the manuscript. Wants to meet us at his shop at four o'clock today.'

Chapter 23

As Laura and Philip left the library the heavens opened. They ran for the multi-storey where Laura had parked earlier. By the time they got there they were both soaked.

'Leave your car at the police station until we get back from London,' Laura suggested. 'We'll take this. It's warmer, faster . . . and a whole lot drier.'

Philip shrugged. No matter what he said, Laura, he knew, could never be made to appreciate the beauty of vintage sports cars like his beloved MGB, a car first built in a tiny workshop off Longwall Street – less than half a mile from where they now stood.

The roads out to Woodstock were barely visible through the downpour. It was not yet midday but the sky was almost black and the street lights had come on. Headlights rushed towards them through the curtains of rain and, to the irritation of those behind her, Laura took things particularly slowly. Forced, as she put it, to drive on the wrong side of the road, she was taking no chances. By the time they reached the house in Woodstock, she felt exhausted with the effort of concentrating so hard on the road ahead. She was seeing white spots in front of her eyes.

She pulled in as close as she could to the back door and made a dash for the shelter of the porch as Philip fumbled for his key. He slipped it into the lock, but the door was already open. They both walked into the kitchen.

'Hello?' Philip called.

'In here.' It was Jo's voice.

A fire was blazing in the living room and a Django Reinhardt track beat melodically from Philip's iPod, which he had hooked up to a pair of speakers. Jo was sitting on the sofa next to another young woman. Philip recognised her vaguely. The girl was sobbing and Jo was trying to comfort her.

'What's happened?' Laura asked. 'Jo?'

'This is Marianne – she's in my topology group.' The young woman looked rather embarrassed and wiped the tears away.

'I don't mean to cause . . .' she began. She had an exceptionally high-pitched voice, the voice of a little girl.

'Don't be silly,' Jo replied. 'Mom, Marianne found this in her pigeonhole at college.' She handed her mother a sheet of paper.

It was a computer-manipulated image, Marianne's

head superimposed on a pornographic photograph of a nude model spreadeagled on a bed. Her hands and feet had been tied to the corners of the bed with thick rope. Using some sophisticated computer software someone had simulated a huge rip the length of the woman's abdomen, and a portion of her intestines was spilling from the gash. Above the picture in bright red lettering was written: *This Is What I'd Like to Do to You.*

'Do you have any idea who might have done this?' Philip asked.

'No, no, not really.'

'Not really?'

'Well, there *is* one creepy guy in our year.'

'He's a real lech – a really serious lech, actually,' Jo added. 'Russell, Russell Cunningham. He's a psychology student but comes to some of our stats classes. Handsome, in a sort of pukey Ricky Martin kinda way, but really creepy. He's always looking at me as if he's mentally undressing me. Not nice.'

'Has this guy ever tried it on?' Laura asked Marianne.

'I don't think he'd have the nerve to actually do anything,' Marianne replied.

'You may be right,' Philip said. 'But I don't think you can go accusing anyone. You certainly have to report this, though, Marianne. I don't want to frighten you,' he added carefully. 'But it may have some bearing on the current murder investigation.'

Marianne turned visibly pale.

'I did think that myself, but I didn't like to say,' Jo said. 'I haven't been into college since the accident, and it's the Easter vac, but everyone left in hall is totally psyched-out by what's happening.'

'I know at least two girls who've gone home to their parents until the whole thing blows over. They would normally have stayed in Oxford to work through the holiday,' Marianne added.

'I can't say I'm surprised,' Laura said with a sigh and sat down in an armchair across from the sofa. 'I think you all have to be especially careful.'

'You kinda get used to this sort of thing in New York,' Jo remarked. 'But I don't know, I thought Oxford would be . . .'

'Oxford's a pretty place, no doubt about that,' Philip said. 'But the people are fundamentally the same as those who live in the Bronx – or in Timbuktu, for that matter.'

'So you think I should take this horrible picture to the police?'

'I think you have to.' Philip did not hesitate. 'It's probably nothing more than a sick joke, but Forensics will want to have a look, just in case.'

Chapter 24

The Public Records Office is a modern brick building surrounded by luxuriant and beautifully maintained gardens in the upmarket district of Kew on the south side of the Thames in west London. Here an average house is worth as much as an entire street of terraced cottages in Sheffield, and the demographic is skewed towards the As and Bs as defined by disposable income and career status. By London standards at least, the tree-lined streets are clean and safe and the cafés and shops are largely frequented by designer families with children dressed from Gap and Kenzo Kids, privately educated and cared for by American and Swedish nannies.

Founded by an Act of Parliament in 1838, the Public Records Office is home to some of the most iconic documents ever penned. These include the original Domesday Book, returns from the parliamentary elections of 1275, an inventory of Elizabeth I's jewels, William Shakespeare's will, the confession of Guy Fawkes, and the minutes of Churchill's

War Cabinet during the Battle of Britain. It is also the repository of many records of criminal investigations dating back to the earliest years of the British police force.

To Laura and Philip's surprise they found that the police archives were indeed stored on computer files and that they could be accessed from a set of terminals in the reading room. The system was similar to the one at the Oxford library, and they found their way around it pretty quickly.

Philip opened the file for 1851 and then put in a search for 'Oxford murder investigations'. There were thirty-seven documents, listed chronologically and dating from the time when each investigation was officially started. He entered 'June'. Two investigations had begun that month. The first was a file only 22K in size, the other was 231K. Philip clicked on the second, reasoning that the serial killings starting that month would have been one of the largest criminal investigations conducted in Oxford for many years.

The file opened and they read the title: *Investigation into the Connected Murders of Molly Wetherspoon, Cynthia Page, Edward Makepeace and Lucinda Gabling, All of Oxford, Between the Dates of 15 June and 9 July 1851*. It was 120 pages long.

'I'll get us some coffee,' Laura said.

Philip tapped her arm and pointed to a sign on

the wall that read: NO EATING OR DRINKING IN READING ROOM.

'Ah,' she sighed. 'In that case, we'd better get started.'

Philip clicked down the file and the first page of text immediately sucked them in. It was entitled CASE SUMMARY and beneath the title was written: STRICTLY PRIVATE. NOT TO BE COPIED. NOT FOR PUBLIC PERUSAL.

Laura felt the hairs rise on the nape of her neck and suddenly all thoughts of coffee were forgotten.

The summary began:

'Our investigation commenced on 15 June, the Year of Our Lord 1851 and it was officially closed on 12 August of the same year.' It then went on to list the names, addresses and some personal details of the victims, as well as some background concerning Patrick Fitzgerald. There then followed three pages describing the murders, each reported in chronological order.

'My God,' Laura exclaimed. 'This is unreal.'

If the style of language was ignored, the locations changed and a few archaisms dismissed, the descriptions that Philip and Laura were reading could almost have been written during the past week. In each case the victims had died from stab wounds or by having their throats slashed. With the one incident that involved a male victim and a female one, the murdered man had been killed and then left, but the girl had been mutilated with surgical precision. In the case of the first murder, Molly Wetherspoon had her kidneys removed. In the second, the female victim, Cynthia Page, had her brain taken from her skull, and in the third murder the liver had been taken from the slain girl Lucinda Gabling.

Here were details that had never been released to the press of the time. At the scene of each murder a coin had been found. The first had been made of copper, the second of silver, the third of tin. Laura felt icy fingers run along her spine.

The commanding officer's summary report read:

After conducting a detailed and thorough investigation into the series of murders committed in this city between 15 June and 9 July 1851 we have reached the conclusion that the murders were committed by Mr Patrick Fitzgerald of Dublin, a labourer, aged 31. This official conclusion was based upon the testimony of three witnesses and later confirmed in a written confession obtained from Mr Fitzgerald on 16 July.

However, I would like to add a personal addendum to the official secret record pertaining to the events described above.

It is my personal conviction (and I feel I must here reiterate that this is an expression of my personal conviction alone) that Mr Fitzgerald was not responsible for the murders under investigation.

Until the time of Mr Fitzgerald's arrest, the press had taken upon themselves the task of inciting public feeling about this case, feeling that was both emotional and volatile. They did this by creating a scapegoat in the sorry form of a young man named Nathaniel Milliner who was accused of murdering all the victims.

However, I believe this to be an entirely erroneous notion. I am convinced that the young boy in question could never have committed these horrendous acts. In each case, the female victims had internal organs removed with expert precision and there were definite, but unreadable occult overtones to all four murders. Nathaniel Milliner is an imbecile with barely the talent to hold a knife and fork at the dinner table. Indeed, my overwhelming suspicions lay entirely elsewhere, and I believe that the murders were committed by a trained and highly skilled individual, possibly a doctor or a surgeon.

After the fourth murder, when the young boy, Nathaniel Milliner, was apprehended at the scene of the killing at Forest Hill, another individual was also present at the scene and was asked to accompany myself and my officers to the Oxford Police Station for further questioning.

This individual is a very senior member of the academic community here in Oxford and so all investigations and questioning were required to be conducted with the utmost probity and attention. The individual was helpful with our enquiries, but I took it upon myself to compose detailed notes on the interview immediately after the individual was allowed to leave our custody. Within these notes I commented upon the following indisputable facts:

1) Stains which looked remarkably like blood were to be found on his jacket and his shirt.
2) When he was encountered close to the scene of the crime, the gentleman in question appeared to be in a highly agitated and anxious state, and he was apparently confused by our presence there.
3) When later interviewed at the station, he told us that he had travelled to Forest Hill directly from a local shoot on the land of Lord Willerby (a close friend) whose estate is indeed in the environs of Forest Hill.
4) Lord Willerby later confirmed this account was entirely true.

To me it seemed undeniable that the gentleman in question was behaving abnormally. Even so, having agreed to return the next day for further questioning, the gentleman was permitted to leave. This individual did not return, nor was he ever asked to return. Instead, on 10 July, the day after the fourth murder,

I was summoned to attend a private meeting with a senior officer who informed me that any further investigation into the affairs of the aforementioned gentleman must be terminated forthwith and that the gentleman was to be left in peace. I was also informed that Nathaniel Milliner should henceforth be left equally unmolested. Five days later, Mr Fitzgerald was arrested by my officers and brought to the police station for questioning.

Here ends my personal addendum.

Signed: Chief Detective Jeffrey Howard.

'Wow,' Laura exclaimed.

'Wow, indeed.'

'So Patrick Fitzgerald was nothing more than a fall guy. And the police knew it?'

'Looks like it.'

'I find that amazing.'

'You shouldn't. Remember, Laura, in 1851 the police force had only been in existence for, what? – twenty years? There have been many similar cover-ups far more recently, I can assure you.'

'And it was one hell of a cover-up,' Laura remarked. 'Neither the boy, Nathaniel Milliner, nor the labourer, Patrick Fitzgerald, had anything to do with it. It was this "gentleman", an "individual" who cannot be named.'

'What I find just as amazing is that this Chief

Detective Jeffrey Howard could be allowed to include this report,' Philip said.

'Classic case of covering one's ass,' Laura responded.

'Yes, but how could a relatively junior investigating officer be allowed to point the finger, however subtly it was done?'

'He must have added this long after the event. Look.' She flicked back. 'It's dated January 1854. Maybe Howard was about to leave the force, or the files were being moved and he knew that no one would be interested in looking at them, until perhaps, one day . . .'

'That has to be it,' Philip replied. 'There's no way Howard could have made his feelings known at the time – he would have been booted out . . . at the very least.'

'The guy found at the scene of the Forest Hill murder was obviously someone important, someone with amazing contacts.'

'I would have thought it's pretty obvious who that was.'

'Nathaniel's father?'

'Our eminent Professor of Medicine, John Milliner.'

'Howard almost says as much in the last line, doesn't he?' Laura responded. 'What did he write?' She flicked back through the text once more: 'Here it is: "The gentleman should be left in peace. I was also informed that Nathaniel Milliner should henceforth be left equally unmolested."'

'So, what have we got here?' Philip said. 'These murders were almost identical to the recent ones – similar mutilations, similar metal coins – and the whole thing was a cover-up: the killings were almost certainly committed by Milliner, an important member of the university, someone with friends in very high places. There's also the fact that the university was the real power-broker in Oxford in 1851. The authorities would have done everything possible to keep the truth quiet. They would have closed ranks, and they would have set up someone they viewed as insignificant trash. So they framed a penniless Irish navvy who had a record. Fitzgerald was just perfect. Poor bastard. Of course, the real clincher will be if we put the exact dates of these murders into almanac.com and find they match with the removed organs and the type of coins found at each scene.'

'It would, but we don't have with us the passwords that Tom gave us, so that'll have to wait until we get back to Oxford,' Laura replied. 'Let's go see what Charlie has to say.'

Chapter 25

The worst of the traffic was around Kew itself. Mothers in four-wheel drives on the school run had no qualms about cutting across lanes, and sales reps racing back to their admin centres to clock off early added their own hazards.

Philip had taken over the driving. 'Getting around this place is like playing fucking Space Invaders,' he complained as a young woman in a Grand Cherokee jeep suddenly appeared out of a side street. 'God, and isn't that just typical?' he yelled, slamming his hand down on the horn. 'Look at that on her bloody rear window – Baby On Board!'

By the time they reached the Westway they had started to make good time, until they crossed over the Baker Street intersection where they got snarled up again. It was almost four-thirty as they turned along Museum Street.

Philip indicated right and was just turning into the narrow street when an ambulance emerged and blocked their way. Philip reversed out quickly and the ambulance sped off in the direction of Tottenham Court Road. Pulling into the lane the first thing they saw were flashing blue lights.

Laura dashed out of the car even before Philip had put on the handbrake. A police car stood directly outside the White Stag bookshop and next to it was a small blue van. A man in a white plastic oversuit was sliding into the driver's seat of the van and another was already seated inside. A uniformed officer stood at the door to the shop, and as Laura ran up two plain-clothes officers emerged.

'What's happened here?' Laura exclaimed. As she reached the doorway she could see a pool of blood on the floor just inside the shop.

'And you are?' one of the officers asked. The other looked on as Philip reached them.

'My name's Laura Niven. I'm an old friend of the owner, Charlie Tucker.'

'Philip Bainbridge. We got a call from Charlie earlier . . .'

The blue van was edging away from the kerb. 'Sanders,' the officer turned to his colleague. 'Tell Forensics home time will have to wait an extra five. I would at least like a verbal from them before they go skipping off.' His voice sounded husky and tired. He extended a hand. 'Detective Jones. I'm sorry, Ms Niven, Mr Bainbridge. I'm afraid I have to inform you that your friend died earlier this afternoon.'

'But that's . . .'

'That's?'

'Well, he texted us, texted me at – I don't know – when was it, Philip? Just before midday?' Laura couldn't hide the shakiness in her voice.

Philip nodded.

'We arrived here about an hour ago,' Jones said. 'The body was taken away just now; after our Forensics chaps were finished.' He pointed towards the opening into Museum Street where the ambulance had nearly collided with them. 'One of the new private ambulance companies. Got here pretty sharpish, I'll give them that.' Then he noticed the Forensics officer walking over from the van. 'Excuse me.'

Out of the corner of her eye Laura could still see the crimson puddle on the bookshop floor. An intense nauseous feeling swept over her. She took a couple of deep breaths.

'You OK?' Philip looked as shocked as she felt.

'I guess,' she replied unconvincingly. 'But this is just madness.'

Jones returned from the van, shaking his head.

'Sorry about that. I know this is a difficult time for you both, but I would be grateful if you could answer a few questions for us.'

'Questions? You don't . . .'

'Ms Niven, you are not a suspect at the moment,

if that's what you're thinking. Mr Tucker died from a gunshot wound, fired at close range. We would like to know more about him. Was he depressed? Can you offer us some background?'

'Shot? I don't . . .'

Philip took Laura's arm. 'Yes, of course,' he said evenly. 'Anything we can do.'

Chapter 26

Oxford: 12 August 1690. Close to midnight.

They were all exhausted. At forty-eight Isaac Newton was the oldest by almost twenty years. Landsdown had seen but thirty summers, and Fatio, the pretty Fatio, was but a score and five years out of the cradle. Newton felt ancient.

They had all the necessary codes and procedures, of course, so they had been able to pass unmolested through the 'Three Stages of Attainment', each one leading inexorably to the next. But the wisdom of the Ancients, thought by most adepts to have been lost to history in the flames of Alexandria, could do nothing to protect them from the stifling heat along the three hundred yards of passageway that led from the college wine cellar to their destination: the secret labyrinth that stretched from a place deep below the Bodleian north to the foundations of the Sheldonian Theatre two score and ten yards distant. Their nostrils were clogged with the stench of old, rotten earth and damp, decaying dead things.

Between the second test and the third, they had rested and drunk wine from a flask. The wine was good but too warm. After the briefest pause they had continued on their way. There was no time to linger tonight.

After completing the third and final test. Landsdown handed the manuscript back to Newton who returned it to safety inside his shirt. This and the ruby sphere were valuable beyond imagining. Newton had toiled for almost eighteen months to translate the coded inscription he had found in the book by George Ripley, and he had reproduced the tiny drawing of the labyrinth so that it could be followed more easily. They would be needing these things again soon, but until then he wanted to keep the precious papers with the orb, next to his own flesh.

Landsdown kept close. The torch was their only source of light. But then, suddenly, the passageway opened up. Newton had already passed alone through some of these tunnels in search of the sphere a few months earlier. In his mind he had also travelled the map while secluded in the privacy of his laboratory in Cambridge. The route was labelled 'The Path to Enlightenment', a title written in Aramaic, a language that had yielded its secrets to Newton after he had spent many years as a young man studying ancient tongues.

As they emerged into a large circular space they could see in the faint light the way in which the ceiling arched and the walls ran smooth and wet. The stone dome above their heads was grey and streaked with mineral deposits that had leached their way into the labyrinth. According to the map they were a little over ninety feet beneath the Bodleian Library.

As the men moved slowly around the room, Newton could hear Landsdown counting paces under his breath. He reached thirteen and stopped. Facing the wall, he repeated what he had done in the wine cellar of the college, running his hands along the wall at waist height. After a few moments he found what he was looking for, another metal ring, a duplicate of the one employed to secure entrance to the first passageway.

Strange shadows lay across their faces. To Newton, Landsdown's eyes looked like fathomless black discs, musket-ball holes in dead flesh. All three of them were sweating profusely and the top of Landsdown's collar was sodden and grey.

'Master . . .' He paused for a moment to catch his breath in the dank chamber. 'I must ask you to prepare yourself for what you will see behind this wall. Fatio and I have been busy in preparation for your arrival and have grown accustomed to it. Please brace yourself.' With that he pulled the ring and they watched as, slowly, a panel opened before them.

Landsdown led the way and turned to secure the torch in a wall bracket. Newton had to duck beneath the stone lintel of the opening and he kept his eyes on the black ground as he walked.

This room was a smaller version of the one they had just left. It was lit only by candles that cast an insipid glow from the far end of the room. But even this seemed intense and dazzling after the nearly complete blackness they had endured for the past two hours.

At first it was difficult for Newton to focus, to understand exactly what he was seeing. In principle, at least, he knew what to expect. He had studied the ancient texts, following carefully the diagrams and the instructions of the Ancients, but it still seemed like something that could not be real.

At the far end of the room a large golden frame had been built in the shape of a pentagram. To each side stood ornate candleholders six feet high; they held huge candles that had burned down to perhaps half their original length. Wax had dripped in piles around the holders and onto the stone floor beneath.

At the head of the golden frame a human brain had been positioned. To the left, on the next apex, a heart had been attached to the gold. As his gaze moved down, Newton saw two kidneys placed at the right apex. Lower down, another organ, what he knew to be a gall bladder, and at the base lay a liver, moist and glistening in the diffused light. A powerful odour reached his nostrils. It was Oil of Turpentine, which, through long hours, Fatio had distilled from the sapwood of the terebinth tree.

Newton looked back at Landsdown and Nicolas Fatio du Duillier. He was breathing heavily and sweating. The cuts on his face had opened so that his sweat blended with blood and ran in dark red lines down his cheeks and neck. His eyes were wide with a demonic excitement that neither of his companions had seen in him before. When he spoke, his voice was cracked with fatigue but it was nonetheless alive with confidence. 'I am pleased,' he hissed, a faint and entirely humourless smile playing across his lips. 'I am exceedingly pleased.'

Chapter 27

Oxford: the evening of 28 March

Sitting alone in the conference room of the Oxford police station, Detective Chief Inspector John Monroe watched the digital clock on the wall flick forward a minute to 10.04 p.m. He was not used to resenting the demands of his job but at this moment he did. By now, on his one free evening a week, he should have been heading home from the Elizabeth Restaurant in a cab with Imelda, the bright, engaging and attractive thirty-something physiotherapist he had met a month earlier. Instead, here he was, picking at the remnants of a Marks and Spencer sandwich that had seen better days and waiting for the arrival of three uniformly unattractive male colleagues.

Sipping at his stewed and bitter coffee, he tossed a screwed-up paper napkin onto the plate beside a half-eaten slice of bread and a few slivers of tomato, pushed his chair back and paced over to a white-board on the nearby wall. The whiteboard was divided into four broad columns. At the head of each a collection of photographs had been taped into place and each column was filled with writing in different-coloured markers. The first column was headed with the words: 'Rachel Southgate'. The second column was titled 'Jessica Fullerton', the third: 'Samantha Thurow/Simon Welding'. At the top of the last column the word 'Miscellaneous' had been written in bold red strokes. He read the words he had put there earlier that evening:

Laura Niven/Philip Bainbridge

Astrology/Alchemy?

1851 /Professor Milliner

Coins

Leather/Plastic

He heard the door open behind him. The forensics officer, Mark Langham, led the way, followed by a tall, thin man in uniform. He was in his late fifties but looked younger. His short white hair, pale blue eyes and chiselled cheekbones gave him a Teutonic look, and he exuded an authority that appeared effortless and had little to do with the bands of ribbon on his chest. Eighteen years earlier, when he had joined the force, DI Piers Candicott, as he was then, had been Monroe's first boss.

'Monroe,' Commander Candicott said as he

entered the room. His voice was deep and surprisingly warm. 'I'm glad you could make this ungodly hour – couldn't do anything about the schedule, I'm afraid.'

The two men shook hands. 'That's quite all right, sir,' Monroe replied.

'John, this is Bruce Holloway, my press liaison officer – spends all his time on the phone to filthy journalists, I'm afraid, poor chap. But he gets things done.'

Holloway looked to be in his mid-thirties. He was a small man, no more than five-six, stocky and with unruly brown hair. He nodded at Monroe, his face quite expressionless, mumbled 'Hello,' and shook the DCI's hand.

Having chucked the remains of his supper into a waste bin, Monroe took the chair nearest the whiteboard. Candicott sat at the head of the table and Langham and Holloway took their places on the side facing Monroe.

'So, what's the state of play, then, Detective Chief Inspector?' Candicott asked.

'My team are working around the clock,' Monroe replied, returning the intensity of Candicott's gaze. 'We've been following a lead from some forensic evidence found at the scene of the second murder.' He glanced at Langham. 'So far, this has just taken us up blind alleys.'

'Nothing concrete, then?'

'Whoever's behind this will make a mistake before too long. They always do.'

'Well, let's hope it's sooner rather than later, John.'

'There is also the fact,' Holloway added, 'that the press are getting jumpy. Another murder and I think Wapping will relocate to the Banbury Road.'

Monroe had never yet met a press officer he liked, and although Holloway was meant to be a cop first and a 'liaison officer' second, to the DCI he had the same demeanour as the journalists and ghastly PR people he had met throughout his career.

'Well, thank you for that little reminder,' Monroe retorted, unable to keep the acid from his voice. 'I'll bear that in mind.' Turning to Commander Candicott, he added: 'Sir, at present I have twenty-two officers and forty-three ancillary staff working on this case. We are sifting through every piece of evidence, following up every lead and brain-storming every possible connection to these murders. After four murders in two days, the last was seven days ago. This has given us a breathing space, but in spite of what I said earlier, we are up against a very thorough, very . . . professional killer.'

Candicott simply nodded wearily.

'Sir, if I might . . .' Langham addressed Monroe as though he was the only other person in the room.

'We have something new from the lab.' He passed a single sheet of paper to Monroe.

'One of my team has found a trace of blood in the upstairs room of the house close to the river, the scene of the second murder. It doesn't match the victim or any of the family.'

Monroe studied the read-out from the DNA analyser.

'Unfortunately, we can't match the DNA to anything on the database either,' Langham added.

'Well, this is something, is it not?' Candicott's cold eyes were bright. 'I assume your team are back at the scene, going over every inch of the place again?'

'Naturally, sir,' Langham said.

'This is good news, Mark.' Monroe looked up from the sheet of paper. 'But no match, so he's not been through the system, never worked for a government body, never been in the armed forces. You don't need me to remind you that we need anything else your team can get – anything.'

There was a sudden knock on the door. Before Monroe could speak, a young officer stepped inside.

'I'm sorry to interrupt, sir.' The officer ignored everyone but Monroe. 'I thought this was too important to wait.'

'Spit it out, then, Greene. What can't wait?'

'It's this, sir. I've been working through the databases for the past two days and . . . well, I got permission from the university to access their systems. It wasn't easy, but . . . I think it was worth it.' He handed Monroe two pages of closely packed writing.

'It's from the Psychology Department,' Greene added. 'A list of forty-seven female students who each attended what the department calls a Trial Day, apparently a set of psychological and physical tests, a week before the start of the academic year – late last September. All three of our dead girls are on the list.'

As Monroe approached the exit, he passed the office of one of his best men, Inspector Joshua Rogers, who was standing in the doorway with a young woman.

'Thank you for this, Miss Ingham,' Monroe heard Rogers say. 'We'll be in touch. One of my men will see you out. You have a lift, I take it?' The girl nodded and pushed open the double doors, heading for the stairs.

Monroe raised his eyebrows.

'That was Marianne Ingham,' Rogers explained. 'A student from St John's. She had this exquisite piece of artwork left in her pigeonhole at college.'

Monroe grimaced when he saw the picture. 'Does she know who did it?'

'She's not sure. Very jumpy – took her a week to

come in to us with it. But she suspects someone in her year – a guy called Russell Cunningham.'

'Good. Check him out and let me know immediately what you find. I'm going home.'

Monroe's mobile rang as he was pulling into the driveway in front of his apartment.

'Thought you would like to see this straight away,' Rogers said.

Monroe switched off the ignition and lifted his phone from its cradle. A picture of a young man appeared on the screen. He was surprisingly handsome with longish curly blond hair, fine eyebrows, a delicate mouth.

'He has form, sir.'

The picture was replaced by a slowly scrolling page of writing.

'Rich kid. Daddy owns a chain of hotels. He was expelled from Downside when he was sixteen. Haven't been able to get to the bottom of why. Family's done a good job persuading the school to keep things under wraps. The father probably helped his son into Oxford – the Cunningham Library at Magdalen was completed last year, six months before the boy came up. There's more, though. Two complaints of sexual harassment from female employees at one of the family hotels in London where Russell was doing a stint. First one when he was seventeen, and then again last year. No charges pressed, cases dropped. Girls no longer employees.'

On screen there were precise dates, places, names.

'Good work, Josh,' Monroe said. 'Is Candicott still there with that goon from the Press Office?'

'No, they left just after you.'

'Good. Well, look, keep this quiet for the moment, but meet me first thing tomorrow at the Psych Department on South Parks Road. Have a word with Greene if he's still there. Get him to bring you up to speed.'

Chapter 28

Oxford: 29 March, 9 a.m.

As John Monroe turned along South Parks Road, he reflected how ugly the building that housed the Psychology Department was.

He had been up since before dawn, sifting through the details of the case. On his home computer he had reviewed, for what must have been the hundredth time, the essentials of the case. Four murders, almost certainly the same killer, someone working alone, almost definitely a man. And what did they have? A scrap of DNA, no match; in fact, no match to anyone on file anywhere, it seemed. And then there were the ritualistic aspects, the coins, the removed organs. Laura Niven and Philip Bainbridge were convinced of an occult connection. And then there were the murders of 1851. There had to be a link.

What did he know about those murders? Monroe had gone back through the files, had spent almost every spare minute for the past week going over all the details. Three girls and a male student had been murdered in the year of the Great Exhibition. An Irish labourer had taken the rap, but it was well known by crime historians that Professor Milliner had been intimately involved, that the man had connections with the occult, that he had been involved in some black-magic group, that the university authorities had closed ranks. Within a year of the murders, Milliner had taken a professorship in Turin and the Milliner family vanished completely from the Oxford scene. Now, with the recent murders, it had emerged that all the girls had volunteered for some tests at the University Psychology Department shortly before the start of the academic year.

Monroe drove into the car park. Ahead of him he saw Rogers getting out of his car close to the main doors of the building. But as he spun the steering wheel to slip in next to the inspector's car he was startled by a Morgan sports car backing out of a parking bay way too fast. Monroe glared at the driver, but he seemed oblivious to anything but the road ahead. With a jolt, Monroe realised that he recognised the face.

'I got his number,' Rogers said, as soon as Monroe joined him.

'It was Cunningham, I'm sure of it.'

Rogers looked startled. 'I'll run a check on the plate.'

'You do that,' Monroe snapped and turned towards the doors.

Outside term time the building was relatively quiet. The reception area consisted of a few chairs arranged around a table. Along one wall ran several rows of lockers and pigeonholes. Next to them there was a large noticeboard covered with posters for forthcoming gigs and sports programmes. Alongside these was an old copy of *The Daily Information* – a news-sheet that went out to every part of the city, announcing entertainments and exhibitions and listing private sales. Monroe strode to the desk where a fat woman in a floral dress sat studying a computer screen. After she had ignored him for twenty seconds he rapped his knuckles hard on the counter. She glared up at him.

'DCI Monroe, Thames Valley Police,' he said, flashing his ID. 'Here to see Dr Rankin – if it's not too much trouble.'

The woman seemed singularly unimpressed. 'C4. Lift over there. Don't think he's here yet . . .'

'Yes, I am, Margaret.'

Monroe turned to see a tall, bony man, a faint smile breaking across his face. 'Arthur Rankin,' he said, shaking Monroe's hand. He acknowledged Rogers with a nod.

'You'll have to excuse Margaret,' Rankin said as he escorted them to the elevator. 'You get used to her after the first five years.' The lift had a strange, earthy smell and it took Monroe a moment or two to realise that the odour was coming from the professor.

'I meant to be here earlier,' Rankin said as the elevator came to a halt on the fourth floor. 'Bloody car wouldn't start. So I walked across the park – quite pleasant, actually. Didn't rain, for a change.'

Rankin's office was tiny, a paper-lined cocoon in white, brown and grey. The single mean window looked out onto a bleak concrete quad. There was not a glimpse of the famous dreaming spires. Rankin took off his coat and cleared some papers and books from the two chairs facing his desk. 'Please, sit down,' he said. 'Apologies for the mess – I can never seem to get things straight in here.'

'That's OK, professor. No need to stand on ceremony. We just have a few quick questions,' Monroe replied as he settled into a chair.

'How may I help?'

'We're interested in the psych tests conducted on a list of forty-seven female students in late September last year. What can you tell us about them?'

For a moment Rankin looked puzzled. He had a high forehead and when he frowned, it looked like he was wearing a headband of worms. Then his expression brightened suddenly. 'Ah, you mean Julius Spenser's tests.'

Monroe said nothing.

Rankin gave a quick cough and began looking through some papers on his desk. Then he stood up slowly and walked over to a wall of shelves. Crouching down, he lifted a huge pile of folders and loose sheets and dumped them on his desk. Licking a fingertip, he began to riffle through the pile. A few moments later he stopped.

'Yes, knew it was here somewhere.' He handed a green folder to Monroe. 'Spenser was a clever chap, had plenty of good ideas.'

'Was?' Rogers asked.

'Yes, left us before Christmas. Got offered a rather tasty number in Boston; MIT, I believe.'

'What was he doing exactly?'

'IQ studies was his thing,' Rankin said and looked out the window to the grey horizon. 'Not my bag, I'm afraid, a bit too dry for my taste.'

'What did the tests involve?' Monroe asked, quickly scanning the pages in front of him.

'He had his own system, quite an unorthodox slant – believed that IQ was directly related to the physical connection between the two hemispheres of the brain, the corpus callosum. You're aware of the idea of the split brain?'

Monroe nodded. 'Vaguely, layman's stuff.'

'Back in the 1960s research appeared to show that the two halves of the brain were very different. The left brain is the analytical side, the right is the imaginative, 'artistic' hemisphere. Roger Sperry won a Nobel Prize for coming up with the idea.'

'And Julius Spenser was developing these theories?'

'He was a Sperry disciple. Studied under him at Caltech in the late 1980s.'

'Dr Spenser did what, exactly?' Rogers asked. 'How did he conduct his tests?'

'Well, it's all there.' Rankin nodded his head towards the papers on their laps. 'He had a sample of around fifty: forty-seven in the end, I think. They were all young women in this phase.'

'This phase?'

'He conducted a similar set of tests on young men the month before. The girls spent most of the day on written IQ tests, then physical manipulation tests, response and reflex analysis, spatial-awareness experiments. They also had full medicals and brain scans.'

'Medicals?' Monroe frowned.

'Yes, it was a key element in Spenser's proposal. He reckons IQ is directly related to physical parameters.'

'What did the medicals involve?'

'Well, now you're asking. I wasn't present myself. In fact, I wasn't even in Oxford that day. But Spenser obviously submitted his research schedule for approval a month or two earlier. Let's take a look.'

Monroe handed back the folder. 'Yes, yes, here we are,' Rankin said after a few moments. 'CAT scan basically, full-body spectrum. The girls did the psych tests here, then went over to the John Radcliffe. Expensive stuff, but Spenser was very good at getting grants.'

Monroe remained silent as he leafed through the material and handed it to Rogers a page at a time.

'So, I take it Spenser wasn't working on his own?'

'No, no. He was always there, of course, a good supervisor with excellent management skills. He had three assistants for the tests and then another three, young female post-docs at the hospital conducting the ah . . . body searches.' He gave the policemen a lopsided grin. 'Analysis of the results was done by young Bridges.'

'Bridges?'

'Malcolm, Malcolm Bridges – on his way to becoming a fine psychologist, that one.'

'And Malcolm Bridges works here?'

'Yes, but he spends all his spare time at the Bodleian with Professor Lightman, the Chief Librarian. He's a dedicated young chap. Don't honestly know how he fits it all in, actually.'

'Is he here at the moment?'

'Should be. Let me think. It's Friday.' He looked at his watch. 'I'll buzz him.' He picked up the phone and tapped in three numbers. 'Nope, not there yet, I'm afraid.'

'No problem.' Monroe stood up. 'We'll get in touch with him. I'd be grateful if we could take this file with us, Dr Rankin. We'll guard it well, and make a copy.'

'Yes, yes, certainly,' Rankin said quickly. 'Is there anything . . . ?'

'Yes, actually, there is one other thing, Dr Rankin. Do you have anything to do with a young man named Russell Cunningham?'

Rankin looked at him blankly.

'I saw him earlier, leaving the car park in a very flash sports car.'

'Cunningham? Yes, yes, indeed. I can't say I know the boy, he's a first-year. Seen him in his car, of course, who hasn't?' Rankin laughed.

'You've probably heard of his father,' Rogers said.

'Quite right, yes . . . the library man, the famous philanthrope. Come to think of it, I think Bridges is Russell's supervisor. But what's he got to do with anything?'

Monroe extended his hand, ignoring the question. 'Thank you very much for your time, Dr Rankin. And for these.' He tapped the folder clutched to his chest.

Monroe and Rogers exited into unexpected bright sunshine. Beyond the car park they could see rugby goalposts and a squad of players in hooded tops running around the field.

'I want to see Malcolm Bridges at the station a.s.a.p.,' Monroe said. 'Get back to the station and drag Greene away from whatever he's doing. I want him to go through this list of girls. I want to know the whereabouts of all of them and I want each of them interviewed, understand?'

Rogers nodded.

'Meanwhile, I'll get a warrant. I think it's time to pay Mr Russell Cunningham a little visit, don't you?'

Chapter 29

Oxford: 29 March, 11.05 a.m.

In the golden days described by Evelyn Waugh, when Sebastian Flyte and his teddy bear Aloysius came up to Oxford they chose to reside in a suite of rooms on the ground floor of Tom Quad, Christchurch, where his lordship had the walls painted in duck-egg blue upon which he placed delicate Chinese lithographs. The best part of a century later, a few undergraduates who came from an entirely different social bracket from the Flytes (but possessed comparable amounts of disposable cash) preferred greater independence from the university. So they had their parents buy them apartments – costing upwards of a quarter of a million pounds – overlooking the Cherwell and located close to the amenities of central Oxford.

Yuppie hutches such as these came with piped vacuuming (to make the maid's life easier) and subterranean garaging for three cars. It was in just such a place that Russell Cunningham was enjoying his first year at Oxford University. He found it a perfect place to entertain, and considered it to be an entirely appropriate pad for the only son of one of Britain's wealthiest self-made entrepreneurs, Nigel Cunningham, who was known among the Oxford snob class (who were happy to accept his multimillion-pound donations) as 'the Library Man'. This was an epithet always delivered with heavy sarcasm because, in spite of the fact that Cunningham had recently financed the building and the stocking of the university's largest library, anyone who was anyone in Oxford assumed that the only books in Nigel Cunningham's home were ones that you coloured in.

Monroe was on his way out of the police station when Inspector Rogers called from his car parked outside Cunningham's apartment. 'I think you'd better get over here, sir. You'll think it's your birthday and Christmas rolled into one.'

Five minutes later, Monroe was pulling up outside an exclusive apartment block just off Thames Street and opposite the Head of the River pub. Rogers met him as he stepped out of the car.

'Just look at this frigging place,' Rogers muttered. 'I couldn't get close to this on an inspector's salary, and some snotty-nosed eighteen-year-old kid brings his girlfriends back here in his sodding Morgan.'

Monroe grinned. 'Never had you down as the bitter type, Josh.'

'Yeah, well,' Rogers replied, shaking his head. 'I think we might bring the little bastard down a peg or two.'

Monroe stared at him, his eyes narrowing. 'Lead the way,' he said and followed his junior officer to the doors of the apartment block.

Two uniformed officers were waiting for them in the hall outside Cunningham's apartment. Monroe and Rogers crossed the polished concrete floor, and entered a vast living room where they could hear an Oscar Peterson track spilling from a pair of over-sized Bang and Olufsen speakers. The wall opposite the entrance was an expanse of glass with views over the Cherwell and the sandstone spires of Oxford. In the foreground, the two detectives could see the sun-splashed tower of Christchurch Cathedral. For some reason, at that moment Monroe recalled a tale about Oxford that he had heard when he had himself been an undergraduate here. Apparently, glider pilots and balloonists loved flying over the city, not just for the views but because there were always good thermals. The jokey explanation for this was that the thermals were produced from the hot air of the dons, but the real reason was the ubiquitous sandstone which reflected the heat of the sun.

Russell Cunningham was reclining in a black

leather George Nelson chair close to the window. A police officer was standing close by. Cunningham was tall, blond, handsome and tanned from what Monroe later learned had been a brief but extremely pleasant skiing holiday in Andorra, from which he had returned two weeks earlier. Dressed in designer jeans and a black V-neck cashmere sweater, he looked every inch the pampered son of a billionaire. He stood up as Monroe strode in, but the DCI ignored him and followed Rogers through the room to a corridor beyond.

Three doors led off the corridor; one of them was ajar. Monroe followed Rogers into a small window-less room lit by a single dull red bulb in the ceiling. Shelves were filled with CD cases. Against the far wall were two flat-screen monitors and in front of them was a small console. Above the monitors the wall was covered with pornographic images, a sordid collage of young women tied up, mutilated, disfig-ured.

Monroe looked at the scene, his face betraying no emotion. Rogers leaned over the console. 'Our boy's certainly having fun here,' he said wryly.

'What exactly is this stuff?'

'State-of-the-art cyber-porn,' Rogers replied. 'He's got web cams set up all over the place – girls' college rooms, the gym showers, ladies' toilets, East Oxford student houses. He keeps careful records, too.' He waved a hand toward the stacks of discs on the shelves. 'Looks like we've struck gold.'

'Maybe,' Monroe replied. 'Let's take him in. We'll leave this stuff here. Get a couple of tech guys to go through it, OK?'

Monroe returned to the living room, his mind racing.

'Perhaps you could explain what all this is about?' The young man had a mid-Atlantic twang to his voice.

'I was rather hoping you could do that, Mr Cunningham.'

Cunningham looked at the floor for a second and then fixed Monroe with a superior glare. 'Detective? Admiral . . . ?' He waved a hand in the air.

'Just a DCI, sir. That is, Detective Chief Inspector . . . Monroe.'

'Well, DCI Monroe, I take it you have a warrant? The other guy . . .'

'Inspector Rogers.'

'Yes, he waved a bit of paper under my nose before stomping all over my place.'

'Oh yes, Mr Cunningham, we do have a warrant. And I'm placing you under arrest. Taylor,' Monroe snapped, turning to the uniform standing over Cunningham. 'Take him in.'

The young man laughed unconvincingly while Monroe read him his rights. 'Terrible mistake you are making. Huge. I assume you know who my father is?'

'Fully aware of the facts, Mr Cunningham. Don't worry yourself about that. I'll be along in ten minutes, Taylor,' Monroe told the constable. 'See that Mr Cunningham is properly looked after.' And he turned back towards the corridor.

Chapter 30

Croydon: 29 March, 2 p.m.

Charlie Tucker's funeral was a bleak, rainswept affair, steeped in suburban misery. The service was held in a concrete chapel built in the early 1980s a few miles outside Croydon, south of London. Fewer than a dozen people turned up. They dashed from their cars across the tarmac of the glistening car park with coats over their heads and umbrellas aloft. In the chapel there was a pervading smell of damp clothes mingled with ageing lilies.

For a short time after Charlie's body had been discovered the police had been working on the principle that he had committed suicide. But then CSI evidence from the scene proved conclusively that he could not have fired the weapon. The investigators began a murder inquiry.

Laura and Philip were the last to arrive and sat together at the back, listening in silence to the taped organ music, each submerged in their own thoughts.

Philip had hardly known Charlie. To him he'd been just another face at Oxford, a friend of Laura's. They had met at parties and had had the occasional argument about politics. Philip had been pretty left-wing, which was more or less de rigueur for students in the 1980s, but Charlie, he recalled, had been rabidly Marxist.

Laura had grown used to the fact that Charlie was dead. Almost a week earlier, when the news had been thrust upon her so viciously, she had been shocked to the core of her being. This wasn't because she had been particularly close to Charlie. But he had been a part of her youth. Perhaps because she had hardly seen him in almost twenty years she still associated him with happy times, with college, freedom, a time just after the end of childhood, a time when, in memory at least, the world seemed to be a more innocent place. Now that he was dead, it felt like a part of herself had been consumed too.

Only later had come the terrible sense of dread that she now felt. The deaths, the slaughter and the violence had started to close in on her. Now Laura could not get it out of her mind that Charlie's death had to be linked in some way with her investigation.

Since returning to Oxford, she and Philip had made precious little progress. They had confirmed that the 1851 murders had been committed on exactly the nights when the relevant heavenly bodies had entered the sign of Cancer and that a five-body planetary conjunction had been expected on 20 July that year. The only difference between those murders and the current ones was that the killers had not started their series of crimes at the vernal equinox because the conjunction of planets had occurred at a quite different time of the year. All this was important, she knew, and it put her theory beyond reasonable doubt. But it still felt as though their search for clues to the identity of today's murderer was running out of steam – and the next killing was scheduled for the following evening, 30 March.

The funeral service was a dismal affair. The sound of a synthesised choir spilling gently from speakers in the ceiling carried the two hymns, and the best anyone in the congregation could muster was a barely audible mumble. As the second hymn petered out, the coffin bearing Charlie's body was lifted carefully by the pall-bearers and carried to a hearse outside. The mourners got up from their pews slowly and drifted towards the doors.

Outside, the hearse pulled away and the group followed, walking past a memorial garden, along a winding lane to an area with fewer graves where the soil had been freshly turned.

Walking back past the chapel, Laura and Philip had almost reached their car when they heard someone running up behind them. Turning, they saw a young woman in a long white dress, slowing to a stop. She looked about twenty-five, short, slim, with dark brown hair falling freely to her waist. She had huge blue eyes, a pixie's face, thin eyebrows and a shapely nose. Laura could see that she had been crying: she wore no make-up but her eyes were bloodshot and the skin beneath her eyes looked bruised.

'You're Laura and Philip, yeah?' she asked.

Laura nodded.

'I, I was Charlie's, er, Charlie's girlfriend. My name's Sabrina.' She extended a hand and as she did so she looked around as if to check that no one was watching them. A middle-aged couple from the service walked past, and Sabrina waited until they were out of earshot.

'I was asked to give you this.' And she slipped a small cold metal object into Laura's hand.

It was a key.

'Put it in your pocket,' Sabrina said quietly but firmly.

'Who . . . ?'

'Charlie, of course. He knew he was in trouble. Please, just listen,' Sabrina whispered. 'Charlie was particularly fond of a biography of Newton. You'll find it in his apartment. Number 2, Chepstow Street, New Cross. You have to go there today. His brother is sorting out his possessions and settling his rent tomorrow morning. The key has a number on it. Now, I have to go. Good luck.' And with that, she turned on her heel and walked swiftly away.

Stunned for a moment, Laura and Philip simply let her go. Then, snapping out of her silence, Laura made as if to go after the girl. But Philip held her back.

'I think we should leave her be.'

Charlie had lived in a tiny two-roomed place in a narrow street off the main road in busy New Cross, South London. It was one of six apartments that made up what had probably once been a rather grand house. Laura and Philip had gone straight from the funeral and parked in Chepstow Street a few doors down from the house. They reached the apartment on the second floor via a dimly lit winding staircase.

The apartment was not as bad as Laura had expected. Charlie had done his best to disguise the crumbling plaster and the general tattiness of the place with a lick of paint and some tasteful framed prints. His furniture was cheap and old. It had probably come with the place when he moved in, but he had invested in a couple of rugs and cushions, which helped a little. The influence of a woman was obvious; Sabrina had smartened things up, Laura thought as she wandered around the main room. There was a rudimentary kitchen at one end and a

TV and bookcases at the other. She peered into the small bedroom that led on to a minuscule bathroom. A strong smell of cigarettes and alcohol pervaded the entire apartment.

'God, I feel like we're trespassing,' Laura said quietly.

'Well, I suppose we are.' Philip grinned.

'Gives me the creeps.'

'Oh, come on. Sabrina made it clear that Charlie wanted us to come here. Don't feel guilty. He trusted you.'

'Yeah, and look what happened after he saw me.' Laura sat down heavily in a swivel chair in front of a small desk. On the desk was a computer and beside it a messy pile of papers and an ashtray filled with cigarette ends. 'The Newton biography.' Laura nodded towards a bookcase next to the TV. 'Do you want to try that one? There's another in the bedroom.'

Philip found it almost immediately. They sat at a tiny wooden table in the kitchen end of the main room with the book opened between them. It was entitled *Isaac Newton: Biography of a Magus* by Liam Ethwiche.

'Charlie was particularly fond of this book,' Laura said recalling the words Sabrina had used. Then she added. 'The key has a number on it.' It was number 112.

'A page number, I would imagine,' Philip said and

flicked through the book until he reached page 112.

As they scanned through the first two para-graphs, they noticed the anomaly at almost the same moment. In the middle of a line, the thread was suddenly lost. The final part of the sentence read: *Paddington Station, box 14, Geoff's party, sweet pea.*

Philip stood up and walked over to the window. Outside, the grey buildings and the grey sky seemed to merge. Rush hour had started and the traffic was stacking up on New Cross Road. At the end of the street, four lines of vehicles were stationary, their exhausts billowing fumes into the late-afternoon air. He did not notice the spotlessly clean black Toyota parked across the street.

'Make any sense to you?' he asked.

'Yeah, it does, actually,' Laura replied. 'Let's go.' She tucked the book under her arm. 'You want to drive, or shall I?'

Paddington Station was no more than six miles from New Cross as the crow flies but it took them nearly ninety minutes to fight their way through the traffic, including a twenty-minute period during which, thanks to roadworks near Piccadilly Circus, they were immobilised on Pall Mall. The sun had set as they approached the Thames from the south some forty minutes earlier, and as they turned along Praed Street the seedy neon red and lemon glow only accentuated the drabness of the crumbling, pollution-stained buildings on either side, home to cheap jean shops and walk-up peep-shows.

Inside the station a human tidal wave washed through the concourse. The personal lockers and security boxes were positioned between a ticket office and a café called The Commuter's Brew. On the front of each box was a small panel containing a numeric keypad.

'So, you going to tell me the combination at last, and what "sweet pea" means, Laura?' Philip asked.

She sighed. 'Do I have a choice?'

'Not really.'

Laura leaned back against the boxes, eyeing the commuters as they streamed past. Turning back to Box 14, she mumbled: 'It's my nickname – well, Charlie's nickname for me, anyway.'

Philip snorted.

'We first met at a party in Oxford in 1982. It was in a big shared house on the Banbury Road owned by the parents of a guy in our year, Geoff . . . Geoff Townsend, I think his name was. Anyway, after that night, Charlie always called me "sweet pea".'

'"Sweet pea"?'

'I wore a jacket made of peacock feathers to the party.'

Philip looked at her in disbelief for a moment, then burst out laughing.

'It was a long time ago.'

Her earnest expression made him laugh even harder. 'I'm sorry,' Philip managed to say, his face straightening. 'It's just the vision of you in a peacock-feather jacket, it's . . .'

'Priceless?'

'Well, yes.'

'The New Romantics were at their height. You remember? You were probably wearing a silk shirt and tucker boots.'

'I never owned a pair of tucker boots,' Philip said indignantly.

Now it was Laura's turn to laugh. 'And you had a horrible little plait when I first met you.'

'It was a real ponytail, actually.' Philip grimaced. 'OK. What's the combination?'

She stared at the keypad and began punching in some numbers. Philip watched. 1 . . . 9 . . . 8 . . . 2. Then she hit the 'enter' button, took the handle and pulled.

Inside the box lay a rolled-up sheet of paper tied with a black silk ribbon. Beside it was a CD in a clear plastic case.

Philip reached in and withdrew the items.

'A DVD, I guess,' he said. He loosened the ribbon on the scroll. 'And what looks . . .' He paused. 'Well, this is interesting. Even I know enough Latin to translate that.'

At the top of the first page was written: *Principia Chemicum by Isaacus Neuutonus.*

Laura and Philip barely exchanged a word as they weaved their way out of London, heading west back towards Oxford. The traffic had lightened a little, and within twenty minutes they had reached the A40 which would lead them to the motorway and the fifty-mile stretch home. They were lost in their own thoughts, each of them working through the threads of what they had learned, neither of them yet ready to talk about it. Philip drove as Laura studied the Newton document. It was covered in tiny, precise calligraphy, most of it written in a strange language or elaborately encoded, giving the appearance of gibberish. This was interspersed with lines written in Latin, along with line drawings, odd-looking symbols, and tables and charts dotted around the page seemingly at random. Then, as they left behind the lights of the city and entered the dark monotony of the motorway and the beckoning countryside on either side of the road, it became too dark for her to read.

'It's obviously a photocopy,' Laura said. 'But what the hell is it about?'

'I wish now I'd paid more attention in Latin lessons when I was thirteen,' Philip said.

'Actually, my Latin's pretty good, but this is a

complete jumble of languages. And what about all these symbols and coded sections? It looks like word soup to me.'

'And what on earth was Charlie Tucker doing with a copy of a document written by Isaac Newton? It's not one I've ever heard of.'

'Me neither. He wrote the *Principia Mathematica*, of course, but . . .' Reaching over to the back seat, Laura grabbed the Newton biography that they had picked up at Charlie's apartment. Switching on the interior light, she began to flick through the pages. '*Biography of a Magus*,' Laura said quietly. 'I remember this book coming out. Caused quite a stir at the time, didn't it?'

Philip looked puzzled.

'It's a revisionist work – Newton as some wacko sorcerer or something . . . Now I remember,' she added and tapped the opened book with her fingers. 'It hinged on the idea that Newton was a dedicated alchemist.'

'Yeah,' Philip replied. 'I remember it too. The book came out a few years back. I read a review in *The Times*.'

'Newton wasn't just an alchemist,' Laura replied and looked up from the book. 'Looks like he was seriously into black magic. Says here: "Newton was an adept in the black arts. Evidence for this aston-ishing fact may be found among the writings he kept hidden until his death. These were held in secret by his disciples for fear of tarnishing the great man's enormous scientific reputation. It was only in 1936 under the auspices of the economist and Newton scholar John Maynard Keynes that these documents were rediscovered – more than a million words on occult subjects ranging from divination to alchemy."'

'So he published the legitimate scientific stuff, but kept the risqué material well away from prying eyes?'

'Apparently. He couldn't have let his interest in the occult become known; it would have destroyed his career.'

'And you think this *Principia Chemicum* could have been one of his secret works?'

'Not sure yet.' Laura flicked to the index of the biography in her lap. 'He wrote all his documents in Latin, it was the standard form of the time.' 'But it's odd that he should use the Latinised version of his name. But . . . Ah-ha,' she said after a moment. 'Listen . . . "Newton's most famous work, his *Principia Mathematica* is sadly not paired with a *Principia Chemicum* – what would have been a definitive work describing his alchemical findings. He leaves us clues and hints, but no manuscript offering an account of success in producing the mythical Philosopher's Stone. This is because, like many hundreds of researchers before and after him,

Newton, for all his extraordinary talents, never did accomplish his ultimate aim. He never did forge the Stone with which he could find the method of producing gold from base metal; he was not offered eternal life, and he never could commune with the Almighty, at least not as a living man."'

A few minutes later they entered the cutting into the Chilterns and began the long, steep descent crossing the border from Buckinghamshire into Oxfordshire. In the dark they could see little of the magnificent panorama that daylight could offer, a patchwork quilt of cultivated fields stretching to the horizon.

Laura closed the book, flicked off the interior light and switched on the radio. 'Fancy some music?'

Pushing a preset button marked '1' all they got was static. '2' and '3' were the same. With '4' the car was filled with power chords, a Van Halen track from the mid-1980s. Philip started to head-bang. 'Yeah, baby . . .'

Laura pushed button number five and turned the volume down. A cacophony of atonal sounds cascaded from the speakers. 'Must be Radio 3,' Philip said. 'Concerto for three sinks and a vibrator, anyone?' he quipped. 'For God's sake, let's have Van Halen.'

'Not likely,' Laura laughed. She switched through a couple of French long-wave stations, some rap coming from a local independent and then found Radio Oxford and what sounded like the tail end of the news.

'. . . The head of the Estonian delegation, Dr Vambola Kuusk, declared that the meeting had been a great success and that he hoped the European commission would abide by their earlier recommendations.' There was a pause.

'And now to some local news. Police are becoming increasingly concerned over the whereabouts of Professor James Lightman, Chief Librarian at the Bodleian Library. His car was found around ten o'clock this morning, left abandoned on Norham Gardens in North Oxford. Police say there was no sign of a struggle and that the professor left his briefcase on the passenger seat and that his keys were still in the ignition. We will be providing a phone number at the end of the programme for anyone with information that may help Thames Valley police.'

Chapter 31

Oxford: 12 August 1690. Close to midnight.

For a few seconds, John Wickins thought he was going to pass out with the heat and the pain. In spite of Robert Boyle's soothing balm and careful ministrations, the burn on his arm was almost as painful as it had been that morning, and the headache he had suffered all day was only a little less oppressive.

He, Boyle and Hooke had passed through the labyrinth, and now they stood gasping for breath in the corridor that led to the chamber beyond. They had glimpsed the three men in front of them just once, as they entered the wine cellar of Hertford College – Newton, du Duillier and another figure, hooded, whose identity they were not certain about, had entered the tunnels ahead of them and disappeared into the maze.

Now the members of the cabal that had formed around Newton, and who shared his dark secrets, had entered the chamber. A faint sliver of light emerged where the door had been left slightly ajar.

Outside, the three Guardians were pressed against the slimy wet wall of the corridor, each of them trying to hold their breath. They had extinguished their single torch and were preparing for action. From the chamber they could hear a man's voice chanting barely discernible words, long monologues that were punctuated periodically by unintelligible phrases intoned by all three voices. A rivulet of sweat meandered down Wickins's back and he tightened his wet palms on the handle of his blade. To his right stood Hooke, cursing under his breath, his face and tunic soaked with sweat. To his left, Boyle had unsheathed his sword. It caught the narrow beam of light from the opening into the chamber and in this reflected light Wickins could see the old man's faint profile. He was staring ahead at the door, every muscle tensed. As Wickins studied him, Boyle moved away from the wall and took three long, rapid, silent strides towards the chamber. Reaching it, he beckoned to the other two. They crossed the space, and Boyle yanked the door wide open. The three men ran into the room with their swords at the ready.

The smell of turpentine, sweat and human flesh, the oppressive wet air and the hum of the unholy incantations assaulted their senses. The three members of Newton's cabal, hooded and dressed in heavy black and grey satin robes, stood before the pentagram at the far end of the room. The central figure held aloft a small red orb.

The Guardians had the element of surprise on their side and Boyle was determined not to squander it. He dashed forward towards the man with the orb, grabbed him around the neck and dragged him away from the pentagram. The ruby sphere fell to the floor and rolled across the stone where it came to rest under the pentagram. Pulling the man to his feet, Boyle pressed his sword to his throat. The other robed figures stood rooted in shock as Hooke and Wickins ran forward and stopped with the tips of their blades only inches from their shrouded faces.

Boyle released his grip on his captive and whirled the man round. They could all hear him snarl from under his hood. But he was powerless. Boyle had his rapier against the man's Adam's apple. 'All three of you, remove your hoods,' Boyle commanded.

None of the men moved. 'Remove your hoods,' Boyle repeated. He had not raised his voice, but there was a new venomous intensity to it.

Slowly, Newton obeyed. His long greying locks were stuck to his damp face. Through the veils of hair his black eyes burned with fury and loathing. 'Who in God's name do you think you are?' he hissed. 'What authority to you have here?'

Boyle did not flinch, but held Newton's gaze. 'Unlike you,' he said, 'I have every right to be here, Professor Newton.'

Newton smirked, the skin of his face folding into moist creases. He looked like a caricature of Mephistopheles. 'You interfering fool!' he hissed, his thin voice trembling with pent-up fury. 'I am the Master here. I alone understand the words of the sages. I am the true inheritor of the Light, the Path, the Way.'

With a faint, utterly humourless smile that summed up how little he cared for Newton's opinions, Boyle said, 'John, Robert, let us see who we have here.'

With the points of their swords never wavering from the throats of the two robed figures, Hooke and Wickins pulled away the hoods and stepped back.

'James? My brother James?' Boyle reeled back. 'What . . . ?' The shock had turned the old man's face into a rigid mask; he seemed lost, paralysed.

It was the opportunity that Newton needed. With a roar he lunged forward, grabbed Boyle's wrist and forced him to drop his sword, which clattered to the floor.

Newton was the only one moving fast. The other five men seemed to be preserved in aspic. But, after a few moments, they began to recover, and suddenly the chamber was filled with flailing bodies, the clang of steel and rasping shouts.

Newton spun round and made a lunge for the ruby sphere. As he did so, Wickins caught him by the ankles and the two men toppled to the floor. In a blind rage, Wickins tore at Newton's hair, making him screech. He brought his sword up to Newton's throat.

'You have betrayed my friendship!' Wickins shouted into Newton's ear. 'I had grown to trust you.'

But, for all his anger, Wickins was not sure what to do next. Isaac Newton was at his mercy. One thrust of his blade, Wickins reasoned, and the man's life would end, his blood would carpet the floor. But that was not what they had come here to do. In spite of the hatred that Wickins now felt for the Lucasian Professor, he was not a murderer. It was at that moment he spotted the orb. He swept it up with his left hand and thrust it into his tunic. Then he pulled Newton to his feet, keeping his blade against the man's throat and began to step backwards towards the others. But he couldn't see where he was going, stumbled into one of the tall sturdy candleholders and went sprawling.

Newton dived for Wickins's sword. In a moment he had it in his hand and had whirled round to survey the room. His eyes were ablaze, every sense sharpened, every self-protective instinct empowering him.

A few feet away Boyle had caught his brother by the throat, forcing him against the wall. At the point of Hooke's sword, Nicolas Fatio du Duillier stood beside him, panting with fury.

'James, James . . . How could you?' Boyle was saying, his voice cracking.

'Big brother Robert,' he sneered. 'Robert, who has always seen himself as my father . . . save me your sanctimoniousness. I need it not.'

'But why?' Boyle whispered. 'Why?'

'You know not, Robert? Truly? You know not?'

Boyle shook his head slowly.

'Where else could I go, dear brother? How could I compete with you? A man who casts such a long shadow.'

Boyle flinched as he felt the point of a sword against his neck.

'Drop your blade,' Newton hissed. 'Now!'

Boyle obeyed and turned around. Du Duillier and James Boyle were still facing Hooke's unflinching rapier and Wickins was scrambling to his feet. He dashed forward and plucked Boyle's sword from the stone floor.

'Another step and I will slice him open!' Newton yelled.

Wickins kept coming.

'I mean it.' And he dug his blade into Boyle's neck, drawing blood.

Wickins stopped. 'You will suffer in hell for this.'

'No, you are wrong, my old friend,' Newton replied evenly. 'For the Lord knows my motives are true.' He took a deep breath. 'Now, give me the sphere.'

Wickins remained rooted to the spot.

'Give me the sphere.'

'Don't, John,' Boyle gasped.

'Ignore this old fool. Hand over the orb. Now. Do it, or I swear I shall kill him,' Newton shouted.

Slowly, Wickins put his hand inside his tunic and his hand encircled the ruby sphere.

'No! Don't!' Boyle implored. 'Better that I die . . .'

Wickins brought out the ruby sphere. As he did so, Hooke, who had been guarding du Duillier and James Boyle, suddenly flicked his blade towards Newton. Newton caught the movement at the edge of his vision and flinched. It was enough. Robert Boyle sank his teeth into Newton's hand. Newton screamed, but somehow managed to keep hold of his sword.

Cursing, Newton whirled around and slashed at Hooke's shoulder. Then he was gone, vanishing into the blackness of the corridor.

Wickins started forward, but Boyle restrained him. 'John, John, let him go. You will never find him in the labyrinth. We must make safe all that is left, the sphere and the documents.' He sounded weary and unbearably sad. 'I must untangle this terrible web and you must make safe the future. As soon as we reach the surface ride with all speed for Cambridge. Get there before Newton – and burn everything.'

Chapter 32

Oxford: 29 March, 9.05 p.m.

Back at the house Philip stoked up the Aga and put the kettle on while Laura went upstairs to find a woollen cardigan. A few minutes later they were in the sitting room with a fresh fire catching hold in the grate.

'The thing is,' Philip said, sipping at a mug of hot tea, 'Lightman's disappearance almost certainly has nothing to do with the murders. It's just a coincidence.'

Laura looked at him blankly. 'I can't see how they could be connected, but it's just so . . . well . . . weird.'

Philip shrugged. 'Did you get any feeling that Lightman was ill, or disturbed? Could he have flipped out?'

Laura shook her head.

'Did he suffer from depression?'

'I don't know. I've only seen him a few times in

recent years. He seemed totally together to me. Why? You think he just left his car and walked off?'

'It happens.'

'Sure. But Lightman?'

'Which means he was abducted?'

Laura looked up from her tea. 'God knows, Philip. But who . . . ?'

'I guess we'll know soon enough. The police won't want to let this one go easily. Lightman's a star in Oxford, and one of the wealthiest men in Britain.' He held up the DVD that they had retrieved from Box 14. 'Shall we?'

There were a few seconds of static before the screen lit up with an image of Charlie Tucker sitting on a chair, staring straight at the camera. They could see bookshelves behind him and an ashtray on the floor beside his chair. He was taking a drag on a cigarette. It looked as though he was filming himself: the angle was not quite right and the lighting was poor.

'Hi, Laura babe. Well, at least I hope it's you watching this.' He gave the camera a brief, nervous smile. 'By the time you get this,' he went on, 'I'll either be dead or abroad somewhere.'

Laura felt a knot in the pit of her stomach.

'The fact is,' Charlie continued, 'my life's in danger. I don't have long to explain and there's so much to say. I hate putting you in danger, but when

261

you came to see me the other day . . . well, I got the feeling you were already in it up to your neck, so . . .'

'OK, where to start? Right, well . . . You've obviously been to Box 14 at Paddington and you have the Newton text. I expect you've been wondering how on earth I could get hold of such a thing. Well, the truth is that for a while I was involved with the group I mentioned – you know, the occultists . . .

'I speak in the past tense because I hope I've got out. You see, I was drawn in by default. They had some incriminating evidence concerning my political activities back in the 1980s and, well . . . the government has a long memory, especially when it comes to the sort of things I was doing.' Charlie produced a conspiratorial grin. 'Anyway, I scarpered when I realised what the group was really up to. I don't want to be part of that.' The cigarette had burned down to the filter, and he paused to take another from a packet in his pocket. Lighting it from the stub, he took a deep drag and exhaled a cloud of smoke.

'Look.' Charlie shifted in his seat. 'This is probably making no sense. Let me start from the beginning.' He coughed.

'Let's go back sixteen hundred years to the Library of Alexandria. A great scholar, who was also the Chief Librarian, was a woman named Hypatia. Now

Hypatia was quite a gal: not only was she one of the most knowledgeable people of the time, but she caused great controversy by rejecting much of the newfangled Christianity that was sweeping across the world. She was viewed as a heretic and was eventually flayed alive by a group of oh-so-pious Christians.' Charlie smirked.

'Hypatia was an adept of the occult. A millennium after her time she would have been called a white witch. In her keeping were some of the most important artefacts known to civilisation. In her library she kept rare manuscripts that dealt with all aspects of the occult, both black and white magic, and she had in her possession the two greatest alchemical treasures known to humankind – the emerald tablet and the ruby sphere.

'The emerald tablet is famous, of course. Over the centuries it's become established as the central pillar of alchemical law. It offers the alchemist a sort of "instruction manual" for their work. Less well known is the ruby sphere. Rumours about this object have circulated in the Hermetic world since Hypatia's time, but few have seen it and fewer still have any idea what power it contains.

'The night the Library of Alexandria was destroyed, on 13 March AD 415, Hypatia made sure that the emerald tablet was taken from the city and transported to Europe, where it was protected by a line of alchemists stretching down the centuries. Meanwhile, she made safe the ruby sphere in a secret hiding place within the foundations of the library. A year later, her father Ecumenius retrieved the precious thing and brought it to England. There he was met by the leaders of a small group of adepts who called themselves the Guardians, a group whose secrets derived from Ancient Egypt and the first alchemists, and in whose arts Hypatia and Ecumenius had been trained.

'The Guardians hid the ruby sphere in a secret vault to which the only access was via an underground labyrinth. They built this close to their meeting place and ensured that the only ones who could pass through the labyrinth were those who possessed the secret knowledge needed to succeed in completing a series of tests. Almost a thousand years later, the city of Oxford grew up on this site.

'The ruby sphere remained in its hiding place until the seventeenth century when Christopher Wren was commissioned to build the Sheldonian Theatre. He discovered the labyrinth, but did nothing about it. However, a couple of decades later Isaac Newton, perhaps the greatest alchemist of his or indeed any age, stumbled across the vital clues about how to find the sphere from a document that had passed through the hands of another alchemist a couple of centuries before him, a man named George Ripley.'

Charlie leaned back in the chair and blew smoke towards the camera.

'This was almost a disaster. The sphere possesses genuinely awesome power and Newton was a genius, obsessed with elucidating the secrets of the universe at whatever cost. With the sphere, he had the chance to fulfil his dream.'

Charlie paused for a moment and stubbed out his cigarette. 'I suppose you're wondering what all the fuss is about? What's so special about this ruby sphere? Why is it so important that people would give their lives to protect it? Murder to possess it? Well, the sphere is the key to finding the Philosopher's Stone and the Elixir of Life, the ultimate dream of the alchemist. No one really knows who made the sphere. It is at least as old as the early Egyptian civilisation and some have speculated that originally it's not from this world. By reading an incantation which is inscribed as one continuous coil around the surface of the sphere, the adept can call upon the Devil to turn the lifeless contents of the crucible into the mythical and most cherished Stone.

'Now, I wouldn't blame you, Laura, if you think this is all a load of crap. But whether or not you believe the ruby sphere can be used to conjure up the Devil, there are those who really do believe, and today, in Oxford, a group of powerful alchemists are trying to prove it. They don't have the sphere, but they do possess some of the secrets they need.

'And I imagine you're trying to figure out what the link is between Isaac Newton in the seventeenth century and this group in the twenty-first. Perhaps you're wondering why I've given you a copy of Newton's secret encoded work, and you must also be trying to understand what I have to do with all this, and why my life is in danger.

'Newton, you see, was the forebear of the present-day group. He called his cabal the Order of the Black Sphinx. This was the name originally used by the early Egyptian alchemists who first used the sphere. He formed what has been called an Unholy Trinity with his lover, the medic Nicolas Fatio du Duillier, and their mutual acquaintance, James Boyle, the younger brother of the great Robert Boyle. The link between Newton and his friends and the present Order of the Black Sphinx is the conjunction of the planets. Newton found a way to obtain the ruby sphere about eighteen months before a five-body conjunction in 1690. The next time the conjunction occurred Professor Milliner had acquired some of the secret lore of the Order and tried his hand. Today, the Order are trying to repeat Newton's experiment.

'And what is this experiment? I'm assuming you have worked that out. The ruby sphere tells the adept to gather five organs, each to be taken from a young woman at precisely documented times. In place of

266

each organ a metal coin is left, an Ancient Egyptian Arkhanon depicting five women – the five victims. These organs are preserved and used at a preordained hour. Placed on the points of the pentagram, they are central to the enactment of a ceremony which, if successful, will call upon the Devil to appear and to impart the secret of how to create the Philosopher's Stone.

'Newton and his friends succeeded in gathering the organs after murdering five young women in Oxford. The organs – a heart, a brain, a pair of kidneys, a gall bladder and a liver – were preserved according to the techniques passed down by the original members of the Order, Egyptian alchemists skilled in the art of mummification and preservation. This was du Duillier's speciality. He had made a detailed study of the processes and had done his best to duplicate the ancient techniques. The ritual was to take place in a chamber beneath the Bodleian Library – a part of the labyrinth of the Guardians. Newton and his friends reached this chamber through a hidden entrance in the wine cellars of Hertford College, close to the Bodleian. It was vital to complete the tests created by the Guardians of the fifth century, but they could do this relatively easily because Newton had the information handed down to him in the manuscript written by George Ripley. It was only thanks to the intervention of the

Guardians in the nick of time that Newton was thwarted.

'From what I've learned of them, the existence of the Guardians is even more secret than that of the Order of the Black Sphinx, and they have been more successful – up until now. In Newton's time, the Guardians were led by Robert Boyle . . . Yes, ironic, isn't it, that James was a key figure in Newton's group. Robert Boyle was helped by Newton's great rival Robert Hooke and a man named John Wickins, who had been Newton's closest associate, his room-mate, a man who had been planted in Cambridge as a young student, specifically to keep an eye on Newton.'

Charlie peered intently at the camera. 'The present-day Order of the Black Sphinx is behind the murders of the young women in Oxford. Their members include a trained killer, a man known only as the Acolyte. They are gathering organs and preserving them, and this time they have twenty-first-century technology at their disposal. Their intention is the same as Newton's and Milliner's – to perform an occult ritual when Mars, Venus and Jupiter are in conjunction with the sun and the moon. This will occur on 31 March, the day after tomorrow, at 1.34 a.m.

'And what did I have to do with all this?' Charlie shifted in his seat before answering his own question. 'Remember my visit to New York, Laura? I was there representing the Order. You see, the Order of the twenty-first century have never had the ruby sphere. Other than the Guardians, Isaac Newton and his companions were the only men to have seen or touched the precious thing since Hypatia's day. And when their cabal was shattered in 1690 the sphere was reclaimed and hidden by Robert Boyle. Furthermore, all Newton's papers on the subject were destroyed. All, that is, except for one, a short encoded document entitled *Principia Chemicum*, a copy of which you now have in your possession.

'This is the document that I obtained for the Order in New York. They knew they could almost certainly never get hold of the sphere in time for the conjunction, and without it their efforts would be futile. However, the leader of the Order, a man I have never met and whose identity has remained a secret, found out about Newton's manuscript and the information it contained – among other things, a linear version of the inscription.'

It was time for another cigarette. 'Let me explain. I said there was an inscription on the sphere. It consists of a single line of Egyptian hieroglyphs etched in a spiral around the sphere from one pole to the other. The makers of the sphere were keen to prevent the knowledge contained within the inscription reaching anyone but the initiated. So they used a cunning form of encryption called steganography – in other words, a physical code. What I mean is that the message, the incantation that must be used in the ritual, had to be read on the sphere by looking at the symbols vertically from top to bottom, not around the spiral. It's an ancient technique called a scytale.

'This is fine if you have the sphere, but only Newton and the Guardians have ever possessed it. The document I found in New York, Newton's manuscript, contains a copy of the inscription translated into Latin, but it was transcribed in linear form, making it more or less useless. I studied mathematics, remember? And I specialised in encryption. The leader of the current Order knew this. I was offered a job that I could not refuse. I had no idea what they were trying to do – well, at least not until I got the manuscript.

'It took me almost a year to decipher the linear inscription. The missing clue was the size of the sphere. If you know that then you can turn the linear inscription into a spiral again and read down the lines to retrieve the message. Newton left no record of the dimensions of the sphere, so you could guess for ever and never get a true interpretation. The only other way to crack the code was by using the most advanced decryption methods and a very expensive computer. I was given the equipment and, well, the rest was up here.' Charlie tapped his head. 'Being a genius has its uses.

'Throughout the time I was trying to crack the code I was under constant pressure from representatives of the Order. But I was also making it my business to find out as much as I could about what they were planning to do with the code. I have never managed to establish who the members are. Nor who their leader is. Everything was done through messengers and by encrypted e-mail. But, having discovered their intentions, I wanted out.

'Just two weeks ago I delivered the decryption. But what the Order have is quite useless. They are not aware of this yet and they are still killing. Two more young women will die in a little over twenty-four hours unless the Order is stopped.'

Charlie took a long contemplative puff of his cigarette. 'Laura, it's up to you now. I hope you can enlist the help of others you trust. There's not much more I can do to help except to tell you what I've learned, so here it is.

'Although Newton did not possess the technology needed to preserve the organs for the ceremony, he did have several advantages over the present-day members of the Order of the Black Sphinx. Most importantly, he had the sphere. Also, when the Order was broken up by the Guardians in 1690 they lost almost all their records – and Boyle and the others made sure that the hidden entrance to the labyrinth through Hertford College was sealed up. The Guardians created a new entry point, the location of which you will have to figure out from other clues I will give you. This leads via a long tunnel to the original labyrinth under the Bodleian.

'This means that Milliner in 1851 was facing three grave problems. He didn't have the sphere but was working from a mysterious copy of the linear inscription, probably a copy that Boyle's brother James had managed to keep from the Guardians back in 1690. He also had no clear idea how to preserve the organs he had started to gather in Oxford and, finally, he did not know how to enter the labyrinth – the Hertford College entry point was no more. And of course he was not privy to the secrets of the Guardians, so he could not have learned of the newer entrance made after Newton's time. To get round this, Milliner did something quite extraordinary. He had known for years about the miles of tunnels under the Bodleian. Even in Victorian times these tunnels were extensive. Through his intimate knowledge of the occult and the traditions of the Order of the Black Sphinx he had a clear idea of the location of the ancient chamber in which the ceremony was to be held. So he financed a little private construction – or, rather, *de*construction – work, which involved linking up the nearest tunnels to those leading to the chamber. The work was carried out in the late 1840s, and the poor architect employed by Milliner was found hanged a month after the job was completed. The police believed he had committed suicide.'

Charlie started to cough and could not stop. 'God,' he said after a while, 'I really must give up these bloody things. I have a strong feeling,' he went on, 'that the present-day members of the Order have no idea how to reach the chamber through the labyrinth of the Guardians, but they have the route that Milliner created which bypasses the labyrinth altogether. It would be impossible to get to the chamber from the surface or to escape the tunnels again without a map, and as far as I know there is only one copy of this and it is kept safely hidden by the Order.

'Well,' Charlie said, with a long sigh. 'I've almost reached the end of this strange monologue. I hope you understand a little more of the background. I wish I could be there with you to help you, but . . . Well, anyway, all I can offer are some clues. This DVD also contains valuable information that will help you. After this message is over, put the disc in your computer. You'll have to decipher my message, a personal one for you, Laura, which will stop anyone else breaking in. Once you are through, you'll find information that will help you translate Newton's manuscript, and from this you will find the current entrance to the labyrinth. Once there, you're pretty much on your own. I have no idea what the Guardians' defences are, nor how you can pass through the labyrinth by completing the three tests created by the ancients. Unfortunately, although Newton had passed through it successfully himself with the aid of Ripley's manuscript, and then later with du Duillier and Boyle the Younger, he left almost no hints about the labyrinth in his document.

'Farewell, Laura. I hope when you see this I'll still be alive and sunning myself on some exotic beach. Maybe when this is all over we can get together and catch up on old times, just like we did when I came to New York. Bye, Sweet Pea.'

The screen went blank. Philip and Laura were both so absorbed with their thoughts that they didn't hear Jo open the front door and come into the room.

Laura looked up. 'Oh, hi, honey,' she said distractedly.

'Good programme?' Jo asked, eyebrows raised.

'It's a message from Charlie.'

Jo looked at her mother with blank incomprehension.

'A recording he made just before he died. It explains an awful lot.' Laura clicked the remote and the DVD began to play again.

★

'So what are we waiting for?' Jo said when it was over. 'Let's try the computer.'

Philip put the DVD in the drive and the screen lit up to display a short message:

Enter '1' and answer.

Philip hit the '1' key and a new line of text appeared:

LAURA, YOU LIKED IT THAT EVENING

Philip turned to look at Laura, an eyebrow raised. 'Well?'

'Well, what? What the hell is that supposed to mean?'

'It's the personal clue Charlie mentioned. The answer will be something obvious only to you.'

'Did you and Charlie . . . ?' Philip said.

'Oh, please.'

'Well, I just . . .'

'He must be referring to New York,' Laura said. 'That's the only time I've seen him in the evening for twenty years. We went to Harry's Grill on West 34th Street.' She stopped for a moment and looked blankly at the screen, trying to recall the evening.

'Was there anything special about it?' Philip asked.

'The crème brûlée was pretty amazing.'

'Let's try it,' Jo said.

Philip typed in 'crème brûlée' and the screen went blank for a moment before a new message appeared.

WARM, BUT SORRY.
JUST TWO TRIES LEFT

'Shit,' Philip exclaimed.

'What? I thought that was it,' Laura hissed and turned to her daughter.

Jo shrugged. 'Too easy, obviously. Then, pulling over a chair, she leaned across Philip. 'OK, we've got two more chances and that's it. We'd better take this a little more carefully.'

'But it's impossible,' Laura said. 'It could be anything.'

'Yeah, but it's a personal code, Mom, something you would know right away.'

'That's why I suggested "crème brûlée", Jo . . .'

'OK,' Philip said. 'Let's think. Charlie's clue is YOU ENJOYED IT THAT EVENING. What else could he mean? You sure he's even referring to the evening in New York?'

'How the hell would I know?' Laura could feel the frustration rising.

'I think you're on the right lines,' Jo said. 'Charlie says as much – warm – which must refer to the evening at the restaurant. But the code could be "crème" or "brûlée" or "cb" . . . anything.'

None of them spoke for a moment. Jo looked lost in thought. Laura ran her fingers through her hair and gazed at the screen.

'I think you're right,' Philip said, eventually. 'It could be anything, but Charlie gave you a clue after the first attempt. Maybe we need more information.'

'Yes, but that would give us just one last try.'

'Any better ideas?' Philip replied.

'Hang on,' Laura said suddenly. 'If we fail after three goes, can't we just reinsert the DVD and start again?'

'I doubt it. It'll wipe itself, I'm sure,' Jo said. 'Or self-destruct like in *Mission Impossible*.'

'Oh, swell.'

'I think Dad's right, though. Without more information we could guess all night. Let's just try something and hope for the best.'

'Doesn't sound very scientific,' said Philip.

'How about just 'brûlée'?' Jo suggested.

Laura shrugged. 'I guess.'

Philip typed in the word. After a moment a new message appeared.

STONE ME, LAURA. THIS IS SUPPOSED
TO BE EASY FOR YOU!
IT'S JUST FIVE LETTERS, BABE

'Damn it,' Laura exclaimed and exhaled through her teeth. Then suddenly she clapped her hands together. 'No, no, of course, that's it . . .'

'What?'

'I remember now. We were just about to eat the crème brûlée when the Rolling Stones' "Brown Sugar" came on the restaurant stereo. Charlie made a joke about the coincidence – crème brûlée – brown sugar?' She leaned over Philip's shoulder and typed in five letters.

'Hang on, Laura,' Philip said, twisting round to face her. 'What're you going to put in?'

'Five letters, of course – Charlie says so – It has to be STONE, doesn't it? And besides, what is this all about anyway? What is the Order of the Black Sphinx after? What was Newton trying to get?' Before either of the others could say anything, Laura tapped in the five letters and hit 'enter'. This time the screen turned black. Then suddenly the word CONGRATULATIONS appeared.

Laura let out a deep sigh. She hit the 'enter' key again and the screen lit up with a new, more elaborate message comprising a line of words followed by a series of numbers:

3.5, 12,
67498763258997
86746496688598
97684795900082
08736047437980
73849096006064
87474877345985
47932768480950

Beneath these numbers was a block of text made up of hundreds of letters without a break.

'Is that it?' Philip asked and scrolled down, but there was nothing more.

'You know,' Jo said, 'your friend Charlie Tucker is something of a legend in the math department.' She gestured to Philip to let her take his seat.

Laura looked round at her. 'Well, he wasn't far wrong on the DVD when he called himself a genius.'

'Tell me about it. Professor Norrington, our Group Theory lecturer, remembers Charlie from when he was first teaching in Oxford. Norrington worked for the CIA and MI5 before he morphed into an academic – he was a code-breaker – and he claims that Charlie was the only mathematician he's ever met who could create codes even he, Norrington, could not crack.'

'Yes, but Charlie wanted us to get this information, didn't he?'

'Sure,' Jo replied, 'But it was in his blood – he couldn't just give it away.'

'Great,' Laura replied and walked over to the sofa.

'But luckily,' Jo retorted, 'you know another genius . . . and my first-year special subject is Group Theory – rather important in cracking codes.' She flexed her fingers and contemplated the screen. 'And I absolutely love a challenge.'

Chapter 33

Oxford: 30 March, early morning

'Mom . . . Mom, wake up.'

Laura opened her eyes to see Jo's face hovering over her. She sat up quickly, putting her fingers to her temples. Sighing, she leaned back onto the cushions of the sofa.

'God, what time is it?'

'Four-fifteen.'

'Where's Philip?'

'Here.' Philip came into the living room carrying a tray. 'I think we all need this.' He put the coffees down on the low table in front of the sofa. 'Well, Jo does, anyway. You've slept through all the action.'

Laura was still half asleep. 'What are you talking about, Philip?'

Philip smiled at Jo. 'Our daughter has cracked Charlie's code.'

'Well, I've cracked *some* of it,' Jo said.

Suddenly Laura was wide awake. Grabbing one

of the coffees, she sat forward on the sofa. 'Start from the beginning, and take it slow,' she said.

Jo had a sheaf of papers in her hand. 'I tried all sorts of things to begin with, but nothing was happening. You have to experiment. Anyway, I started to think about what Charlie said about the ruby sphere. He mentioned the scytale and it suddenly occurred to me that this code he used on the DVD was also a scytale. Another clue came from the number 3.5 he wrote after the list of colours. Then there's the block of numbers,' she continued. 'Seven rows of fourteen apparently random integers. It seemed likely that there was a number combination there, some sequence that would be relevant. So I decided to print out the numbers. Then I made a tube of paper that was exactly 3.5 centimetres in diameter.'

'And the numbers fitted?'

'No.'

'What?'

'It wasn't as simple as I'd thought it would be. I was stumped. But then I looked again at the message. After the number 3.5 there was 12, New York. I'd assumed that New York referred to Charlie's visit in some way and that it might be relevant later.'

'But then,' Philip interrupted, 'Jo demonstrated true genius.'

Jo smiled at her father. 'Flattery will get you

everywhere, Daddy. But, actually, it was obvious now I think about it. New York is a font. I had to print out the numbers using New York, size twelve.'

'And that worked?'

'Like a dream.

'So there's another scytale.'

'Problem was, though, I just had the same ninety-eight numbers – the seven rows of fourteen. I tried to see if there were any obvious patterns that popped up, you know – numbers one to seven or something straightforward like that, but that didn't work.'

'So what did you do?' Laura asked.

'I wasted a good hour chasing up a blind alley looking at number relations, like doubling the first number – 3.5, 7, 14 – I'm sure Charlie did that deliberately to throw people off the scent. But, after I realised that this was going nowhere, I started to think about the other part of the message – the colours. That's where Dad helped out.'

'I can do more than make the coffee,' Philip said.

'Glad to hear it. This tastes awful,' Laura retorted, pulling a face. 'Just kidding . . . Go on.'

'Dad was on the computer trying to find out anything he could about the alchemy stuff that Charlie had described, and I was at the table over there using reliable old pen and paper.'

'By happy coincidence, just as Jo got stuck I found out some stuff about the emerald tablet and what alchemists tried to do with the inscriptions on it. There is absolutely nothing on the Net about the ruby sphere, but I guess you would expect that.'

'Come on, then. Tell me. What did you find?' Laura asked impatiently.

'Pretty crazy, most of it,' Philip replied. 'There was no consistency in the work of the alchemists. They were all obsessed with secrecy. You can see why Charlie was attracted to this stuff. It was all about codes and secret languages, one alchemist keeping secrets from another. They certainly didn't like to share, and they each interpreted their findings differently. More often than not the accounts they left of what they discovered contradict each other completely. However.' He took a deep breath and rubbed his eyes. 'There were a few things they all had in common. First, they all started their experiments with a simple set of chemicals which they mixed together and heated to see what would happen. Second, almost all alchemists used the emerald-tablet texts as their source of information; and from this they followed a sort of "recipe". In almost all accounts, they saw the same thing happen when they heated their mix of chemicals. They saw them change colour. The pattern was always the same – the mixture started off black, turned white, then yellow, then red.'

'Ah.'

'Ah indeed,' Philip said.

'Still didn't get me anywhere,' said Jo, with a grin. 'Except that it made me focus on the colours in Charlie's message, and how they might relate to the table of numbers – Charlie was obviously tying them together. In cryptanalysis everything has a purpose, and Charlie is – was – a master.'

'OK, so what did you do?'

'Nothing much, just stared at the cylinder of numbers,' Jo said. 'And then suddenly I saw it.'

'Saw what?'

'The numbers 5,5,6,3 in one of the columns along the scytale.'

'The word black – five letters, white – five letters, and so on?' Laura asked.

'Precisely. And that, Mother, is called a key.'

'Well, thanks, Jo. I'm not Homer Simpson.'

'The block of text is a set of instructions,' Philip interrupted. He showed Laura a printout.

FIRST OFF. USE THE SAME KEY TO DECODE NEWTON'S DOCUMENT. INTERPRET THE INCANTATION – IT MIGHT INTEREST YOU. THE DIAGRAM SHOWS THE LABYRINTH UNDER THE BODLEIAN. YOU ENTER IT VIA THE TRILL MILL STREAM, DOOR IN WALL SIXTY-THREE PACES IN FROM WEST ENTRANCE. AT THE BOTTOM OF THE

PAGE IS AN ESSENTIAL QUOTE: YOU
WILL NEED IT LATER. GOOD LUCK!

'Fantastic, Jo!' Laura exclaimed. 'OK. My turn.'
She jumped up from the sofa. 'Newton document,
Philip, please,' she said. 'And *lots* more of your
excellent coffee.'

Laura laid out the single page on the table in the
dining room. Charlie had used a high-res colour
photocopier and every crease and crinkle of the original could be seen on the reproduction. It had a dark
ochre tinge and was skirted with white where Charlie
had mounted the document on a modern card
backing. The lettering was in different shades of grey.
Laura assumed that Newton had used different inks
and added to the text over a period of time. Around
the edges of the page were roughly drawn diagrams
and images, symbols and formulae. Laura wondered
about the significance of a ram's head, a sun symbol
and a few Greek letters . . .

At the top it said: PRINCIPIA CHEMICUM by
Isaacus Neuutonus and beneath that were two lines
of Latin.

'The subtitle is just about the only thing that makes
any sort of immediate sense,' said Laura, leaning over
the paper with her arms crossed on the table. 'I read
that much in the car coming from London.'

'It does?' Philip and Jo said in unison.

'God, where were you two educated? It says "From the Manuscript of the Adept Ripley and Supplemented by My Own Researches and Explorations. Translated from the Original Egyptian Text."'

The rest of the page was divided almost evenly into two. The first section consisted of lines of writing, made up from a block of letters similar to the text that Charlie had put on the DVD. Under that was a roughly drawn scratchy-looking diagram – a network of interlocking lines that resembled a complex maze of corridors. At the base of the diagram a series of lines threaded their way almost to the foot of the page. Beside this was a single line in plain Latin:

ALUMNUS AMAS SEMPER
UNICIUM TUA DEUS

'Over to you again, Mom,' Jo remarked wearily.

'Yes, it's a bit of an odd sentence. Literally, it translates as: "Pupil love always . . . er, uniquely, I guess . . . thy, your . . . God." Which is very clumsy, so I suppose it would better read as something like: "Adept", yes, adept is better for alumnus . . . "Adept, love always thy God."'

'"Adept, love always thy God"? A sort of signing-off? A signature at the end of the document?' Philip speculated.

'Could be. Perhaps a sort of general statement for the alchemist, like "God Bless You" or "Best Wishes", maybe.' Laura shrugged. 'Doesn't seem to help much. Let's get to work on this first block, using the key.'

'5 5 6 3,' Jo said. 'So, fifth letter, tenth, sixteenth, nineteenth.'

As they went methodically through the text Philip wrote down each letter on a fresh sheet of paper. After a few minutes they had distilled nine lines from it.

'It's Latin again,' Laura noted. 'I can translate the first few words, but there are no breaks.'

After twenty minutes, between them they had arranged the string of letters into a paragraph of Latin words which Laura translated and wrote out on a separate sheet.

You are Mercury the mighty flower,
You are most worthy of honour;
You are the Source of Sol, Luna and Mars,
You are Settler of Saturn and Source of Venus,
You are Emperor, Prince and most regal of Kings,
You are Father of the Mirror and Maker of Light.
You are head and highest and fairest in Sight.
All praise thee.
All praise thee. Giver of truth.
We seek, we beseech, we welcome you.

'Twaddle,' Philip snorted.

'Maybe, but it's obviously some sort of incantation. I can only assume this is what the Order of the Black Sphinx use to conjure up Old Nick.'

'And this is what the present-day Order need to carry out the ritual.'

'And what Charlie gave them in altered form,' Philip said.

'Why did he bother changing it if it's all nonsense?' Jo asked.

'Because he's a believer. Never quite understood how someone so intelligent could be taken in by this stuff, but there you are. To Charlie, this incantation was a real way to conjure up the Devil, and to the members of the Order it is too. Newton believed it – but then, he did live in an entirely different age, an era during which magic and witchcraft were accepted in the way that we accept the principles of science.'

'They can believe in the Loch Ness Monster for all I care,' Philip added. 'But we have to do everything we can to stop them committing more murders. And we have just over twelve hours before the next one.'

Laura turned her attention to the diagram. 'This must be the labyrinth,' she said.

'Which you can reach from . . . where was it?' Jo asked.

'The Trill Mill Stream.'

'What on earth is that?'

Laura looked at Philip and they both laughed. 'She's only been here a few months, poor love,' Philip said.

Jo rolled her eyes. 'Oh, wise ones, please impart your ancient knowledge.'

'It's quite famous, Jo. A stream that runs under the city from Christ Church Meadow. Its about a mile long. When T. E. Lawrence was young he used to row through it.'

'Really?'

'Yeah, and legend has it that in the 1920s someone found a punt down there with a couple of skeletons in Victorian dress – they had got stuck there and died.'

'Spooky,' Jo said. 'It all sounds like some third-rate horror movie.'

'But I'm afraid it's all horribly true,' said Philip.

'And I think it's time we looked down there for ourselves,' said Laura.

Chapter 34

Oxford: 30 March, noon

The police station was abuzz with activity as DCI John Monroe swung open the doors and strode in. In the reception area two officers were trying to restrain a drunken youth wearing a yellow-and-black football scarf and bobble hat.

'Coachload from Watford. Drunk as skunks,' explained PC Hornet as Monroe approached the desk. Monroe said nothing but slid some papers across the counter towards the duty officer. 'And there's a Mr Bridges in Room 3. Been here half an hour,' Hornet added. 'Also, a witness has come forward about the Lightman disappearance. Old lady reckons she saw the professor being dragged from a car by two men, just outside her house on Norham Gardens. Here's the report.'

Monroe waved a silent thanks and headed along the corridor off the main reception area. He glanced at the report but decided to save it for later. Entering

Interview Room 3, he saw Malcolm Bridges sitting at a table placed under a window on the far side of the room.

'Mr Bridges, I'm sorry for the delay.'

The young man began to get out of his seat.

Monroe lowered himself wearily into the chair opposite. He leaned forwards with his elbows on the desk and rubbed his eyes. 'Professor Lightman . . . you know him well?' he said.

Bridges looked uncomfortable. 'Yes, yes. I, er, help him out at the library.'

'And at his home?'

'Yes, he pays well.' Bridges allowed himself a brief smile.

'Quite,' Monroe said, his face blank. 'When did you see him last?'

'Last night, about seven o'clock, at his house in . . .'

'I know where he lives, Mr Bridges.'

Bridges gave a nervous cough. 'Do you have anything new on his disappearance?'

Monroe appraised the young man on the other side of the table. He was neatly dressed in a dark suit, but his long greased-back hair only emphasised his cadaverous look. He was unhealthily thin and his skin was exceptionally pale, as though he spent more time than was good for him in libraries and laboratories.

'How long have you known Professor Lightman?'

'About two years. I met him when I was working on my PhD. Before that I was at Cambridge.'

'I see. And Russell Cunningham? How well do you know him?'

'He's a first-year in the department, one of my charges for practical work. Not a terribly good student, to be honest – too many distractions. What's Cunningham got to do with anything?'

'How well do you know him?'

Bridges paused for a second. 'Not well at all. We meet up in my office once a fortnight so that I can assess his progress. Apart from that I see him around the department sometimes. I can't say he's my type, really.'

Monroe raised an eyebrow. 'That's an odd thing to say.'

'To be honest, I think he's wasting his time in Oxford. Should be doing something in the City. I think he's here because of his daddy. Men like Nigel Cunningham send their sons to Oxford to enhance their own image. He's a trophy son.'

'So, you don't really like the boy?'

'I didn't say that. I just . . .'

'Resent people like him.'

'I wouldn't even say resent . . . I find people like Cunningham uninteresting.'

'OK,' Monroe said, with a sigh. 'Can you account

for your whereabouts at the times of the recent murders?

'WHAT?' Bridges looked utterly shocked. 'I thought you asked me here to help find Professor Lightman.'

'I did. But we're exploring any possible connections. Russell Cunningham is a suspect . . .'

'He is?'

'. . . And you work with him. You also work with Professor Lightman. Can you tell me where you were on 20/21 March between 7.30 p.m. and 3 a.m.?'

Bridges fiddled with his ear lobe. 'I was in London throughout the day on the twentieth – a Monday, yes? I went to the Royal Society of Psychologists meeting on Pall Mall.'

'And you were back in Oxford when?'

'Around ten or ten-thirty, I think. I was in a room with at least fifty other psychologists at 7.30 p.m.'

'What a dreadful thought. And what about the night of Wednesday, 22 March? Were you in Oxford then?'

Bridges glanced down at the table. 'Wednesdays I supervise a 7.30 p.m. practical group, so I would have been working late at the Psychology Department, until about eight-forty-five, nine maybe.'

'You had a class the Wednesday before last?'

'Yes.'

'And the class lasts an hour?'

Bridges nodded.

'Did anyone else see you there after eight-thirty?'

'There were still a few people about after the class ended. Rankin left earlier, about eight, I think. He passed by the lab for a few words. The students always vanish almost immediately the class is over, but a few of the other post-docs were around.'

'I see. So, technically, you could have killed the second and third victims.'

Bridges turned pale. 'Why do you even suggest something so ridiculous?'

'Your office is only a five-minute drive away.'

'But that's absurd! Lots of places are only a five-minute drive away. Why would I murder anyone? What possible motive . . . ?'

'Calm yourself, Mr Bridges. I didn't say you *did* commit the murders. I simply remarked that you *could have* committed them.'

Bridges eyed Monroe with growing hostility. 'Is there anything else you want to ask me, Detective Chief Inspector?'

'No, thank you, Mr Bridges. Not at this precise moment. You've been most helpful.' Monroe stood up. 'There is just one more thing you could do for us, though. Would you be so kind as to provide a DNA sample?'

★

As Monroe left Interview Room 3, a junior forensics officer came in with a DNA test kit and walked
over to where Bridges was sitting.

It was quieter now in the corridor. Two football
fans were being held in the cells and the rest had
been sent back to Watford three hours before the
game was due to start in Headington. On the way
to his office, Monroe stopped at the main desk.

'Hornet?' he called to the young PC who was
sitting at a computer terminal.

'Yes, sir?'

'How are the interviews going with the female
students?'

Hornet checked a large notebook on the counter.
'Greene, Matson and Thompson are running parallel
interviews in 4, 5 and 7. We've had in . . .' he ran
his finger down the page, '. . . let me see . . . ten,
eleven . . . fourteen girls, including the three in there
at the moment.'

'OK.' Monroe tapped the book with the tips of
his fingers, lost in thought.

Back in his office, Monroe was glad to close the
door on the outside world. He felt unsettled by what
was happening. His junior officers had been elated
by what they had found at Cunningham's apartment
the day before, but there was something not quite
right about it. The kid was obviously disturbed, but
that didn't make him the killer. Whoever had

murdered the three girls and Simon Welding was a pro, not some pervy rich kid with too much time on his hands. And what was he to make of Bridges? The man was as jumpy as hell, but that just seemed to be the way he was. He didn't feel convinced that Bridges was hiding anything.

Bridges could have committed the later murders, Monroe reasoned. But that didn't help; all the murders had been committed by the same person, surely? If Bridges hadn't carried out the first killing then he must be in the clear.

And then Monroe started to think about what Forensics had thrown up. A piece of leather and some plastic. No leads had come from those. Then there was the blood trace found at the scene of the second murder, but it couldn't be matched with anything on the police databases.

Moving some papers from his desk, Monroe tried to find the report from the lab. It was at the bottom of a pile. The second page showed the read-out from the spectrum analyser, the DNA fingerprint from the tiny speck of blood found in the house close to where Jessica Fullerton's body had been found. He stared at the collection of lines and blocks of colour on the page. This was someone's profile, he thought to himself, the unique DNA signature of someone in this world, someone who was probably not far away from where he was sitting – someone living in this city. But without a record to match it against, it would be of little or no help.

Monroe tossed the paper onto the desk and reached for the phone.

'Hornet,' he snapped. 'Get me Howard Smales at MI5, a.s.a.p, and route the call through to my office.'

He picked up the read-out from the DNA analyser again and was following the pattern of peaks and troughs when the phone rang.

'Howard,' he said warmly. 'Yes, yes, it has been a while . . . Oh, you know, same old thing . . . Yes, I heard . . . congratulations. So look, Howard, I was wondering if I could ask a favour . . . Between you and me it is to do with the mur— Yes.' He laughed mirthlessly. 'Well, yes, I have a sample, but it doesn't match with anything on our . . . No, I know . . . Well, would you? No, no, I can get it over right away . . . And . . . yes, there is some urgency . . . I know, but that's the way the old team operates, I'm afraid. None of your government love-ins and not much dosh either . . . No . . . That would be great . . . Thanks, Howard, I owe you one.'

Chapter 35

Near Woodstock: 30 March, 2 p.m.

Philip only managed to grab a couple of hours' sleep before he was needed at the police station in Oxford. Four hours later, after snatching a take-out chicken sandwich from a bakery near Carfax, he was driving back to Woodstock when his mobile rang.

'How's it going?' It was Laura.

'Oh, awake, are we?'

She sighed down the line. 'Actually, I was up and about soon after you left. I went to James Lightman's house. I was hoping to catch Bridges, but he wasn't there.'

'Apparently, Monroe's found a new link between the victims,' Philip said. 'I didn't see him myself, and everyone I spoke to was very cagey – seems like the DCI has locked down on this one. But all the murdered girls were the subjects of some sort of psychological profiling carried out by a research team at the uni last year.'

'Really?' Laura sounded excited. 'Profiling? What kind . . . ?'

'I couldn't get many details. Apparently, it was a voluntary thing, a day of tests in exchange for a fifty-quid book voucher or something like that. Forty or so girls took part.'

'No names?'

'Only Monroe and a couple of other officers have the list . . . couldn't find out a thing. Everyone's clammed up. Where are you, by the way?'

'Near your place, just coming into Woodstock.'

'I'm not far behind you. See you at home.'

A few minutes later Philip pulled into the drive. He was surprised to see Laura standing at the kitchen door. She looked harried.

'What is it?'

'You've had a break-in.'

He followed her quickly through the dining room into the living room. His computer was in pieces that were scattered across the floor. Papers were strewn everywhere, bookcases had been overturned, a couple of his mother's paintings hung at odd angles. Philip sat down on the back of a sofa with his arms folded and surveyed the damage in silence before letting out a heavy sigh as he felt his anger mount.

'I'm sorry, Philip,' Laura said suddenly.

'Sorry? Why?'

'I was the one who dragged you into this mess.

Me and my crazy ideas. And now everything Charlie left us has gone.'

'What makes you think that?'

'Well, just look,' she replied and waved at the mess. 'This wasn't done by a bunch of kids or an opportunist thief, was it?'

'I'm sure you're right,' Philip replied. 'But you don't have to worry about Charlie's stuff. I had a feeling something like this might happen . . . and I took the precaution of keeping it all with me. It's in the car.'

Chapter 36

Victoria Coach Station, London: 30 March, 5 p.m.

Gail Honeywell, skin tanned, hair bleached blonde by Greek spring sun, dumped her rucksack on the floor of the waiting room at Victoria Coach Station, carefully avoiding the still-moist chewing gum and the dark smudge of what she hoped was chocolate. Fishing out her phone card she took two paces to the nearest payphone. Surprised to hear a dial tone, she keyed in her boyfriend's number and waited as the connection was made.

'Ray,' she said excitedly. 'Hi, I've made it to London. Listen, I haven't got long on this card. No, it was great. Professor Truman is just so relaxed, and I think we did some good work. It's just . . . six weeks away is too long. I can't wait to get home. I can't wait to see you . . .' Through the filthy, semi-opaque glass she could see coaches turning and reversing, passengers getting on and off. A uniformed driver passed by the door; the room was empty.

'I'm catching the five-thirty from here. Should get into Headington about six-forty. No, look, you don't have to come to meet me – it's football night, isn't it? . . . Yeah, yeah. No, Ray, I haven't . . . what murders? No, God, really? Shit, you're kidding. And he knew her? Yeah, yeah. No, OK, if you really don't mind . . . No, silly. God, I've missed you too. I loved it, but I'm glad to be back.' She was quiet for a moment, listening. Then she said. 'Yeah, no, cool. Look, OK . . . See ya . . . love y—' And the card expired.

Gail replaced the receiver and picked up her bag just as a uniformed driver stuck his head round the door. 'You catching the five-thirty for Oxford, love?' he asked.

Gail nodded.

'Got a seat on the five-oh-nine if you want it. Old lady feels sick, decided to 'ave a cuppa tea and catch a later one – want it?'

'Thanks,' she said. 'Great.'

The Acolyte sat in the black Toyota outside the house where Raymond Delaware lived. That afternoon he had made the final decision to use Gail Honeywell. She did not have the ideal medical profile, but the other two choices were more problematic. Ann

Clayton was in France for the Easter vac and at 7.14, the precise time for the procedure, Sally Ringwald would be in a room with six hundred other people during an award ceremony organised by the university's Theology Department.

An archaeology student, Gail Honeywell had been in Greece for the past six weeks on a dig, but an hour earlier the Acolyte had confirmed that she had arrived back in Britain that afternoon. The admin officer of the Archaeology Department had verified that the entire team was returning today, and he had seen the record on the cross-channel-ferry database to which he had quite easily gained access. Then, using the tap he had planted two weeks before, he had listened to the call Gail Honeywell had made to Ray Delaware from a callbox in London. She would be getting off the coach at the junction of Headington Road and Marston Road in St Clements at around six-forty. That, the Acolyte knew, would give him some leeway. The coaches were fairly reliable, and he would be prepared.

At 6.09 Raymond Delaware left the house on South Parks Road, earlier than the Acolyte had expected. It was no more than a mile and a half from the house to the bus stop, a route that would take him across the University Parks and along a quiet leafy lane called Mesopotamia Walk, which skirted a narrow tributary of the Cherwell. It was a favourite walk for the couple, and the Acolyte knew it well. On more than one occasion he had followed them along the path.

The Acolyte watched Raymond Delaware head east along the street and cursed aloud. The young man wanted to get to the bus stop early. 'Missing his girlfriend, no doubt,' the Acolyte thought with disgust as he pulled away from the kerb and drove dangerously fast along South Parks Road. At the end, he turned right into St Cross Road and then into Manor Road, a dead end which led through an iron gate onto a meadow to the west of Mesopotamia Walk.

He had less than ten minutes to prepare. Jumping out of the car, he had the presence of mind to make sure that he did not catch the pocket of his Ermanegildo Zegna jacket on the door handle. Then he paced round to the boot and withdrew a large zippered bag and an organ-carrier identical to the one he had used to transport Samantha Thurow's kidneys a week earlier. Keeping his head down to avoid being identified precisely by any nosy residents who might happen to be looking out of their windows, he headed for the gate.

The Acolyte was exceptionally fit and although the organ-transporter weighed more than fifteen kilogrammes and the field was waterlogged he made good speed and found shelter among some trees. It was silent except for the sound of distant traffic and nearby birdsong. He checked his watch. It was 6.14 and the insipid sun was low in the cloudy sky. It would be dark within half an hour, but he didn't have that long. He would have to take some risks.

He placed the box on the damp earth and unzipped the bag. It took him no more than a minute to dress in the plastic suit and to pull on the gloves and visor. The Acolyte checked his watch again and waited silently, slowing his breathing and calming himself by using the tantric exercises he had practised for many years.

On the coach, squeezed in next to an overweight man in a business suit, Gail Honeywell had grown steadily more bored and uncomfortable. She read a novel half-heartedly and stared out of the window at the grey London suburbs before the coach reached the motorway, and then later at the green fields under a dull sky smothered by heavy dark clouds.

Ten minutes onto the motorway and the man sitting next to her dozed off to sleep. He had a newspaper on his lap, and Gail lifted it gingerly and began to read. The big news story of the day was a threatened rail strike. This competed for attention with another scandal brewing in the royal family and the sexual indiscretions of a backbench Labour MP. On the dig, they had hardly seen a newspaper and had

had no TV. The radio was all in Greek and none of the other students or lecturers had cared to know what was happening in the world beyond their little heaven in the dust of Athens.

On page four she found a brief mention of the murders that Ray had described on the phone, but it told her little.

Gail put the paper back in the man's lap and went back to staring out of the window. For a moment she missed the sunshine of Greece and the work she loved. But then she thought of Ray – kind, gentle Ray. If ever a man was husband material, he was, she mused. She couldn't wait to see him again.

Raymond Delaware crossed the bridge over the Cherwell close to Parson's Pleasure, a gated and fenced-off stretch of the river which, for more than a century, had been reserved as a nudist sanctuary for the private use of the dons. It was quiet at this time; a dreary Friday evening. The clouds were heavy with rain and most of the students still in Oxford were either watching early-evening soaps on TV, making for the pub or grabbing a snack on The High or along Cornmarket Street.

Ray had missed Gail more than he'd ever believed he would. The six weeks they had spent apart had seemed like an age. He knew now that she was someone special, someone more important than the other girlfriends he had had during his first two years at university. He didn't like to think too far ahead or to get too serious, but at the same time he could not deny his emotions.

Within a few moments he had reached the wide tree-lined path that ran between the river on one side and the sodden fields on the other. Ray and Gail had walked along here on so many occasions. They loved it most in the deep winter, in January when it was freezing cold and they had to wrap up against the wind and the sleet. Last winter, Oxford had seen the heaviest snowfalls in anyone's memory and parts of the Cherwell had frozen over. This path had looked like a fantasy landscape, and even now, with the trees dripping wet and the air heavy with an approaching cloudburst, it still possessed an indefinable charm.

There was a sound behind him like the crack of a twig. Turning round, Ray felt a sudden burning sensation in his neck. Startled, he grabbed at his throat. Blood gushed between his fingers and for perhaps a second he simply stared at the red liquid. Then his head was yanked back. The branches of the trees whirled through the air in front of him and he began to choke. Blood ran across his face and into his nose and eyes, blinding him. He lost his balance and seemed to float in the air for a brief moment, a moment filled with a blend of panic and confusion before he landed heavily on the ground, his head smashing painfully against a rock. He tried to turn, to scramble to his feet, but a hand was pushing down on his face. Then came another stab from what felt like a molten hot dagger. It sent more tremors through him, screaming around inside his head.

Somehow, Ray managed to lift a hand and wipe it across his eyes. He caught a glimpse of a figure leaning over him but its face was a featureless mask. He began to shake uncontrollably. The shadowy figure straightened up and peered down at him. Then everything went black.

Gail watched the coach pull away and checked her watch. It was 6.21. She was twenty minutes early. Her legs felt stiff and it was good to fill her lungs with fresh air. Too excited to wait at the bus stop for Ray to arrive, she decided to head for the lane leading to Mesopotamia Walk. Ray was bound to be early and she would meet him on the path – it would be romantic. Maybe they would have a real Hollywood moment of kissing under the trees, she thought, and smiled to herself as she heaved the rucksack onto her back. She turned from Marston Road left into the lane, a short walk that would take her to the first of two small bridges across narrow tributaries of the river. Passing the old mill on her right, she would soon be on the broad path alongside the river, where she was bound to see Ray heading towards her.

It started to rain and Gail quickened her pace. Crossing the second bridge, she ran for the cover of the trees and then made a dash for the mill. The huge wooden wheel, a relic of the Industrial Revolution and now part of an English Heritage site, stood still, and water swept through the unmoving blades. The rain was falling in great torrents now, spattering on the path and the trees, competing with the sound of the water racing by through the lock and the narrow waterway that ran beside the mill. Pulling her rucksack up a little to relieve the ache in her shoulders, Gail turned a sharp bend on the path and kept her head down against the driving rain.

Something made her look up. Ten yards ahead was a surreal tableau. What looked like a sack smeared in red lay on the ground, and standing over the object was a man in a glistening wet one-piece plastic suit. A perspex visor obscured his face and a hood covered his head. She could see in the man's hand a tapered metal object that glinted in the feeble light.

For perhaps two seconds Gail stood frozen to the spot. Then, in a sudden rush of understanding, she realised that the sack on the floor was Raymond – his body, lifeless, soaked in blood. The man in the plastic suit had spotted her.

Gail Honeywell yanked the rucksack from her

shoulders and let it fall to the ground. Turning on her heel, she was driven by a primal fear, horror welling up in her throat. She ran as fast as she could back towards the path beside the mill. It was almost enough to save her. But the Acolyte's reactions were faster. In the time that it had taken Gail to realise what was happening and to shrug off the heavy rucksack, the Acolyte had almost covered the ten yards between them.

Gail made it to the bridge. Drawing in huge breaths, she ran faster than she had ever run before in her life. Adrenalin pumped through her veins. She leaped onto the bridge, grabbing for the rail to steady herself. But the wooden slats of the structure were soaked with rainwater. Halfway across, her right foot landed on a patch of mud and she slid along the planks. She almost managed to retain her balance, but just as she thought she would make it to the grass on the far side her legs gave way. She crashed down onto her back and felt a shudder of pain rip through her as she collided with the railings.

The Acolyte was on her in seconds. He grabbed her wrists as she kicked and struggled. Gail managed to bite his arm, but her teeth met only resistant plastic. He pinned her to the floor with his knee. She tried to scream, but she couldn't gather her breath. A raw animal grunt came from the pit of her stomach. Rifling through his oversuit pocket, the

Acolyte pulled out a roll of thick tape. With practised fingers, he wound the tape roughly around the girl's wrists and slapped a strip across her mouth. With his knee still pushing down hard on her chest, he wrapped more tape around her ankles.

Standing up, the Acolyte looked down at Gail Honeywell, a satisfied smile spreading across his face. At this close range she could just see it through the visor. Then he looked at his watch. It was 6.31. He had to wait forty-three minutes before he could begin the procedure, which meant that the girl could be allowed to live a little longer. He felt a thrill of excitement shoot up his spine. 'Time enough to have some fun,' he said under his breath.

Chapter 37

Oxford: 30 March, 9.15 p.m.

Laura and Philip could see thin shards of a dark purple sky behind the terraced houses of Botley as they drove along Oxpens Road. Both were lost in their own thoughts. Philip contemplated the task ahead of them with a growing sense of dread, while Laura couldn't dismiss the knowledge that somewhere not far from where they were now, another girl was lying dead, her gall bladder removed.

Turning off the main road, Philip pulled into a free parking space close to Littlegate to the southwest of the city centre. This was about twenty yards from the less conspicuous of the two entrances to the Trill Mill Stream, at the edge of a small patch of lawn close to a modern office building. From there the stream ran east underground for almost a mile, following a path some thirty feet under Oxford until it emerged in the grounds of Christ Church College close to a walled path called Deadman's Walk.

Stepping out of the car, Philip pulled a large canvas bag from the boot and handed it to Laura. He then took out a rucksack which he shouldered before shutting the boot. It was quiet, not a soul in sight as they made their way along the street and through a gate onto the lawned area. A row of bushes screened the entrance to the stream from the road.

Parts of the Trill Mill Stream had once been an open sewer and consequently a health hazard. But during the middle of the nineteenth century the sections above ground had been covered over and built upon. It had been something of an attraction for intrepid explorers until the 1960s when Oxford City Council had closed it off to the public and blocked both ends with heavy metal grilles.

There was a small gate in the grille that was used to gain access for inspections and maintenance work. A heavy-duty chain and padlock were draped around the bars. The tunnel was about ten feet wide and perhaps five high. The walls were slimy and wet. The water was no more than eighteen inches deep, and as it trickled from the opening it flowed into a large metal pipe that ran into the ground at a slight angle before disappearing under the grass.

Laura threw down the canvas bag and Philip eased his rucksack onto the grass.

Laura made a face.

'I can't say I relish the idea of going in there

myself,' Philip said. 'But we don't have any choice.' Then he pulled open the top flap of the rucksack.

Laura squatted down beside him.

'Two torches, plus spare battery packs. Matches. Our mobiles plus spare batteries – although I'm not sure that we'll get any signal once we're through the Guardians' entrance. A length of rope, a Swiss Army knife, water, biscuits, two spare sweaters.'

'And two pairs of waders and the all-important bolt-cutters,' Laura said, unzipping the canvas bag.

Philip picked up the bolt-cutters and strode over to the grille. Laura looked around, suddenly anxious. Within a few seconds, the chain had been sliced in two. Philip swung open the gate, then returned to where Laura was pulling on her waders. He yanked on his own pair and tucked their boots inside the rucksack.

Between the grille and the tunnel opening stood a small caged area which allowed them to stand upright for what would be the last time until they found the entrance to the Guardians' tunnel. Even then they could not be sure what they might find behind the concealed opening. Laura positioned the ends of the broken chain to make it look untouched and they concealed the canvas bag just inside the shadow of the entrance, placing a couple of bricks and a length of metal pipe over it.

'Ready?' Philip asked.

'I guess.' Laura could feel her heart beginning to pound.

Philip switched on the torch and took a few tentative steps into the tunnel. Bent almost double, his head was just a few inches below the curved roof. Laura looked out at the haze of city lights and took a deep breath. 'Au revoir,' she said quietly and followed Philip into the darkness.

After the first sharp bend, the only light came from their torches. Laura had never experienced claustrophobia before, but now she was beginning to feel the dank walls closing in on her. According to Charlie's map, access to the Guardians' tunnel should be on the left, sixty-three paces from the entrance to the Trill Mill Stream. But paces were a rather inaccurate way of measuring, so they would have to keep their eyes peeled.

After a few minutes, their backs were aching and the smell was almost overpowering. The walls were covered in mould and slime. The tunnel widened suddenly, but its ceiling was still bearing down oppressively.

'Can't be far now,' Laura announced.

Philip stopped for a moment and leaned back against the slimy wall, lowering himself a little to relieve the strain on his back. He was breathing heavily. 'Yeah, you're right. I made it fifty-five, but my strides are longer than yours. I suggest we shuffle along with our backs against this wall. We'll have to move forward slowly and scan the far wall with our torches.'

Arching their backs against the wall offered some relief, but not for long: its surface was jagged, and sharp edges dug into them. They took it as slowly as they could, searching the far wall. But after ten paces their torches had failed to reveal any abnormality in the ancient wall.

'This is no good,' Philip muttered. 'Damn. We must have missed it.'

'I feel like Quasimodo,' Laura replied. 'OK. I'll lead the way.'

Shuffling slowly back towards the open air, Laura saw something. 'What's that?' she said, her voice echoing along the tunnel. In the torch's beam they could see a red smudge the size of an apple, placed about a foot above the water. Training both their torches on it, they searched around the mark for any other anomalies. Something glistened inside the red circle. Philip waded nearer. Close to the centre of the circle was a fleck of silver.

'What is it?' Laura asked.

'Not sure. A tiny fleck of metal. Hang on.'

Philip struggled to fish out the Swiss Army knife from his back pocket and banged his head on the roof. 'Ow . . . Fuck!' he exclaimed. 'That hurt.'

Ignoring the pain, he crouched down and began

to dig the blade into the powdery stone of the wall inside the red circle. It came away with surprising ease, exposing a silver-coloured disc about two inches in diameter. On the disc they could see five female figures holding aloft a bowl containing the sun. It was an exact copy of the image on the coins found at each murder scene.

Laura ran her fingers over the glistening surface. 'No doubts about that, then,' she said, with a grin. Philip was about to respond when suddenly the metal disc gave way beneath Laura's fingers and a low rumbling came from the wall. They both took a step backwards. As they watched, a black line appeared. It ran down to the disc, ran around it, and carried on to a point about six inches above the water. Slowly, it widened as the stone slid away into a recess. A few moments later the rumbling stopped and they were peering at a pitch-black rectangle the width of Philip's shoulders. They shone their torches into the opening, and in patches the blackness gave way to reveal stone walls receding into a featureless void beyond.

Laura stepped into the opening, shining her torch around and above her head. The ceiling arched several feet above her. Philip followed, and they both straightened up.

Laura sighed with relief. 'God, that was even harder than I thought it would be.'

'Ought to be grateful you're not six-two . . .' Philip stopped mid-sentence as the rumbling sound began again. They whirled round to see the stone begin to slide back into place. Philip reacted with surprising speed. Picking up a large rock, he thrust it into the opening. But the door kept on and the rock crumbled.

Laura felt a tremor of panic.

'I think it's OK,' Philip said as reassuringly as he could. He played his torch beam along the walls, which were surprisingly dry. 'The air is fresher here than it was in the stream. And at least we have some headroom. Come on.'

He edged forward slowly, scanning the floor and the walls as he went and brushing aside the cobwebs. The darkness was terrifying and it was taking all his concentration to hold down the unnamed things that his imagination was trying to dredge up to the surface. To stay focused, Philip studied the walls and the limited universe illuminated by the light from his torch. Laura was immediately behind him and she had gripped his hand. He could hear her breathing.

The walls were smooth and much drier than in the Trill Mill Stream tunnel. The smell now was more musty and earthy; the odour of rotting garbage and mould had been left behind. Philip picked his way very carefully. Anything could lie ahead of them –

a hole in the floor, a mantrap, any number of dangers. The biggest mistake would be to get overconfident. They had to take their time and watch where they stepped, he thought to himself.

The tunnel seemed to go on and on, unchanging. It was about ten feet wide, the walls curved and quite featureless. The floor was compacted soil, dry and flat. Then, suddenly, the tunnel opened out so that the beams from their torches produced only dispersed puddles of faint light on the walls to left and right. Taking a few more paces forward, they realised that they had entered a circular expanse.

'What's that?' Laura shone her torch at a point on the nearest wall at about head height. It revealed a small metal bracket extending from the wall and atop it was an old cream-coloured candle half burned down. Philip ran the beam of his torch along the wall to left and right and they caught sight of several more candles placed at intervals of about ten feet.

'You think they'll still work?' Laura asked.

'Only one way to find out,' Philip replied. 'Matches are in the left-hand back pocket of the rucksack.'

Laura struck one and stood on tiptoe to light the nearest candle. It spluttered and sparked for a few seconds before catching to produce a steady yellow flame. A few moments later they had twenty or more candles alight.

It was only then that they could fully appreciate the size of the chamber. But more importantly, the light from the candles revealed decorations on the floor, on the walls and on the ceiling. The inside of the room was covered with elaborate images. Across the ceiling ran a picture of a huge white stag, its antlers at least ten feet long. Around it other animals leaped and danced. A wolf skulked close to the bottom of the domed ceiling while a flock of birds – giant golden eagles – emerged from the rim of the ceiling to hover over the stag. And around the perimeter ran a fresco depicting a menagerie of creatures all painted in rich colours: ambers, crimsons, ochre and the richest, most royal blue.

Around the walls ran streams of alchemical symbols of different sizes, painted in silver and gold. Some were as tall as a man, running from the floor halfway to the ceiling, others were crowded tight and small. On the circular floor, some forty feet across, was one single image – of five robed maidens holding aloft a bowl containing the sun.

Philip lowered his rucksack to the ground and walked slowly around the room, touching the symbols before squatting down to study the image on the floor. Laura sat on the floor in the centre of the chamber and stared up at the ceiling.

'It's absolutely incredible,' she said after a few moments.

'It's like something out of *Indiana Jones*,' muttered Philip wryly.

'And to think probably only a handful of people have ever seen this.'

'And less than a hundred feet above our heads buses are running along St Aldates.'

'What do you think it's for?' Laura mused.

Philip shrugged. 'I guess it is – was – a meeting place for the Guardians. What do you think?'

But she had just noticed something. 'Look,' she said, 'there's a door.'

It had been easy to miss because there was little more than an outline in the stonework.

Philip pulled out the Newton photocopy. 'This must be the entrance to the labyrinth itself,' he said.

Laura turned to look at the manuscript.

'Here is the passageway that led from the wine cellar of Hertford College.' Philip ran a finger from the foot of the page up to a doorway that joined a complex tangle of interlinking lines. 'We've come in a different way because the old tunnel was sealed off. The Guardians must have built this room after 1690. I reckon that behind this door we'll be at this point here . . . and beyond that must be the labyrinth.'

'But first we have to open it.' Laura bent down to examine the symbols in front of her. Philip loosened the catches of his rucksack and pulled out their boots. He sat down and pulled off his waders. Laura removed hers but was concentrating on the markings around the door. Philip then handed her a pair of boots. She slipped them on and laced them up without even looking at what she was doing.

'It's the Guardian statement ALUMNUS AMAS SEMPER UNICUM TUA DEUS: "Adept, love always thy God,"' she said, pointing to a single sentence among the collection of symbols and illustrations.

'And what's this?' Philip said, pointing to a small aperture that curved upwards into the doorway like a tiny chimney. He lowered himself almost to the floor and looked inside. 'It's full of cobwebs but there's a row of what look like coloured pulleys.'

'Let me see.' Laura crouched down and brushed the cobwebs aside with her torch. She counted ten brightly coloured tags.

'They must be linked with the colours in Charlie's code – the colour changes that the alchemists followed,' Philip said.

Laura reached in and gripped the black tag halfway along the row. It was made from very soft leather. She pulled. It came towards her easily, then clicked into place a foot down from its original position. She looked up at Philip and raised an eyebrow. 'Well, nothing's exploded.'

'Yet . . .' he retorted. 'Try the others – white, yellow, red.'

She followed the sequence, pulling down the white tag, then the yellow. Finally her fingers tightened around the red leather strip and she gave it a gentle tug. There was a hollow click. But nothing happened.

Laura got to her feet as Philip picked up the rucksack and kicked the waders away from the door. For several moments nothing happened, then they heard a creaking sound. It grew louder and they stepped back as the stone slab pivoted into the room, revealing a black hole beyond.

'Here we go,' Philip said.

Immediately inside the doorway, they saw two ancient-looking wood-and-rag torches in wall brackets. Laura reached for her matches. The old torches cast a poor light and the electric flashlights were still needed to dispel the gloom. Philip took a cautious step forward.

They were in another stone-walled room, but it was much smaller than the chamber they had just left; and this one was rectangular and low-ceilinged. Directly ahead stood an archway draped in massive cobwebs. They trained their torch beams on the opening. Beyond it a corridor fell away into the darkness. Two feet ahead of them, the floor of the room simply disappeared. Laura gasped and Philip gripped her arm.

'Wow,' she said.

They directed their torches towards the gaping

hole. A chasm at least twenty feet across, it took up most of the room. On the far side there was another two-foot-wide platform before the archway, and to left and right the hole stretched to the walls of the chamber. It was a yawning black pit, the bottom invisible. But as their eyes adjusted to the light they could make out the faint outline of sixteen coloured circles like stepping stones across the chasm. Each circle formed the top of a narrow pedestal that thrust up from the blackness of the pit.

'What do you reckon?' Philip said.

'I can see the black, white, yellow and red at just the right intervals. Come on.' Before Philip could say anything, Laura had stepped onto the black-topped pedestal in the first row.

With one foot on the strip of floor close to the door and the other alighting on the black circle, it looked for a second as though she had made a good decision and that they would soon be across the void. But as she lowered her full weight the pedestal began to crumble. Laura screamed and lost her balance. The pedestal powdered beneath her feet. She spun round and Philip saw her blind panic as she flailed at the dead air, clutching at nothing. Missing the edge of the pit by at least six inches, she crashed downwards into emptiness.

Chapter 38

Oxford: 30 March, 9.35 p.m.

Monroe felt utterly depressed as he drove along The High, heading out of the city centre towards Headington Hill. Another couple had been murdered. Although it vindicated his suspicions that Cunningham could not be the killer, it also meant that two more young people had died and he was no nearer finding the maniac who was responsible. It also proved beyond doubt that Laura Niven and Philip Bainbridge had been right all along about the astrological connection; this latest abomination had been committed exactly when they had predicted it would.

He punched a key on his car phone and the duty officer at the station answered almost immediately. 'Any luck contacting Bainbridge?' Monroe asked.

'Nothing sir, just his voicemail again.'

'OK, call his mobile every five minutes and keep trying the house. I want to know the moment you reach him.'

Just before Headington Hill, Monroe turned off into Marston Road. A few hundred yards down on the left he swung the car onto a muddy track called Kings Mill Lane. He saw immediately, fifty yards ahead, the floodlights and the reflective jackets of his team. Three police cars and an ambulance were parked to one side of the lane. As he drew closer, he could see an elderly man sitting just inside the ambulance with a red blanket over his shoulders. An oxygen mask was strapped to his face.

Monroe pulled the car over beside the other vehicles, and walked over to the ambulance. 'What's happened here?'

The paramedic took Monroe to one side. 'Old boy found the bodies about forty minutes ago. He's in shock.' Monroe raised an eyebrow. 'Says he walked right past them on his way towards Mesopotamia Walk from Headington but then realised something was up when he saw them again on his way back home. Take a look – you'll see what I mean.'

The lane was soaked from the heavy rain and Monroe's shoes squelched in the mud. It was all he could do to keep his balance. But a few yards further on, the track led onto a narrow tarmac path that ran on towards an old mill and the river walk.

Ten yards ahead, Forensics had just finished erecting a white plastic screen across the path. As Monroe approached, a young constable held a flap open for him and he ducked under the retaining bar to emerge on the other side.

Two floodlights had been set up and they produced a harsh lemon light. Another wall of white plastic stood twenty feet away along the path. It started to drizzle again and the floodlights caught the droplets of water, making them glisten in the pallid night. To his right, Monroe could see a bench beside the path. He caught a glimpse of two figures seated there, but they were partially obscured by someone dressed in a Forensics suit. As the man stood up Monroe recognised a grim-faced Mark Langham, who stepped back to allow Monroe his first clear look at the dead couple.

They had been positioned to appear as though they were embracing, their faces close together, lips almost touching. A passer-by giving them a casual glance would think that they were simply a couple in love. Monroe felt a momentary frisson of disgust.

He bent down to take a closer look. In the floodlight beams the skin of their faces and hands had taken on a puce hue. Their dead stares were fixed ahead. Both of them were fully dressed but their clothes were dishevelled and stained. Gail Honeywell had her left palm at Raymond Delaware's neck as though pulling him towards her lips. Monroe felt his jaw clench as he spotted the black and red gash of the victim's ripped throat.

Langham crouched down beside Monroe. 'They've been dead for at least two hours,' he said. 'And if you look here' – he pointed to a blood-soaked area just above the hem of the girl's opened jacket – 'I would imagine this is where the murderer removed an organ . . . assuming it's the same killer, with the same MO. And then there's this . . .' He gently turned Gail Honeywell's head.

The side of the girl's face was a patchwork of deep gashes. Broad streaks of blood ran down her neck and across her right shoulder, drenching her blouse red. Her right eye was missing.

'The amount of blood would indicate that these injuries were sustained pre-mortem,' Langham remarked. 'This is different from the earlier murders. Really weird.'

Monroe made no comment. He straightened, staring at the lifeless faces of the young couple. Then he noticed a dull and faded metal plaque screwed to one of the wooden planks across the back of the bench. It must have been there for as long as the bench had stood in this spot. It said: 'Oh Rest a Bit for 'tis a Rare Place to Rest At.'

'How very droll,' he said under his breath.

Monroe was a few paces away from the car when his phone rang.

'Rogers, sir. I thought you wouldn't mind being

disturbed. Just got the report back from the lab on the blood sample from the second murder.'

'And?'

'A perfect match – it belongs to Malcolm Bridges.'

Chapter 39

'You fool!' The Master was glaring at him, his eyes bulging, sweat running down his cheeks. 'You moronic . . . you could have destroyed everything.' He slapped the Acolyte hard across the face.

For an instant the Acolyte almost lost control. His right hand twitched.

The Master noticed the involuntary movement and smirked. He fixed the Acolyte with a look of unalloyed menace. 'Do you not want to strike me? I sense that you do. Or do you prefer to take your pleasures only with young girls?'

The Acolyte said nothing but stared rigidly ahead of him.

The Master slapped the Acolyte's face again. A red welt appeared on the man's cheek. The older man hit him again, harder still.

Taking a step back, the Master appraised the

trained killer. His face contorting with contempt, he spat in the Acolyte's face.

The Acolyte did not react even as spittle ran down his cheek.

'Get out of here . . . you barbaric pig,' the Master said. 'If you fail me again I will treat you worse than you treated Gail Honeywell.'

Chapter 40

Oxford: 30 March, 10.18 p.m.

With lightning reflexes, Philip hurled himself forward to catch hold of Laura's arm as she fell. Bracing himself on the edge of the pit he helped her scramble to safety. She was shaking as she sat on the narrow strip of floor. Philip found a space beside her. 'A little silly,' he said, putting his arm around her shoulders. Laura was speechless.

He reached for the water bottle in his rucksack. 'Here, have a drink.'

'Shame you don't have anything stronger.' She grinned and took a long swig, wiping her mouth as she handed it back. 'Christ . . . thanks,' she said, lowering her head onto her knees.

'Any time. I don't want to do this on my own, now do I?'

Laura gave him a weak smile. 'So, what now?'

'Good question.'

'I was sure the route had to be linked with the alchemical colours.'

Philip shrugged.

'Maybe it's backwards? It doesn't make sense otherwise.'

'OK, but how are we going to find out?'

'Use the rucksack.'

'But that's not heavy enough, and if we lose it . . .'

'Better than one of us going down.'

Philip reached for the bag. Stepping to the edge of the chasm he placed it gently on a red circle next to where the black pedestal had stood. He let go slowly and stepped back. Nothing happened.

'Right,' he said and pulled the bag back. 'But I'm still not convinced. Let's use the rope. Tie it around your waist and I'll use the wall bracket to brace it. If it holds your weight, then fine. If not, I'll catch you.'

Laura wound the rope around her waist in two loops and Philip knotted it tightly. Then he swung the other end over the iron wall bracket and stood on the edge with his feet well apart. Laura moved forward carefully to place one foot slowly on the red pedestal. She was breathing heavily and beads of sweat appeared on her forehead. 'Here goes.'

It held. She turned to face Philip with a look of triumph on her face and he gave her the thumbs-up.

'Try the next one,' he called to her. 'I'll give you some slack.'

Laura inspected the pattern of circles in front of her. In the second row, second from the left, stood a yellow platform. Moving as light-footedly as she could, she hopped onto the yellow stone and let out a deep sigh of relief.

'I'll go the whole way,' she announced. 'It's too dangerous for both of us to be on these things at the same time.' Then, turning to look again at the 'bridge' of pedestals, she stepped onto the white one in the third row. There she paused for a moment, took a deep breath and then moved onto the black circle in the final row. A few seconds later she was on the other side.

'OK, your turn,' Laura called, her heart racing.

She untied the rope and paid it out so that Philip could approach the bridge with it hooked over the bracket and then tied to his waist. On Laura's side of the pit she looped the rope over another torch bracket in the wall near the archway. If one of the pedestals should give way Philip could pull himself over along the rope.

Moving as quickly but as carefully as he could, Philip followed the same route that Laura had taken – red, yellow, white and black, and in a few moments he was on the far side standing next to her.

'Phew,' he said and wiped the sweat away from his eyes. 'I'd like to say that was fun. But in all honesty I can't.'

★

Through the archway was a short corridor which twisted to the left and then sharply right. As Laura and Philip took the second bend they emerged into a circular room. It was lit from the ceiling. In fact, the whole ceiling seemed to glow.

It was made of solid rock but the light seemed to be emanating from the stone itself.

'My God,' Philip said, looking up at the rock over his head. It was lumpy and mottled, and on closer inspection he could see a dusting of yellow crystals covering the entire surface. 'Must be some sort of natural light-emitting crystal,' he added.

'Clever alchemists.'

'I guess so. Makes you wonder, doesn't it?'

The room was bare except for another opening in the wall opposite the archway that they had come through. Laura peered in. Corridors led off left and right. On the wall ahead were two metal discs, each about the size of a CD. Etched into the left-hand disc were two concentric circles. The disc on the right carried another symbol, a circle with what looked like a pair of horns on top and a cross at the base.

'Any ideas?' she asked.

Philip peered at the Newton document. 'They're both on here – look, next to the labyrinth.'

'The one on the left is the symbol for Sol, the sun; the other one is Mercury, isn't it?'

Philip nodded.

'So, do we follow the sun or Mercury?'

'What relevance do either of them have?'

'Mercury is the winged messenger. The sun . . . what? Light . . . the surface, maybe?'

'Doesn't help much. Mercury was the most important metal to the alchemist, though, right? One of the three basic elements used to create the Earth.'

'So we should go this way, then?' Laura pointed to the corridor on the right.

'Maybe. But the sun is the centre of all things in astrology.'

The ceilings of both corridors were illuminated in the same way as the chamber behind them. 'I would go for the left, the sun.'

'OK.'

Laura led the way. They took it slowly. A few yards in, the corridor curved to the right and then to the left, and soon they came to another fork. Here the path split into two smaller passageways, each one heading off at an angle, ten o'clock and two o'clock. Between the openings stood a rock column. There, at Laura's head height, they found another disc. It was divided by a vertical line. To the left of this they saw again the symbol for the sun, the circles they had seen earlier, and on the right, etched into the metal, was another symbol. It looked like the letter 'h' with a horizontal line through it.

'Does this mean we just keep following the symbol for the sun? That can't be right.' Laura frowned.

'No, it doesn't feel correct,' Philip confirmed.

'Which either means we go this way' – she pointed to the right-hand passageway – 'or we go back to the first pair of symbols and take the other route.'

Laura took the Newton document from Philip's hand and sat cross-legged on the floor with her back to the rock column that divided the pathways. The light from the ceiling was bright enough to read by.

'So, what information have we used so far?' Laura said. 'The colour code? We've used that twice, haven't we? And it doesn't seem relevant here. Mercury is a metal, but the other symbols are Saturn and the sun, so the Mercury symbol must refer to the planet.'

Philip squatted down beside her. 'What about the positions of these symbols?' he mused. 'Maybe they're telling us something.'

They both stared hard at the paper, trying to match the positions of the symbols with the schematic of the labyrinth that Newton had reproduced from the original.

'It's not their positions,' Laura said suddenly. 'It's their relationship to the incantation – this.' And she pointed at the lines of Latin they had obtained using

Charlie's code. Philip rifled through his pockets to find the translation they had written out the night before.

You are Mercury the mighty flower,
You are most worthy of honour;
You are the Source of Sol, Luna and Mars,
You are Settler of Saturn and Source of Venus,
You are Emperor, Prince and most regal of Kings,
You are Father of the Mirror and Maker of Light.
You are head and highest and fairest in Sight.
All praise thee.
All praise thee. Giver of truth.
We seek, we beseech, we welcome you.

'Yes . . . "You are Mercury the mighty flower,"' Laura read aloud. 'Third line . . . "You are the Source of Sol, Luna and Mars . . ." That's it. We took the wrong corridor at the start. We should have followed Mercury, the right-hand passageway.'

Back at the archway leading from the circular stone chamber, they paused at the two discs on the wall for a moment and then headed off along the corridor straight ahead of them, the right-hand turning off the chamber. A few moments later they reached a T-junction. On the wall ahead of them were two more discs. The right-hand disc carried the symbol for Venus, a circle with a cross at the bottom.

Into the left-hand plate had been etched the symbol for the sun.

'There should be four more junctions in the labyrinth,' Philip added, 'and symbols for the moon, Mars, Saturn, and Venus, in that order. It would be absolutely impossible to get through this without the document.' And he led the way along the left-hand passageway.

The corridor to the next junction twisted and turned and seemed to go on for miles before hitting a steep upward incline. By the time they reached the top they were sweating and panting. Philip bent over with his hands on his knees. Laura wiped the sweat from her eyes and looked at the two plates on the wall designating another choice of route. The right-hand disc carried a crescent, the symbol for the moon. In the centre of the left-hand disc was the sign representing Mercury.

They paused for a moment to catch their breath and this time Laura led the way to the fourth fork. Here they found the symbol for Mars, a circle with an arrow pointing diagonally away to the right, and they took that route, which ran steeply downhill. At the bottom, they found themselves in a broad corridor some four yards across. At the far end of this section there were three openings in the wall: to the left of the first one there were three discs on the wall. This time the three symbols were for Mercury, Saturn and the sun.

'The middle one,' Laura said confidently, and they followed a narrow passageway just wide enough for Philip to pass through without his shoulders grazing the walls. It sloped downhill, and at the far end they emerged into a circular room with a domed ceiling. Placed evenly at six points around the room were six archways. To the left of each they found the usual discs. Each disc contained a different symbol representing the planets listed in the incantation. The opening labelled with the symbol for Venus was second to their left.

Philip took off the rucksack and passed the water bottle to Laura. As she drank, he checked his watch. It was 10.43. He unzipped another pocket in the bag and tried his mobile.

'No signal, of course,' he said and stuffed it back inside.

Laura checked hers. 'Ditto. Not a great surprise. There must be – what? Eighty, ninety feet of rock over our heads?'

Philip shouldered his rucksack. 'OK?' he asked.

Laura nodded.

'Ever onward, then.'

The corridor was extremely narrow at first. Philip had to take off the rucksack again and his elbows scraped painfully against the jagged rock face. But after about ten yards the passage widened and there was enough room for them to walk side by side.

Here the crystal lights were more densely clustered along the ceiling, and the tunnel was much brighter than the others had been. They quickened their pace. Immediately ahead they could see an archway leading to another chamber. Philip stopped abruptly and peered down at the ground. Laura was a few yards behind and she could see him looking at something on the dirt floor. He began to walk slowly forward, half crouching to the ground while studying the marks. 'Hey, look,' he called back to her. 'Some writing in English. It says . . .'

Laura heard the swishing sound before she saw anything move. It seemed to be coming from inside the wall to their right. Then came three more thuds. Something hit Philip and two other speeding objects flashed past him and struck the wall to their left. He fell to the floor and the sounds stopped immediately. Laura dived to the ground and crawled along until she reached him. 'You OK?'

'I think so. What the hell happened?'

On the floor to his left Philip could see two shattered arrows, each one just a few inches long. Two more were stuck in his rucksack. 'Stay low,' he hissed, as they crawled slowly towards the opening.

On the other side of the archway Philip sat up slowly and pulled out one of the arrows. 'That could have been a bit nasty,' he said and threw it to one side.

'Looks like that rucksack saved your life.' Laura examined the sharp tips of the other arrows. 'What were you looking at on the floor?'

'Some words in English. In gold letters: "Only the pure may pass."'

Laura stared into his eyes and was about to say something when they both felt rather than heard a low rumble. For several long seconds the walls seemed to vibrate. They scrambled to the far wall, clutching at each other. Dust fell from the ceiling and powdered their hair. Before the sound died completely they felt a wave of air rush past them, and it seemed as though every molecule of oxygen was being sucked from the room. A massive block of stone crashed down from the lintel of the archway, landing squarely with a thump on the dusty floor. They were sealed in.

Chapter 41

Oxford: 30 March, 10.38 p.m.

Monroe looked at the clock on the wall of his office and watched the seconds click by. He had just sent out a dozen officers to three different locations in Oxford to try to track down Malcolm Bridges – his tiny flat on Iffley Road, Lightman's house in Park Town in the north of the city, and his office at the Psychology Department. He had little hope that the man would be found at any of them.

So, Bridges had been at the scene of the second murder. He had no watertight alibi for the time of that murder, but he did have one for the first, which meant that he had to be working with someone. But to Monroe this instinctively felt wrong; and besides, there was absolutely no evidence to support the idea.

So what was the situation? Another murder, four separate incidents, six dead kids, and what did he know for sure? Bridges was involved somehow, but couldn't have been working alone, and another murder was due to be committed tonight, just after midnight. How would he be able to stop that unless he had Bridges? And, even then, would the man's arrest stop the killing? Rubbing his eyes, Monroe suddenly felt incredibly tired.

The phone rang. 'Monroe,' he said wearily.

'It's Howard.'

'I hope you have some good news for me.'

'Well, I do have some news,' Smales replied. 'But I don't really know what to make of it. It's just, well, the sample has thrown up a . . . how shall I put it? A rather sensitive ID.'

Chapter 42

Oxford: 30 March, 10.43 p.m.

Laura and Philip were in total darkness. There were no crystals in the low ceiling of this chamber, and when the stone had crashed down it had blocked out the meagre light that had penetrated from the corridor. Philip swung his rucksack off his shoulder and found the main zipper. Slipping his hand inside, he felt around for the torches. He flicked them on in the bag and pulled them out, handing one to Laura. They both sat back against the wall and trained the spots of light around the room. Then Philip stood up and went to inspect the place where until a few seconds earlier the doorway had been. He ran his torch's beam over the smooth rock surface. In this light he could see no trace of a join. The stone block must have fitted almost perfectly.

Laura walked over to the far wall and ran her torch beam over the surface, then across the floor and ceiling. The room was no more than twelve feet square and the ceiling was very low. She wondered suddenly if they might run out of air. And then, with a jolt, she spotted an anomaly in the otherwise smooth rock. It was an inscription, the now familiar phrase: ALUMNUS AMAS SEMPER UNICUM TUA DEUS.

'Philip, look.' She bent down to examine the markings more closely, feeling the letters with the tips of her fingers. The words were made of metal, raised a millimetre or two above the surface of the rock. As she touched them they sank into the wall, springing back when she removed her fingers.

'Curiouser and curiouser,' Laura said.

Philip pushed a few of the letters and watched them rise up again. 'Do you think it's some sort of lock, a combination lock?' he mused. 'If we get the right sequence maybe we can find a way out.'

'I bloody well hope so,' Laura replied grimly. 'But how on earth can we figure out the combination? We can't guess – there are literally billions of possibilities.'

'Well, no, obviously we can't just take a guess. The words must have some hidden meaning. "Adept, Love Always Thy God" must have something to do with it.'

Laura pinched the bridge of her nose and closed her eyes. When she opened them again her eyes were bloodshot and Philip realised how hard she had been pushing herself.

'OK, we have to figure something out. How long before we suffocate?' Laura asked.

'I thought the same thing the moment the stone came down,' Philip replied. 'Did you feel the air rush out? I reckon we could last hours in here if that hadn't happened. But, to be honest, I feel the air is getting pretty thin already.'

'I do too.'

'We have to try to slow our breathing and stay calm. The last thing you want is to increase your heart rate.' He looked round at Laura; he thought she looked pretty frayed.

'I *am* calm,' snapped Laura. 'OK, let's concentrate on this darn inscription.'

Methodically, she tried a series of different combinations. Nothing worked. Suddenly she felt a tightening in her chest, and before she knew what she was doing she was punching viciously at the metal. 'Damn you!'

Philip was next to her in a second and pulled her hands away from the letters before she could injure herself. Laura collapsed into his arms, sobbing. He held her to him and kissed her gently on the cheek. He could feel her shaking and knew that he had to let her get it out of her system. After a few moments, he guided her to the wall close to the sealed doorway and lowered her to the floor before sitting down next to her.

'We're not going to get out of this one, are we?' she sobbed.

'Of course we are, you daft—'

'Philip . . . the air is going. It's going, I can feel it.'

He couldn't deny it. In just the past minute or two, the air seemed to have grown much thinner and he was finding it harder to draw breath. He pulled her closer.

They were quiet for a moment. Laura stopped sobbing but kept her head close to Philip's chest. 'I really am sorry, you know,' she added quietly.

'Sorry for what?' he replied, but he knew exactly what she was referring to.

'You know what I'm talking about, Philip. I don't need to spell it out, not to you.'

He said nothing.

Laura pulled her head away from his shoulder. 'I . . . I just thought it was the right thing to do at the time. I didn't think we had a future. I was wrong. I should have stayed. I should have married you.'

Philip suddenly felt lost. For days the two of them had been preoccupied with solving the mystery of the killings and then they had been put through the wringer here in this stinking hole under the Bodleian Library. But it took no time at all for the old emotions to come flooding back. For almost twenty years he had tried to bottle them up, and for the most part, he told himself, he had succeeded. But every time Laura had come back to England or he had gone to New York the same old wounds had reopened. He hated it – but then, he simply could not go through life without seeing Laura and Jo whenever possible. For a moment, he was lost for words. What could he say?

He studied Laura's face. In the sparse torchlight he could see the streaks of her tears. They had made her mascara run. Then, suddenly, her mouth was on his and he could feel her melt into him, feel her hair brushing his cheek, feel her warmth, her familiarity. He had missed that so much. Then, all too quickly, she pulled away and they looked into each other's eyes.

'What . . . ?' he asked.

'I just wanted to steal your air.'

Philip laughed. 'You're welcome, Laura.'

She put a finger to his lips and smiled. Then she leaned forward to kiss him again.

A second later she yelped, her lips still fixed to Philip's. 'That's it.'

Without saying another word, Laura walked over to the far wall, crouched down and began to stab at the letters. She hit five of them, her hand moving quickly from left to right until she reached the 'M' in 'UNICUM'. She drew her hand back and punched at the letter with a grandiose gesture. Philip couldn't suppress a small laugh.

For long, agonising moments they waited. Then there was the faintest squeak followed by another creaking sound in the wall perpendicular to the original opening. A few nervous heartbeats later, the first crack began to appear in the wall and gradually two huge slabs of rock started to slide upwards into recesses in the ceiling. Philip grabbed the rucksack and they scrambled through the new doorway as quickly as they could.

Chapter 43

Oxford: 30 March, 10.45 p.m.

Just as Monroe put down the receiver there was a knock at his door. He was so amazed by what he had just heard that for a few seconds he could barely focus on the bulky form of PC Steve Greene as he walked up to his desk.

'Sir, this arrived about an hour ago. Chatwin apologises . . . he forgot about it . . . busy night . . . he just gave me it . . . Courier dropped it in, apparently.'

On the front was typed: *DCI Monroe, Oxford Police Station*. Below that was the word URGENT, written in red capitals. Seeing this, Monroe sighed and shook his head. Then he ripped open the envelope. Inside was a single sheet of paper. He glanced quickly at the illustration showing a complex array of interlocking lines like the schematic for a complex electrical current. Beside this was a jumble of Latin words and bizarre-looking symbols. He began to read the message written in English at the top of the sheet.

Chapter 44

They stood in the corridor, bent almost double with their hands on their knees, trying to breathe normally again.

'How did you do that?' panted Philip.

'It was obvious really . . . Gold.'

'You may have to be a bit more precise.'

'"Aurum", the Latin word for gold. It was spelled in the Guardian's mysterious statement. ALUMNUS AMAS SEMPER UNICUM TUA DEUS. A and U in "ALUMNUS", R in "SEMPER", U and M in "UNICUM".'

'You're a genius, Laura,' Philip said.

'I know.'

'And it's nice to know that your mind was on the job back there.'

'I'm a woman, Philip, I multi-task,' she replied, with a grin.

Ahead of them, some twenty yards away, stood a

door. It was slightly ajar and light spilled out into the corridor.

Reaching the wall to one side of the opening, they peeped inside.

The room was lit by a cluster of candles in a chandelier that hung from the centre of a domed ceiling. At the far end stood a huge gold pentagram. It was at least seven feet across and rested on a platform a short way from the far wall. To the right of the pentagram Laura could see a glass door set into the wall. It looked like a huge refrigerator, the glass opaque with ice.

Two men stood close to the pentagram. They were wearing long black robes, their hoods thrown back. The man to the right was leaning forward, making adjustments to the metal structure.

Laura was about to turn to whisper something to Philip when the torch that she had been holding suddenly slipped from her grasp. It clanged across the floor. She stepped back quickly and cursed under her breath.

'Laura, I'm so pleased you could join us,' came a familiar voice from the chamber.

She felt a jolt of horror pass through her, a definite physical reaction, immediate and powerful. She turned to Philip, who looked stunned. Closing her eyes, Laura felt the pain of realisation sweep through her. Philip thought she was going to cry, but instead she turned on her heel and walked into the chamber.

James Lightman looked ridiculously relaxed, as though they were meeting in the drawing room of his house or at a tea shop on The High. He stood with his hands clasped in front of him and appeared to be filled with self-confidence and energy. His intense brown eyes glinted in the candlelight. Beside him stood Malcolm Bridges, his eyes expressionless. The shadows that fell across the young man's face made him look like the Grim Reaper.

'You've arrived at a most auspicious time,' Lightman said.

Laura felt sick to her stomach. 'What the hell is this?' she demanded, her face flushing. 'How could you . . . ?'

With a hint of a smile, Lightman said: 'Surely you suspected, Laura? With your vivid imagination?'

'I could have believed it of *him*.' She glared at Bridges who returned the look with blank eyes. 'But you, James? Why on earth?'

'Why on earth would I want eternal life, Laura? Now, let me think.'

'But occult rituals . . . ?'

'It would be a dull world, would it not, if we all believed in the same things? But come . . . enough. I must congratulate you both on passing the tests of the Guardians. Few have ever managed it. I would have been keen to see the document that you used

355

to guide you, but I no longer need such things. My task will soon be complete.' He gestured towards the Pentagram.

'As you know from your intrepid investigations, this evening the final organ will be in my possession and the real work will then begin. The final piece will soon be here.'

Laura was about to say something, but Lightman raised his hand. 'I'm sure what you have to say is very important, Laura my dear, but please, let me just finish what I was starting to explain. I think you'll consider it of value. You see, the two of you' – he glanced briefly at Philip – 'will never again see the light of day. It is impossible to retrace your steps through the tunnels of the Guardians and there is only one other way out. That is the route that takes us from here to the library, and only I have the map.' He tapped his breast.

'The route created by John Milliner,' said Laura.

'My predecessor in more ways than one.'

Laura looked puzzled.

'Ah, another piece of the jigsaw puzzle that the two of you missed,' Lightman said. 'John Milliner was not just a Professor of Medicine at the University, he was also Chief Librarian. The Chief Librarians of the Bodleian have been leaders of my order, the Order of the Black Sphinx, for at least a dozen generations. Each of us has added something to the vast network of tunnels beneath the library. Building work stopped a long, long time ago, but we have each added decorations or some other refinement. My contribution has been this ingenious refrigeration unit.'

'And I suppose he's been your executioner.' Laura nodded towards Bridges.

'Oh no, my clever Laura,' Lightman said. 'I'm afraid that there you are quite wrong. Malcolm here has many talents, but he is not your killer. That is the responsibility of another young colleague. He has used many aliases over the years, but the university authorities knew him as Julius Spenser. Officially, he's a high-flying psychologist who is now working in America. At least, that's what the police know of him. I'm afraid poor old DCI Monroe has been less than inspired in his efforts of late . . . But as it happens, dear girl, there *is* something I would like to explain about my colleague.'

Lightman took a step back and pulled a revolver from under his robe. Pointing it directly at Bridges, he said coldly: 'Malcolm, maybe you could tell us something about your role in all this.'

The room was as still and silent as a mausoleum. Situated as they were, some hundred feet beneath the Bodleian Library, all the usual sounds of the everyday world were excluded: the rumble of traffic, the noise of people – all these things had been left on the surface. The four of them could have been transported back in time. Ignoring Lightman's refrigeration unit, they might have been standing in this room when Milliner was surveying it for the first time, or when Newton was studying an entirely different set of human organs.

Bridges's eyes now widened in alarm. He put his hands up slowly and deliberately, looking from the old man's face to the gun and back again. Laura could see beads of sweat on his forehead.

'What?' he said, shaking his head slightly. 'What exactly . . . ?'

'Well, naturally, you would not like to admit . . .'

Philip was about to interrupt when Lightman glared at him. 'This has nothing to do with you, Mr Bainbridge.' He gestured at Bridges with the gun. 'Well?'

'I don't . . .'

'Malcolm, Malcolm,' Lightman sighed and shook his head. 'Please don't waste my time. Let's start at the beginning, shall we? I'll help you. You see, I know very much more about you than you might imagine. I have many, many useful contacts in all sorts of interesting places. I know, for example, that you were present at the scene when my colleague . . . shall we call him Julius? Yes, when Julius was harvesting the brain. The police found a tiny sample of your blood in the girl's house. Then two weeks ago you were caught on film, searching through my study at home. I have records of the most incriminating communications between you and your employers.'

Bridges seemed suddenly transformed. Gone was the pallid academic, the vampiric accessory to a series of horrendous crimes. He suddenly looked more ordinary. 'You know who I work for,' he said, fixing Lightman with his stare. 'Your taxes pay my salary. And if you really have tapped my communications, which I actually rather doubt, you'll know they end up at Millbank. I was at the dead girl's house hoping to get in Spenser's way. Unfortunately, I was too late to save her life – I saw him slice her open. I'm here now to prevent you from finishing your task.'

Lightman gave him a brief, icy smile. But Laura could sense that some of the sheen had gone from his seemingly impervious confidence.

'Ah, the self-assurance of youth,' he said. 'How I admire it so. But I think you have left things a little too late, dear boy. Of course you could not have done much to stop us earlier – there was nothing to go on, was there? Julius is very thorough. What would your superiors have thought if you had gone to them with some cock-and-bull story where the Chief Librarian, who has mysteriously disappeared, is in fact the head of an occult group seeking to employ the services of the Dark Lord in some nefarious ritual? As we speak, Julius is preparing to harvest the final item.'

Bridges said nothing and slowly lowered his hands.

'Don't do that. I think you should keep them there,' Lightman snapped, gesturing with the gun again. Bridges did as he was told. 'Now,' Lightman added and glanced quickly at Laura and Philip, 'you may think I'm a frail old man, but please do not entertain any thoughts of trying to overpower me. I am a superb marksman and a great deal more agile than I might appear.' He took a deep breath. 'I would very much like all three of you to sit down over here, please.' He waved the gun in the direction of the pentagram.

'James, don't you think this has gone far enough?' Laura said.

'You don't really understand, do you, Laura?' Lightman replied. 'This is not a game. This is deadly serious. I have spent the last ten years of my life planning this most delicate process, and tonight will be the climax and the fulfilment of that work. You cannot be allowed to interfere. Now, please, do as I ask.' He put a hand to Laura's shoulder to guide her across the room. But she shrugged him off angrily.

'I can't believe this of you,' she hissed.

Philip took her arm and Lightman herded the three

of them to the platform where the pentagram stood. On the floor lay a toolbox. Lightman opened the lid. Inside lay a wrench, some screwdrivers, an assortment of spanners, nuts and bolts, and a roll of duct tape. He picked up the tape and handed it to Laura.

'Tie their wrists to the pentagram. You, sit down, over there,' he said to the two men. He held the gun to Bridges's back, pushing it just hard enough for him to feel it between his shoulder blades.

Philip slipped off his rucksack and laid it close by before lowering himself to the stone floor. Lightman walked around the back of the pentagram, keeping his revolver trained on them. He kicked Philip's bag across the floor and watched as Laura crouched down and wound the tape around Philip's wrists. He checked it as she moved on to do the same to Bridges.

'Sit down, please, Laura,' he said when she was done. He then taped her wrists to the pentagram.

'Now, I have much to do.' Lightman looked from face to face. Laura turned away in disgust.

'You really are wasting your time, you know.' Bridges's voice was quiet but authoritative.

'Don't make me angry, Malcolm,' Lightman snapped. 'Although you are going to die anyway, there are ways to die that you would not like to contemplate, I assure you.'

'The inscription is a fake.'

'Is it, now?'

'Charlie Tucker learned what you were trying to achieve and altered the decoded inscription. He was obviously a believer. You killed him too soon, Professor.'

Lightman stared at Bridges for a moment. When he eventually spoke his voice was strangely subdued. 'I didn't have Tucker killed.'

'Well, whoever did take out Charlie Tucker has left you with a useless inscription that wouldn't conjure up a pixie, let alone Mephistopheles.'

Lightman's eyes were dark with fury. 'You think what you like, Malcolm,' he sneered. 'I imagine you are merely following your training. I can see the training manual now – Technique No.72: Try to intimidate your adversary with potentially threatening but quite spurious information.'

Bridges simply shrugged. 'OK . . . we can wait.'

'Can you?' Lightman barked and took a step forward. 'Perhaps I can rectify that.' He raised his gun to Bridges's head.

'No!' Laura screamed. Lightman turned on her and Philip, the gun waving around in front of their faces.

Lightman laughed and stepped back to survey the three of them tied to the pentagram. 'What a pathetic sight you make.'

'Oh, do shut up, James,' Laura snapped back. 'If

anyone's pathetic it's you – you must have lost your mind.'

Lightman walked over to where Laura was sitting between Bridges and Philip. He lowered himself so that his face was level with hers. She could feel his breath on her cheek.

'You don't have the faintest suspicion, do you?' he said.

'Suspicion of what?' Laura hissed. 'What the hell are you talking about?'

'Why, the identity of the final victim, of course.' He smiled.

It took a moment for his words to take shape in Laura's mind.

'Ah, now you understand,' Lightman said coldly. 'Your daughter will be killed in . . .' He looked at his watch. 'About forty-five minutes. Julius will then remove her liver and bring it here.'

Laura went cold. It swept over her like an Arctic wave. She felt Philip beside her trying to yank himself free from the tape that bound him to the pentagram.

'Don't tell me, Mr Bainbridge,' Lightman said softly. 'I won't get away with this? But who is going to stop me? Monroe? He hasn't got the foggiest.'

Laura was speechless with horror. Through her mind raced images of Jo alone at the house in Woodstock and the cold-hearted Julius Spenser creeping in through the back door. Philip had his eyes closed and his lips pressed firmly together. He looked very pale.

'Now, I expect you are wondering how Monroe could not have known Jo was my final subject, are you not?' No one answered Lightman and he seemed quite content to talk on. 'Well, although our DCI is a bit of a clod, this was not entirely his fault. You see, Jo – may I call her Jo? – Jo used her stepfather's name, Newcombe. That, as you know, Laura, is the name she uses for all official purposes and it is the name on her university admission forms. It's the name she used for the psychology tests. How could Monroe have worked that one out?'

Bridges let out an exaggerated sigh, and Lightman snapped his attention back to him.

'I'll say it again, Professor. You're wasting your time.'

Lightman levelled the gun once more at Bridges. They could all see the old man's hand shaking, and Laura suddenly remembered her visit to Lightman's office at the Bodleian a week earlier. She remembered the odd gripping device he had used to alleviate his arthritic pain. But she could do nothing. Her hands were bound so tightly that she could hardly feel her fingers.

Lightman switched hands, and as his right hand fell to his side he shook it as if to relieve some pain.

'You know, Malcolm,' and his voice trembled slightly, 'I'm getting rather tired of you repeating yourself.' They all watched him bring the gun up to Bridges's forehead. Slowly, almost sensuously, Lightman caressed Bridges's face with the cold muzzle. He moved it across his skin, leaving white marks. 'We are such frail things, are we not?' Lightman whispered. He lowered the gun slowly to a point a few inches above his victim's chest, then slid it along each arm, the left, then the right. Bringing it back to Bridges's torso and down to his groin, Lightman let the gun hover there for a few seconds. Still slowly, he ran it up the young man's right leg, then his left. Reaching the knee, he paused for a second. He seemed to be studying Bridges's leg, tilting his head slightly to one side, considering it. 'So very frail.'

He looked into Malcolm Bridges's eyes and fired.

The sound slammed around the room, ricocheting from the stone walls. The bullet shattered Bridges's knee. He screamed and spasmed violently, crashing back against the metal framework of the pentagram.

Lightman's face was expressionless. He ignored the young man's writhing body and turned his attention to Laura and Philip. They were both paralysed with shock.

'As I say, I have much to do,' Lightman muttered. There was a polite cough from the main doorway.

DCI Monroe stood there, flanked by two police officers. They were dressed in helmets and bulletproof vests. The two uniformed officers had their guns pointing at Lightman's head. 'Freeze! Lower your weapon,' Monroe said.

Lightman took a step to his right and grabbed Laura by the hair, making her scream with pain. Bringing his gun up to her right temple, he said. 'I rather think you should lower your weapons. I do so hate a mess.'

Laura's mind was racing. She refused to let panic overwhelm her. That would not help the situation and it certainly would not help Jo. Monroe and the two policemen stepped forward into the room. In response, Lightman pushed the gun harder against her temple, sending waves of pain through her head.

Without thinking exactly what she was doing, Laura twisted her head and pushed back hard against a crossbar of the metal pentagram immediately behind her. Another wave of pain shot through her, but it must have hurt Lightman even more because his fingers were crushed between the metal and the back of Laura's head.

He yelped, tried to free his hand and lost his balance. It was all the police marksmen needed. Two shots rang out and Lightman fell to the ground, clutching his chest.

Monroe was across the room in an instant. As he

reached the pentagram two more officers arrived.

'Jones, get me the paramedic kit,' Monroe shouted.

The other policeman ran over to Lightman's body.

'See to this man immediately.' Monroe pointed to Bridges. 'Get him to the surface and call the paramedics on the way – as soon as you have a signal.' Then he turned to Laura and Philip. 'You two OK?'

Laura's face was drained of blood and her whole body was shaking. 'Jo . . . You've got to save Jo,' she gasped.

Monroe looked confused. 'What . . . ?'

'Jo's the last target,' Philip said, his voice shaky. 'Our daughter – she'll be at my house in Woodstock. The killer's on his way.'

Monroe didn't hesitate. 'Harcourt, Smith,' he yelled to the two officers who had entered the room with him. 'You need to get back to the surface immediately.' He turned to Philip. 'What's the address?'

'Somersby Cottage, Ridley Street. It's directly off the High Street, two down from the post office.'

'Tell all units: extreme caution,' Monroe snapped. 'The suspect is armed and highly dangerous.' Then he walked round the back of the pentagram and cut the tape. Laura and Philip jumped to their feet, rubbing their wrists.

'We've got to get out of here,' Laura croaked, her heart thudding in her chest.

'We can deal with this, Laura,' Monroe insisted.

'I hope so. But there's no way I am hanging around here.'

One of the policeman crouching beside Lightman straightened up. 'He's dead,' he announced.

Laura didn't even stop to look at Lightman's corpse as she ran for the door, followed by Philip and Monroe. On his way Philip caught a glimpse of Bridges struggling to sit up. Jones had a tourniquet above the man's knee and an oxygen mask over his face.

'Thank you,' Philip said as he rushed past.

Monroe led the way, turning left through an archway with a curved ceiling illuminated by crystals.

'How did you manage to find us?' Philip asked as they ran.

'You have to thank our friend Malcolm Bridges for that,' Monroe replied.

It took them several minutes to reach the surface. Monroe had to stop a few times to check the map that Bridges had sent him earlier. The tunnels twisted and turned but followed a gentle upward slope. It was exhausting, but they couldn't waste a second. They kept going even as Monroe took out his intercom. One green light showed on the signal indicator. He stabbed at the call button.

'Harcourt? You on the road? Good. All units

heading for Woodstock. Right, listen, the suspect is one Julius Spenser. Get Smith to run a profile en route. We know he's a highly trained assassin. He'll be well armed.' Monroe took several deep breaths as he ran and felt a pain in his chest. Must get back to the gym, he thought. 'We'll be there as quickly as we can. Jenkins will supervise until I get there; he's on his way.'

As they turned the final corner they were confronted by a heavy oak door. But there was no need to follow any unlocking code: it was open. Monroe led the way into Lightman's office. They traversed the room with barely a glance around them, passed two police officers standing in the corridor beyond, and a few seconds later emerged into the chill night air. Monroe's car was close to the main doors. Philip and Laura jumped into the back as the DCI took the wheel and raced onto Parks Road, heading north towards Woodstock. Behind them they could see the lights of an ambulance pulling up outside the main entrance to the library.

Chapter 45

Woodstock: 30 March, midnight

The house was in almost total darkness as the Acolyte parked his black Toyota in the driveway that curved round the back of the house. A light was on in the kitchen and this cast a faint glow across the path that ran under the window. He knew that the only people in the house were Tom and Jo. Almost three hours earlier he had seen Laura and Philip enter the Trill Mill Stream, then he had met with the Master before leaving for St Giles and Jo's college. He had watched Jo emerge from the main gate with her boyfriend at 10.45. Then he had followed their car north out of the city and along the road to Woodstock. There he had observed them entering the house before he'd driven a short distance to wait in a nearby lane.

This would be the final harvesting: a liver from Jo Newcombe. With this task accomplished he would make all haste to Oxford where he would stand beside his Master as they performed the ritual. By the morning, their work would be complete.

The Acolyte turned the handle of the kitchen door. It was locked. Lowering the organ-transporter to the floor he opened a pouch in his plastic oversuit, removed a long needle-like implement and slipped it into the lock. A moment later the door was open and he stepped inside.

He could hear sounds coming from a nearby room. He had been here earlier in the day and knew the layout of the house. He crept across the darkened dining room to a door that led onto the narrow hallway. He opened the door very carefully. Everything seemed to creak and groan in this old house. In the hall he could hear more clearly the sound from the TV in the large sitting room directly ahead. To his left there was a winding narrow staircase. He traversed the hall. The door to the living room was open, but only a crack. He eased it back on its hinges.

A lamp glowed in the corner near the door, but the flickering light from the TV was the only illumination at the far end of the room. Jo and Tom were sitting close together on the sofa, lost in an old movie. The Acolyte caught a glimpse of the actors, black-and-white images, a couple kissing through the window of a train carriage, steam billowing around them. *Brief Encounter*, he thought. How apt.

He checked his watch. It was time. He lowered the transporter to the floor with exaggerated care and silently withdrew a scalpel from a pocket in his sleeve. The long, horribly sharp blade caught the light and glistened for a fraction of a second. He took a step forward, but as his foot came to rest on the floor an old wooden board creaked. Jo and Tom spun round.

The Acolyte was fast, but Jo and Tom were faster. They were off the sofa before the killer had taken two steps. Jo screamed and fell back behind Tom who was gripping a cricket bat. The Acolyte did not pause. He came straight for them, the scalpel held out in front of him. Tom and Jo backed against the wall. Jo was ashen-faced, her eyes wide. Tom was trying desperately to keep his nerve and took a wild swing at the Acolyte. He missed. Jo screamed again and grabbed at Tom's shirt, ripping it. They started to back towards the door. The Acolyte grunted with impatience and made another rush towards them. Tom swung the bat again and it came down hard on the Acolyte's arm. The killer howled and the scalpel dropped to the floor.

Jo and Tom had gained a second and dashed for the hall. Jo grasped the handle to the front door and tugged. It was locked. She cursed.

'Upstairs,' Tom yelled and he pushed her ahead of him. He started to back towards the narrow stairs just as the Acolyte emerged from the living room. The killer now had the scalpel in his left hand. His right arm hung limp at his side. Tom caught a glimpse of the face behind the perspex visor. The eyes were featureless black circles, the face a waxwork doppelgänger of a living human.

Jo sped to the stairs and Tom was close behind. They took the stairs two at a time and Tom swung again at the Acolyte who expertly dodged the bat, letting it slam against the banisters and the wall, where it took a chunk out of the plaster.

'The bedroom,' Tom shouted as they reached the landing.

The Acolyte was at his shoulder and Tom swung at him once more. This time the bat made contact with the Acolyte's shoulder, a glancing blow that barely slowed him. Tom flailed again. He missed and the bat caught between two banister struts and slipped out of his grasp. In the split second before he started to run, Tom looked again into the eyes of the Acolyte. All he could see there was his own death.

Jo was at the door of the bedroom and rushing inside as Tom sped along the corridor. Tom was super-fit and fast, but as he hurtled down the corridor his pursuer was no more than a pace behind. Jo held open the bedroom door and slammed it behind Tom, but instantly the Acolyte was forcing it back inwards with all his strength.

'Bolt it!' Tom hollered as he pushed his body against the wood. Jo just managed to slip the bolt home. She was shaking and on the verge of hysteria; her eyes were wild, her cheeks drained of blood.

The Acolyte began to hammer on the door with incredible force. A panel shattered. Jo screamed.

'Get out of the window,' Tom shouted. 'Get out . . . jump . . . whatever . . . just get out.'

'But—'

'Go!'

Jo was at the window and trying to work the latch, but her hands were shaking uncontrollably. Nauseous with terror, she managed to unfasten the window just as a plastic-clad hand thrust through the splintered door panel and reached for the bolt. Tom grabbed the nearest thing to hand, a heavy glass vase, and brought it down on the Acolyte's plastic-covered fingers. He felt gratified to hear a muffled groan from behind the visor as the gloved hand was pulled back.

Tom backed away towards the window as the door shattered from a furious kick. The Acolyte knew that his moment had passed – the astrological conditions had changed – but he was now driven on by sheer bloodlust. He rushed towards the young couple.

Monroe turned off the High Street into Ridley Street. Ahead were three police cars, their lights off. He switched off his own lights and eased forward.

Four officers dressed in full body armour and with high-powered rifles were moving to the side of the house. Two of them dashed forward as the others covered them.

Laura was pushing open the door even before the car had stopped.

Monroe grabbed her arm. 'Don't be bloody stupid. My men are going in . . . they can't do their—'

Laura yanked her arm away. 'If you think—'

'If you go in there you could get yourself killed,' Monroe shouted. 'You could be responsible for your daughter's murder. Think, woman – is that what you want?'

Laura went limp suddenly and her hands went up to her face. 'Oh, my God,' she said. Philip put a comforting arm around her.

Monroe ran over to the nearest squad car. PC Smith was there, talking into his radio. Monroe was about to instruct him to go around the other side of the house when a loud crash made them look up to the bedroom windows. There was a piercing scream. Monroe yelled into his radio. 'Jenkins – report!'

There was no reply.

'Smith, follow through, round the side there.' Monroe took out his own gun and ran to the rear of the house.

As they entered the shadows at the side of the house,

an upstairs window swung open. It was pushed outward with such force that it shook on its hinges. Laura saw it from inside Monroe's car and she was running towards the front lawn before Philip could stop her. Looking up, she saw Jo's petrified face appear. She was pulling herself up onto the window ledge when three gunshots rang out. They came from inside the house. Another shot followed, then a fifth. Laura flinched and closed her eyes for a fraction of a second. When she opened them again, Jo had disappeared.

The Acolyte's body lay face down in the bedroom; it looked like a red and white mannequin. The back of his hood was shredded and crimson-splashed, and two gaping holes marked a pair of bullet wounds between his shoulder blades. All around lay chunks of shattered wood.

Tom and Jo were talking to Monroe as Laura and Philip rushed into the room. Laura gathered her daughter into her arms.

Philip placed a hand on Tom's shoulder. 'Well done,' he said.

'Nothing like a good piece of willow to get you out of a spot,' Tom replied, his voice a little shaky.

Philip looked puzzled.

'I kept a cricket bat on my lap all evening. After the break-in I wasn't taking any chances,' Tom explained.

'Good for you, Tom,' Philip replied, walking over to where Laura and Jo were hugging. Embracing his daughter, he kissed her on her tear-streaked face. Then he placed one arm around Jo's shoulders and pulled Laura close with the other. 'Happy families,' he said.

Chapter 46

Los Angeles: two days later.

A tall, slender man wearing baggy cargo shorts and a fedora stepped out into the blazing sun of a perfect Californian morning. It was quiet along the beach strip and still too early for the stalls to be open.

Crossing the boardwalk, he strolled barefoot through the powdery warm sand of Venice Beach to the water's edge. He turned and looked back at the spacious beach house painted brilliant white and girdled by steel and glass balconies, before settling himself down onto the sand to stare out at the ocean.

His mobile bleeped. He looked at the screen and read the text. It said: 'Task completed. Last girl saved. Master and servant both dead. I wish you eternal happiness. Bradwardine.'

Charlie Tucker smiled and pondered the waves. It had not been easy faking his own death in London, but as the leader of the Guardians he had many resources at his disposal. The police and ambulance crews at the scene of his 'murder' had been loyal members of the fraternity. They had performed their tasks perfectly and, even as he had begun to acclimatise to the Californian sun, others had arranged his funeral in Croydon. He had felt bad about leading Laura into danger but, as he had told her on the DVD that he had left behind, she was immersing herself in the mystery anyway.

He had much to thank the twenty-first-century Bradwardine for. Bradwardine had been the code name used by his most trusted companion and fellow Guardian, Malcolm Bridges. Malcolm had had the most dangerous job of all, and he had risked everything. He had been planted in MI5 and at Oxford to monitor occult activities, just as John Wickins had been placed in Cambridge almost three and a half centuries earlier to watch over Newton. There was little that Bridges could have done to alert the authorities. Instead, he had acted in the way all Guardians had acted through the centuries: he had watched and waited, befriended and interfered as best he could without drawing attention to the ancient organisation of which he was a part. Charlie understood this because he had done exactly the same thing – he had used others, manoeuvring them to do the things that he needed them to do.

And from across the world, Bradwardine/Bridges had kept him appraised of the whole sequence of events. He had been informed when Lightman went underground, literally. The Professor had used tactics similar to his own and had faked his disappearance even down to the detail of having a witness claim that they had seen his abduction. He also knew that Laura and Philip had penetrated the labyrinth. From six thousand miles away, he could do little more than wait, hoping he had given them enough information to get through safely without blowing his own cover. Now he knew that Jo was safe and Lightman and Spenser were both dead.

With a sigh, Charlie reached into his pocket and pulled out the precious object he carried with him everywhere now: a perfect ruby sphere. He held it up to the light, considering the fine lines of hieroglyphics that ran in a closely packed spiral from pole to pole. The sun caught in its fathomless depths. Returning the orb to his pocket, he looked out at the glassy blue ocean, feeling content with the world.

The Facts Behind
the Fiction

Equinox is of course a work of fiction but some elements of the story are based in fact. What follows is a selection of these elements and the truth behind them.

Alchemy

Alchemy is considered to be the predecessor of modern chemistry. It has been practised for thousands of years and still has its followers today. Some say that the art has its roots in truly ancient times and that such figures as Moses were adepts. But this is almost certainly an exaggeration.

We do know, though, that alchemy goes back at least two thousand years, because there are records of the work of early alchemists from ancient China, and from the city of Alexandria, much of which was destroyed in the early fifth century AD by Bishop Theophilus. The ancient Chinese were very keen alchemists, and it has been suggested that they discovered gunpowder centuries before it was redis-covered in Europe by the great thirteenth-century philosopher Roger Bacon. The ancient Chinese also kept records of alchemical experiments that they performed on human guinea pigs – convicted crim-inals.

The alchemists believed that they could find a magical material called the Philosopher's Stone, a substance that could convert any base metal to gold. To this end many thousands of men and women laboured for years in dark and dingy laboratories, chasing their elusive goal.

The alchemists were true believers in what they were doing and many became completely obsessed with the art. The great psychologist Carl Jung was fascinated with alchemy, and realised that the processes the alchemists employed in their laboratories were really rituals linked to a form of religious obsession. The alchemists were actually trying to transmute their own psyche, or 'soul', as they attempted to change base metals into gold. This is a little like any religious process in which the adept attempts to achieve perfection or to find the 'gold' within themselves. The alchemists were only partially aware of this aspect of their endeavours but realised that they had to be 'pure of spirit' to achieve their goal. Many spent years in mental preparation for their task.

Some modern occultists still insist that alchemy is a true science and they try to draw parallels between alchemy and modern quantum mechanics, the scientific theory which describes the subatomic world. However, there really is no link. Quantum mechanics is a rigorous science that has been supported by almost a century of experiment, whereas alchemy is based on the false idea that transmutation from base to precious metal can be achieved in a crucible. Most importantly, quantum mechanics gives us real, tangible technology such as lasers, television and microelectronics. Alchemy is entirely subjective and has no logical foundation.

Alchemy is a very confusing subject to study because it was such an idiosyncratic practice. Each alchemist had his own methods for finding what he thought was the Philosopher's Stone. The earliest-known documents on the subject were kept in Alexandria. From those manuscripts that survived the destruction of the famous library, the Arab philosophers of the seventh and eighth centuries AD developed a more advanced alchemical lore. This was imported into Europe around the eleventh century, and alchemy soon became popular throughout the Continent. By the sixteenth century there were hundreds of peripatetic magi who found employment with gullible wealthy merchants and European nobles.

Hundreds of alchemists wrote books about the techniques they used, but they deliberately obscured their meaning with codes or poetic language so that other alchemists could not copy them. Another reason why they hid their findings in this way was to cover up the fact that they were totally unsuccessful in achieving their objectives.

In 1404, the English king Henry IV made the practice of alchemy a capital offence because it was thought that, if an alchemist could succeed, they would disturb the status quo by producing vast amounts of gold and destabilising the financial system. But later, Queen Elizabeth I employed alchemists in an attempt to boost the royal coffers. One of her favourites was John Dee, who was a gifted natural philosopher as well as an occultist.

Alchemists could never have hoped to succeed in

turning base metal to gold because they were attempting to transform the basic fabric of matter by using nothing more powerful than a furnace and a mixture of simple chemicals. Transmutation is only possible today in the heart of nuclear reactors, where large atoms are split into smaller particles in a process called 'nuclear fission'. However, although it is now theoretically possible to produce gold from other metals, the amount of energy needed (and therefore the cost involved) exceeds the value of the material produced at the end of the process.

The methods of the alchemists were very basic. They usually began by mixing in a mortar three substances: a metal ore, usually impure iron, another metal (often lead or mercury), and an acid of organic origin – most typically citric acid from fruit or vegetables. They ground these together for anything up to six months to ensure complete mixing, and the blend was then heated carefully in a crucible. The temperature was allowed to rise very slowly until it reached an optimum, which was maintained for ten days. This was a dangerous process that produced toxic fumes, and many an alchemist working in cramped, unventilated rooms succumbed to poisoning from mercury vapour. Others went slowly mad from lead or mercury poisoning.

After the heating process was completed, the material in the crucible was removed and dissolved in an acid. Many generations of alchemists experimented with different types of solvent, and in this way nitric, sulphuric and ethanoic acid were all discovered.

After the material from the crucible had been successfully dissolved in the solvent, the next step was to evaporate and reconstitute the material – to distil it. This distillation process was the most delicate and time-consuming step, and often took the alchemist years to complete to his satisfaction. It was also another dangerous stage – the laboratory fire was never allowed to go out, and there were frequent accidents.

If the experimenter was not consumed by flame, and the material was not lost through poor experimental technique, then the alchemist could move on to the next stage, a step most clearly linked with mysticism. According to most alchemical texts, the moment when distillation should be stopped was determined by 'a sign'. No two alchemical manuals agreed upon when or how this should happen, and the poor alchemist simply had to wait until he deemed that the most propitious moment had arrived to stop the distillation.

The material was then removed from the distillation equipment and an oxidising agent added. This was usually potassium nitrate, a substance certainly known to the ancient Chinese and quite possibly to the Alexandrians. However, combined with sulphur from the metal ore and carbon from the organic acid, the alchemist then had, quite literally, an explosive mixture – gunpowder.

Many an alchemist who survived poisoning and fire ended his days going up with his laboratory in a detonation.

Those who survived all these steps were then able to move on to the final stages where the mixture was sealed in a special container and warmed carefully. Then, after cooling the material, a white solid was sometimes observed which was known as the White Stone, capable, it was claimed, of transmuting base metals into silver. The most ambitious stage – producing a red solid called the Red Rose, by warming and then cooling and purifying the distillate – was supposed to lead to the production of the Philosopher's Stone itself.

All of these stages in the process were described in the literature allegorically, and were enveloped in mystical language and secret, esoteric meaning. For example, the blending of the original ingredients and their fusion via the use of heat was described as 'setting the two dragons at war with one another'. In this way the male and the female elements of the substances, symbolised by a king and a queen, were released and then recombined or 'married'. This was the concept behind one of the most famous of all alchemical books, the allegorical romance *The Chemical Wedding*, which, on one level, has been interpreted as describing the transmutation process.

Alchemy was fantastical but it did bear fruit. Alchemists invented or improved many techniques, including heating methods, decanting, recrystallisation and evaporation. They also pioneered the use of a vast range of chemical apparatus, including heating equipment and specialised glassware.

Successive generations of alchemists refined the technique of distillation first developed by the magi of Alexandria almost two thousand years ago. Today, no chemical laboratory would be complete without distillation apparatus. Indeed, the same kind of equipment, albeit on a much grander scale, is used to refine oil, separating it into its components.

Further reading: *Isaac Newton: The Last Sorcerer*, Michael White, Fourth Estate, 1997.

Astrology

According to most historians, the origins of modern Western astrology date back to the city of Mesopotamia around 4,000 BC. The ancients devised the system of star signs more or less as they are known today – dividing the sky into twelve constellations.

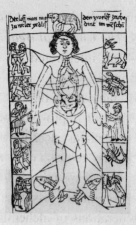

The basic tenets of this ancient art were later adopted by the early Greeks, and took root to become an important part of the philosophical mélange of the era. Socrates, Plato and Aristotle all practised astrology, and it was of particular interest to the great Hellenic conqueror Alexander the Great, Aristotle's pupil.

With the coming of Christianity, astrology was sidelined, although some early Church leaders supported, astrological thinking and even tried to form an amalgam of astrology and Christian theology. But for a period during the early Middle Ages the Church vilified astrologers, and many practitioners were burned at the stake as heretics.

Perhaps as a consequence of theological opposition astrology went underground, becoming an anti-establishment practice akin to many other areas of the occult tradition such as alchemy and divining. Many alchemists were also astrologers and the two subjects were largely intertwined – as they are for the members of the Order of the Black Sphinx in *Equinox*. Most alchemists explored links between alchemical discovery and the signs of the zodiac, and believed that alchemy and astrology had common origins in the teachings of the ancient Egyptians.

The science of astronomy should really have sounded the death knell for astrology. It is certainly true that the development of scientific knowledge, and a growing realisation that humankind is an insignificant species in an almost infinite universe, has stolen astrology's thunder, but there are still many people who believe in the relevance of star signs, and that their lives are in some way guided by the stars. Indeed, astrology is probably the most popular aspect of the occult in the twenty-first century. Many people read their horoscopes or talk about their star sign at dinner parties, never really associating the subject with the occult tradition.

According to some statistics, ninety-nine per cent of people today know their star sign, and an esti-mated fifty per cent of the population consult horo-scopes regularly. But the majority of scientists dismiss astrology as nothing more than wish-fulfil-ment. They point to the fact that experiments have shown that there is no correlation between a person's birth date and their character, or the course that their life follows. They highlight the fact that most horoscopes contain what have been called 'Barnum statements' (after the man who coined the phrase 'There's one born every minute'). Barnum statements are very vague pronouncements such as: 'You like a challenge' or 'Sometimes you feel extroverted, at other times you feel introverted.'

In one famous experiment to show how such statements can be and are interpreted to suit the individual reading the horoscope, a French scientist, Michel Gauquelin, placed an ad in the magazine *Ici Paris* offering free horoscopes to anyone who responded. He received a hundred and fifty requests and duly posted the horoscopes. He then asked each applicant what they thought of theirs. Ninety-four per cent of them said that they believed it accurately portrayed their personality. What Gauquelin did not tell them was that they had received the same horoscope – that of Dr Petroit, an infamous French mass murderer.

The other serious problem with astrology is the one put forward by Jo in *Equinox*, when she points out that the stars are not fixed in the sky and that during the six thousand years since the star signs were first postulated the stars have moved out of their positions in the night sky.

However, the most important objection to astrology is simply one of logic. The entire concept was first postulated by relatively primitive people who had no concept of the nature of the universe. To the people of 4,000 BC the Earth was a special place and humanity was unique. To them the gods controlled every facet of human life, and the heavens were little more than a backdrop to humanity's existence. Today we have the lessons of Darwin, and astronomers from Galileo to twenty-first-century researchers working with the most advanced radio telescopes, have taught us that humankind is not cosmically important, and that the Earth is an insignificant speck in a spiral arm of one ordinary galaxy among billions. In view of these facts it is hard to believe that distant suns, some of which are thousands of light years from our world, can have any influence at all over our tiny lives. To believe otherwise is perhaps the ultimate example of egotism.

Further reading: *Pseudoscience and the Paranormal*, Terence Hines, Prometheus Books, 1988.

The Bodleian Library

The Bodleian is the largest academic library in the world and perhaps the oldest. It has its origins in a collection of books owned by Thomas Cobham, the Bishop of Worcester, which was donated to Oxford University in the 1320s. When Cobham died, his books were pawned to pay his death duties but were later bought by Oriel College, Oxford, where they remained for almost four hundred years.

A Fellow of Merton College named Sir Thomas Bodley (1545–1613) was responsible for finding the funds to build an independent library for the university. Cobham's collection became the core of this new library, which was opened in 1602 and named after its founder, Bodley, in 1604.

Today the Bodleian Library is housed in a collection of buildings in the centre of Oxford, and includes the New Bodleian, which was completed in 1939. The majority of the library's five million books are stored in over one hundred kilometres of tunnels under the city of Oxford.

Little is known about the origin of these tunnels, but it is believed that they were first built in the eighteenth century, and have been extended gradually ever since. During the Second World War the tunnels were used to house precious art treasures and ancient artefacts in order to protect them from the danger of Luftwaffe bombs. As far as I'm aware, the tunnels have never been used for occult rituals.

Robert Boyle (1627–1691)

After Newton and Galileo, Robert Boyle was perhaps the most important scientist of the seventeenth century. He was principally interested in what would later be called chemistry, but he was also an adept of the alchemical tradition. In many ways we may think of Boyle as a man who bridged the ancient art of alchemy and the modern science of chemistry.

ROBERTVS BOYLE ARM:

Born in Ireland in 1627, as one of the founders of the Royal Society Boyle was something of an elder statesman in the world of seventeenth-century science. His most famous contribution to scientific knowledge was his book *The Sceptical Chymist*, published in 1661.

An aristocrat, Boyle was the fourteenth and youngest son of the Earl of Cork, and therefore had no younger brother James as depicted in *Equinox*. However, he was the most renowned scientist in Oxford and had a laboratory at University College on the High. Today, a plaque on the wall of the college facing the High Street reads:

In a house on this site
between 1655 and 1668 lived
ROBERT BOYLE

Boyle is also known to have been a member of secret cabals who met to discuss alchemical lore and share occult knowledge. He knew Isaac Newton well, and was one of the few men whom the Lucasian Professor admired. It was Robert Boyle who educated a young Newton into the idea that he must keep secret his alchemical researches, for fear of ridicule within the scientific community and possible clashes with the Church and the Crown.

Further reading: *The Aspiring Adept: Robert Boyle and his Alchemical Quest*, Lawrence Principe, Princeton University Press, 2000.

Thomas Bradwardine (c. 1297–1349)

Thomas Bradwardine's exact birth date is open to conjecture and has been guessed at by historians, based on the fact that he was awarded his MA at Oxford in 1321. He became a distinguished figure at the university and held several important positions there before leaving for the royal court in 1337. He was appointed Chancellor of St Paul's Cathedral, and later he became the king's chaplain. For the final two years of his life Bradwardine was Archbishop of Canterbury. He fell victim to the Black Death that swept through Europe in the late 1340s.

Bradwardine was not only renowned as a theologian, he was also a very talented and forward-thinking mathematician. He lived in a time during which most intellectuals followed unquestioningly the teachings of Aristotle, but he challenged many of the Greek philosopher's ideas. In Oxford, Bradwardine was known as 'Doctor Profundus' – the profound doctor – and he left a body of pioneering work in logic and problem-solving.

The Bear Inn, Oxford

In *Equinox*, this is the inn at which Newton stays before joining the gathering of the Order of the Black Sphinx under the Bodleian Library. It is a real pub, and according to legend it received its name because it was built over a bear pit. It is one of the oldest pubs in Oxford and dates back to 1242.

Cooper's Bookshop

William Cooper owned a bookshop in an area of London called Little Britain, which was famed for its literary tradition. Isaac Newton really did frequent this shop and made special trips to London to buy books there. William Cooper was a respected figure but he was also known by insiders as a dealer in illegal occult texts. He was an important contact for Newton and procured many forbidden books for him, when the scientist began experimenting with alchemy during the 1670s.

The Emerald Tablet

For the alchemist, the text of the Emerald Tablet is one of the most sacred. The fabled tablet is said to have belonged to the mythical Hermes Trismegistus, the godfather of alchemy, and all later alchemists had to work from copies of copies of copies of the original text. Not surprisingly, the various versions altered dramatically down the ages.

The reason why the text of the emerald tablet was so important was that it gave what purported to be a tried and tested method for producing the Philosopher's Stone – something like an incredibly complex recipe passed from generation to generation. The first known copy of the text appeared in the West around the middle of the twelfth century, in editions of what is known as the pseudo-Aristotelian *Secretum Secretorum* – which was actually a translation of the *Kitab Sirr al-Asar*, a book of advice to kings translated into Latin by Johannes Hispalensis. The *Kitab Sirr al-Asar*, the oldest known version of the text anywhere in the world, is thought to date from about AD 800, but some scholars claim the precedence of another work, *Kitab Sirr al-Khaliqa wa San 'at al-Tabi'a* (*Book of the Secret of Creation and the Art of Nature*) written as early as AD 650.

The ruby sphere described in *Equinox* is completely fictitious.

Liam Ethwiche

The name of the author of the Isaac Newton biography mentioned in *Equinox* is an anagram.

Nicolas Fatio du Duillier (1664–1753)

Fatio de Duillier was born into a wealthy family who mollycoddled him for most of his early life. He became quite well known for a while among the intelligentsia but his reputation did not last. The seventh of twelve children, Fatio grew up in Switzerland, the son of a wealthy landowner.

By the time he was eighteen in 1682, Fatio was living off a generous allowance in Paris. He was quite a talented mathematician, and he impressed a succession of eminent philosophers with his youthful precociousness. In 1687 he travelled to England specifically to meet Newton.

He succeeded in ingratiating himself with the great scientist, and between 1689 and 1693 they shared an intense relationship. At one point, Newton wanted Fatio to move into his rooms in Cambridge, but the plan never came to anything. What is certain is that Fatio was deeply involved with the occult tradition and encouraged Newton to delve further into magic. Together they conducted many alchemical experiments, and it is possible that Fatio nurtured in Newton an interest in the Black Arts.

Fatio was never trusted by the scientific establishment in England and he had many enemies. He and Newton parted acrimoniously in 1693. Fatio lost his protector, and the younger man's capital plummeted.

Little is known about Fatio du Duillier's later life. He was one of those strange figures who remained on the periphery of the scientific community of the time. He was known to have been involved with the Rosicrucians and other outlandish fringe groups, and on at least one occasion he was put in the stocks at Charing Cross for antisocial activities. He lived until his ninetieth year, but died in poverty and almost complete obscurity.

Robert Hooke (1635–1703)

Born in 1635, Robert Hooke was the son of a clergyman. His father had committed suicide by hanging himself in 1648, when Robert was still in his early teens. As a boy he had displayed an aptitude for drawing and painting, and after receiving a modest inheritance of one hundred pounds he had been packed off to London to be taught by the painter Sir Peter Lely. By good fortune, he came to the attention of Richard Busby, a master at Westminster School, who realised that the boy's intellectual capabilities extended beyond his ability as an artist. Under Busby's tutelage, he received the best education available at the time and secured a place at Christ Church College, Oxford, where he obtained his MA in 1663.

Hooke had to make his way through his undergraduate studies by working as a servant. After graduating, he became Robert Boyle's paid assistant and worked in his Oxford laboratory. From there he became involved with the Invisible College (the precursor to the Royal Society), and began to associate with the influential thinkers of the day. It was Boyle who later secured for Hooke the position of Curator of Experiments in London in 1662.

Hooke possessed a restless energy and flitted from one enthusiasm to another. He could never give his undivided attention to anything for long and so, to many, he appeared something of a dilettante. His greatest work, *Micrographia,* was ostensibly a treatise about microscopy, but it also included a number of original theories concerning the nature of light. Published in 1665, it was a book that Newton knew well and secretly admired.

Hooke and Newton were bitter enemies. They were also very different characters. Hooke loved the coffee house, the gossip of his friends over a bottle of port, and the attentions of at least one mistress at a time. He was a man who recorded his sexual exploits and the quality of his orgasms in his diary. Newton lived a life of monkish austerity and isolation at Trinity College, Cambridge. Beyond this, though, Newton had only contempt for anyone who merely dipped into a subject, as Hooke appeared to do.

For his part, Hooke saw Newton as a dried-up husk of a man who was, admittedly, brilliant but was also obsessive and self-opinionated, and had an excessively rosy self-image. Their egos exaggerated their differences, so that each subconsciously defended their own way of working and neither was able to give the other credit. They remained bitter enemies until Hooke's death in 1703.

Further reading: *The Curious Life of Robert Hooke: The Man who Measured London*, Lisa Jardine, HarperCollins, 2005.

Hypatia (c. 380–415)

As Charlie Tucker said, Hypatia was 'quite a gal'. Little is known of her life. She is thought to have been born around AD 380, and her father, Theon, was a distinguished mathematician who taught at the great school at the Library of Alexandria.

Hypatia is known to have travelled widely, and later became a respected scholar who was best known for her work in mathematics and natural philosophy. She is credited with three major treatises on geometry and algebra, and one on astronomy. According to some accounts, she also became the last Chief Librarian of the Library of Alexandria.

Hypatia met a violent end. She was suspected of witchcraft and a Christian mob pulled her from her classroom into the streets, where they flayed her to death with oyster shells.

Hypatia was remarkably modern in her thinking, claiming that: 'All formal dogmatic religions are fallacious and must never be accepted by self-respecting persons as final.' Elsewhere she commented: 'Reserve your right to think, for even to think wrongly is better than not to think at all.'

No wonder the early Christians hated her.

Further reading: *Hypatia of Alexandria*, Maria Dzielska, Cambridge: Harvard University Press, 1995.

The Library of Alexandria

The library is thought to have been founded as early as the third century BC, and it has been suggested that its original 'core' was a collection of books once owned by Aristotle.

The Library of Alexandria was certainly the greatest repository of books in the ancient world; at its height it contained an estimated half a million scrolls. It was a royal library, having been founded at the decree of Ptolemy III of Egypt. It is said that Ptolemy ordered any visitors to Alexandria to hand over books in their possession so that they could be copied. The original building storing the collection was built on the site of the Temple of the Muses, the *Musaeum* (from which the word 'museum' is derived).

It is unclear who was responsible for the destruction of the library in AD 415. The Roman scholar Plutarch blamed Julius Caesar, but more recently the renowned historian Edward Gibbon pointed the finger at Theophilus, the Christian Patriarch of Alexandria.

Ever since the destruction of the library, scholars and philosophers have mourned this terrible loss to the world of learning. No one knows how many manuscripts were destroyed when fire razed the library, but it is certain that some were saved and preserved for future generations. The fragment of learning that survived was later unearthed by Arabic scholars, and some of these texts found their way to Italy and Spain during the fourteenth and fifteenth centuries, helping to lay the foundations of the Renaissance. Other remnants fell into the hands of Arabic alchemists who passed on their knowledge to their European counterparts, fuelling the development of mystical and occult knowledge.

Further reading: *The Library of Alexandria: Centre of Learning in the Ancient World*, Roy MacLeod, I.B Tauris Publishers, 2004.

Isaac Newton (1642–1727)

When people think of Isaac Newton they usually associate him with an apple that fell from a tree and sparked off his discovery of the theory of gravity. But actually there is compelling evidence to suggest that he did not come by the theory at this particular moment. Instead, the true inspiration setting him on the road to one of the most important theories in science came from his involvement with the occult.

Isaac Newton as born in 1642 into a relatively wealthy family who lived in the village of Woolsthorpe near Grantham in Lincolnshire. He was always a rather detached, introverted boy who did not do particularly well at school, until about the age of fourteen when he was noticed by his headmaster, Henry Stokes.

Newton went to Cambridge University in 1661, and very soon came under the influence of other, older scholars who saw something in him and encouraged him. Most important among these were two Cambridge Fellows, Henry More and Isaac Barrow. Both these men were natural philosophers, but they also dabbled in the ancient art of alchemy, an interest that they passed on to Newton.

For Isaac Newton, alchemy was a means to an end. He was a puritan who believed in the idea of God's word and God's works. In other words, he was devoted to the teachings of the Bible, and believed that it was his duty to unravel the puzzle of life, to investigate everything that there was to know about the world – in other words, to study God's works.

During Newton's lifetime, alchemy was an illegal pursuit and was punishable by death. It would also have destroyed his academic reputation if he had been discovered. But he still spent far more time on alchemical research than he did on orthodox scientific practice. In fact, when Newton died in 1727, it was discovered that he had owned the largest library of occult literature ever collected, and that he had himself written over 1,000,000 words on the subject.

At the same time that Newton was studying alchemy, he was of course following a conventional scientific career. He became the second Lucasian Professor of Mathematics at Cambridge (the seat that is held today by Professor Stephen Hawking), succeeding his friend and mentor Isaac Barrow in 1669 at the tender age of twenty-seven. From the early 1670s he began to gain recognition beyond the confines of Cambridge University, and was accepted as a Fellow of the Royal Society.

According to the history books, Newton's great achievement – his elucidation of the theory of gravity in 1666 – occurred to him while he was staying at his mother's house in Woolsthorpe. It is true that Newton, along with the rest of the academic community, fled Cambridge during the plague years of 1665/6, and he did indeed return to live with his mother at their rural home. It is even possible that Newton did one day sit under an apple tree as he mused upon the meaning of gravity, and could have seen an apple fall. This might have pushed his thinking along, but it is ridiculous to believe that the whole concept of gravity came to him then in one great rush. Newton probably made up this story to conceal the fact that he had used alchemy to help develop his famous theory.

The working-out of the theory of gravity took Newton almost twenty years, and did not really take shape until he began his great book, the *Principia Mathematica*, published in 1687. During the two decades between the first inspirational spark in the garden in Woolsthorpe and the appearance of this work, many influences shaped the theory.

First there was mathematics. Newton was a supreme mathematician. By the age of twenty-four he was the most advanced one of his time. He was also a born natural philosopher, and had absorbed the entire canon of science up to that date. By the plague year of 1665, and his time in the country, he had already surpassed the great thinkers of the day, including Robert Boyle and René Descartes, and was beginning to synthesise his own ideas. With these talents he was able to begin to understand that gravity was responsible for keeping the planets in motion, and he was even able to suggest a relationship between the distance separating two bodies (such as planets) and the force of gravity between them, the 'inverse square' law.

At the time, the idea that one object could influence the movement of another without actually touching it was unimaginable. This behaviour is now called 'action at a distance' and we take it for granted, but people in Newton's day could not understand this and saw it as magic or an occult property.

Through his experiments in alchemy, Newton was

able to approach gravity with a more open mind than most of his peers. He began investigating alchemy in about 1669. He travelled to London to buy forbidden books from fellow alchemists, and carried out his private experiments, hidden away from the authorities and his rivals within the scientific community. His earliest experiments were very basic, but after reading everything he could about alchemy he soon pushed the art beyond the limits set by his predecessors. In true scientific fashion, he approached each experiment logically and with great precision, meticulously writing up what he had discovered. Whereas the alchemists of yore had fumbled around for years not really knowing what they were doing, Newton approached the work systematically.

Another great difference between Newton and his predecessors was that Newton was never interested in making gold. His sole purpose in studying alchemy was to find what he believed were hidden basic laws that governed the universe. He might not have realised that he would come to a theory of gravity through alchemy and other occult practices, but he did think that there was some basic law or hidden ancient knowledge to be found from his researches.

The breakthrough from alchemy came when Newton observed materials in his crucible, and realised that they were acting under the influence of forces. He could see particles attracted to each other and other particles repelled by their neighbours, without there being any physical contact or tangible link between them. In other words, he saw action at a distance within the alchemist's crucible. He then began to realise that this might also be how gravity worked and that what happened in the microcosm of the crucible and the alchemists' fire could perhaps also happen in the macrocosm – the world of planets and suns.

But there were other occult influences at work. From the mid-1670s, when Newton was in his early thirties, until the day he died in 1727, he was obsessed with religion, and spent years investigating the Bible. He believed that the origin of all true knowledge derived from the ancient peoples described in the Old Testament, and he considered King Solomon to be the ultimate authority.

Newton called King Solomon: 'The greatest Philosopher in the world', and spent years studying the design of Solomon's Temple as described in the book of Ezekiel in the Old Testament.

Originally built around 1,000 BC, on a site then already sacred to the Jews, Solomon's Temple was the most hallowed symbol of wisdom and faith long before Newton put his own personal interpretation upon it. Almost from the time of its construction until the Enlightenment, the greater part of three thousand years later, it was as revered as the

Pyramids or Stonehenge had been by the pagan faithful who had built them.

Newton believed that Solomon had encoded the wisdom of the Ancients, that lay at the heart of the Old Testament, into the design of his temple. Furthermore, he believed that by analysing the Bible, using Solomon's floor plan as a key, he could prophesy future events. According to Newton, the design acted as a template: the dimensions and geometry of the temple offered clues to timescales, and to the pronouncements of the great Biblical prophets (especially Ezekiel, John and Daniel).

Combining this floor plan with his interpretations of Scripture allowed Newton to produce a detailed outline for an alternative 'world chronology'. To this he assigned dates for such events as the Second Coming of Christ and the Day of Judgement.

But the configuration of Solomon's Temple helped Newton in other ways. He described the ancient temple as '. . . a fire for offering sacrifices [that] burned perpetually in the middle of a sacred place', and visualised the centre of the temple as a central fire around which the believers assembled. He called this arrangement a *prytaneum*.

The image of a fire at the centre of the temple, with disciples arranged in a circle around the flame, acted as another trigger in moulding his concept of universal gravitation. Key to this is the idea that instead of simply seeing the rays of light radiating *outwards* from the fire, Newton might instead have visualised them as a force *attracting* the disciples *towards* the centre. In this scheme, the parallels between the solar system and the temple are apparent: the planets were symbolised by the disciples and the temple fire (sometimes called 'the fire at the heart of the world') was the model for the sun.

Combined with the action of forces that he had observed in the crucible and his elucidation of the inverse square law, Newton was able to come up with the idea that there was an invisible force that acted between all objects, and whose power diminished as the objects were moved further apart. The way this force changed was governed by the same inverse square law.

All these influences, combined with experiments that Newton conducted in his rooms, and observations he made of planets and comets, convinced him of his theory. This work came to fruition in the *Principia*, now seen as probably the most important scientific treatise ever written. Ironically, this is a book that came not just from Newton's genius for science but also from his obsession with the occult and the lore of the Ancients.

Isaac Newton was a very unpleasant man who was scarred by childhood unhappiness. His father died before his birth and when he was three his mother, to whom he was very close, remarried and left him with his grandparents. He never recovered from this – as he saw it – rejection, and became an introverted and insular individual who found it almost impossible to make friends.

In 1692, when he was fifty, Newton suffered a nervous breakdown. This came immediately after his deepest involvement with the occult, and the end of a homosexual affair with Nicolas Fatio du Duillier. Newton gave up science almost overnight. In 1696, he left his home in Cambridge and moved to London. He became the Master of the Royal Mint at the Tower of London, and he sent many men to the gallows for the crime of clipping (removing little pieces of coins and melting down the gold and silver). He became a Member of Parliament for Cambridge University and an influential and very wealthy Establishment figure, famed and lauded for his contributions to science and state. Newton's occult interests remained secret until after his death.

Further reading: *Isaac Newton: The Last Sorcerer*, Michael White, Fourth Estate, 1997.

The Order of the Black Sphinx

Like the Guardians, the Order of the Black Sphinx is a fiction. However, both organisations are based on real secret societies and occult groups that have existed for many centuries.

The most famous of these are the Freemasons and the Knights Templar. Others include the Illuminati, the Rosicrucians and, more recently, the Hermetic Order of the Golden Dawn. A quick search on Google reveals the existence of many strange and obscure secret societies. Most of these are made up of harmless fantasists, but conspiracy theories abound that groups such as the Illuminati and the Freemasons are actually agencies for shadowy figures who are the real power-brokers of the world, men who control the financial and political levers of the modern world.

Further reading: *Secret Societies*, Nick Harding, Pocket Essentials, 2005.

The Royal Society

Originally known as the 'Invisible College', the Royal Society began life in 1648 at Wadham College, Oxford. In those days it was little more than an informal gathering of academics brought together by the inspirational figure of John Wilkins, an acclaimed mathematician. The founders included such luminaries as Robert Boyle, Henry Oldenburg and the astronomer and bishop Seth Ward.

By 1659, the Society had moved to rooms in London (at Gresham College), and three years later it was awarded a charter from King Charles II, who was a great supporter of science and philosophy. Henceforth, it was called the Royal Society.

In 1672, a decade after the Society's official foundation, Isaac Newton became a Fellow. By this time some of the most famous men of the day had joined the Royal Society, including Samuel Pepys, Christopher Wren and Robert Hooke.

The remit of the Royal Society was to study what was then called natural philosophy (now defined as 'science'), and to this end members conducted experiments and demonstrations, read their work to gatherings of Fellows and published some of the first known scientific papers. At the same time, many of the Fellows pursued an interest in matters that would now be considered occult, and there is evidence to show that some of them were deeply involved with the Freemasons and the Knights Templar.

These proto-scientists, including some of the greatest names of the age – Isaac Newton, Robert Boyle, Robert Hooke – led double lives. On the surface they appeared to be conventional philosophers and scientific researchers, but behind closed doors they pursued an avid interest in alchemy, astrology and other aspects of the occult tradition.

Further reading: *The Invisible College: The Royal Society, Freemasonry and the Birth of Modern Science*, Robert Lomas, Headline, 2003.

The Sheldonian Theatre

This was designed by Christopher Wren. Work began on the building in 1664 and it was completed in 1668. It was originally built as part of Oxford University, and was used for lectures and special events. Today it is open to the public and is a venue for concerts and conferences. The theatre lies very close to the Radcliffe Camera, the Bodleian Library and Hertford College, and its foundations are almost certainly interlaced with the fabled tunnels fanning

out from beneath the Bodleian. However, in reality Christopher Wren did not report finding a strange labyrinth as the foundations were being laid.

The Scytale and cryptography

There are two ways in which codes may be used. These are called *steganography* and *cryptography*. Steganography is the physical concealment of a message. The most famous example of this comes from the writings of Herodotus, in which he describes a method of encoding used by the Persian, Histiaeus. Histiaeus is said to have sent a message to Aristagoras, the tyrannical ruler of Miletus, by tattooing it on the scalp of a slave and waiting for the hair to grow back. He then sent the slave to Aristagoras with instructions to shave the man's head.

An ingenious variation on this idea was the *scytale*, first used by Greek commanders. This involved writing a message mixed in with random letters or words on a piece of papyrus. If this is wrapped around a stick, the message may be read along the length of the stick. The message is then sent without the stick. The recipient would have to know the size of the original stick and how to correctly wrap the scroll in order to decode the message.

Cryptography, a far more versatile code system, has been favoured by military planners, commanders and governments since the earliest days of writing. Julius Caesar is said to have been one of the first soldiers in the field to employ a code, sending messages from his campaigns in Britain back to Rome using the simplest of all cryptographs, namely shifting the letters of the alphabet by three, so that an A becomes a D, and a B becomes an E, and so on. Only those who knew the shift could translate the code. This appears remarkably unsophisticated today, but because it was one of the earliest codes to be used, the sheer novelty of the encryption kept the secret safe – at least for a while.

In Dark Age Europe codes fell out of favour, along

with reading and writing, but Renaissance military men and philosophers rediscovered encryption. Leonardo da Vinci concealed his most clandestine researches by composing his notes using mirror writing. Roger Bacon was obsessed with codes and ciphers, and during the middle of the thirteenth century he wrote a widely read treatise on the subject entitled *Secret Works of Art and the Nullity of Magic*.

The polymathic genius Leon Alberti, who greatly influenced and inspired Leonardo in so many areas, has become known as the 'Father of Western Cryptography' because he introduced many of the key ideas still used by analysts today. These ingenious ideas include *frequency analysis*, a technique used to detect and define patterns in a text, which then give important clues to the code key. Alberti also made the first polyalphabetic ciphers and the earliest cipher wheel, using a series of wheels engraved with numbers and letters that could be used to substitute the letters in any given message.

Alberti's ideas for polyalphabetical coding systems were further developed by the German scholar Johannes Trithemius, who published the *Polygraphiae* in 1518. Alberti's cipher wheels were also adapted by Thomas Jefferson, who used an elaborate set of twenty-six of them to create a code machine used from the early nineteenth century until it was retired by the American military in 1942.

Perhaps the most famous code story of modern times is that of the Enigma Machine, an encryption device developed by the Germans before the start of the Second World War to encode field operations and to communicate with their submarine fleet. The cracking of the Enigma code became a high-priority operation for the Allies, and led to the establishment of a specialised team of British cryptographers and mathematicians at Bletchley Park in Buckinghamshire. They began decoding Enigma messages in April 1940 and continued to operate throughout the war. Their work not only saved thousands of Allied lives, it greatly accelerated the development of the first electronic computer. Most crucial was the construction of a machine called Colossus, a project led by Alan Turing and a small group of analysts who became the world's first computer specialists. Their work paved the way for the massive expansion of computing that followed the war. It is therefore not surprising that the development of the computer has been inextricably linked with codes ever since. Today the lessons learned from cryptographers are of profound importance to business and science, and cryptography remains a valuable tool for military strategists and politicians.

Further reading: *The Code Book,* Simon Singh, Fourth Estate, 2000.

The Trill Mill Stream

The Trill Mill Stream exists just as it is described in *Equinox*, but today it is a pale shadow of the original stream. It is a small tributary of the Thames, and during the Middle Ages it flowed as an open waterway through the centre of Oxford and was used as a thoroughfare for small boats. By the middle of the nineteenth century the Trill Mill Stream had become so polluted that it was more or less an open sewer. Eventually it was considered such a health hazard that it was diverted underground and built over.

Both the story of T. E. Lawrence and the Victorian skeletons mentioned in *Equinox* are true, but as far as I'm aware there is no secret entrance to a hidden underground labyrinth via the Trill Mill Stream.

John Wickins (1643–1719)

Isaac Newton met John Wickins eighteen months after arriving at Trinity College, Cambridge, and they quickly became room-mates. Wickins, the son of the Master of Manchester Grammar School, entered Trinity in 1663. According to his own recollections, whilst out walking he encountered Newton looking miserable and lonely, the two of them struck up a conversation and soon found that they had much in common.

It is one of the great mysteries of Newton's life that,

although he and Wickins shared a suite of rooms for over two decades, Wickins left almost no record of their close association. They separated in 1683 under a cloud, and despite the fact that Wickins lived for another thirty-six years the two men never met again.

For many years Wickins worked as Newton's assistant. He regularly transcribed experiment notes and helped to set up apparatus and monitor investigations. Their rooms became a live-in laboratory. At first it was strewn with documents and simple home-made optical instruments, but later it was crowded out with furnaces and bottles of chemicals. After leaving Cambridge, Wickins became a clergyman, married and started a family. Many years after they parted Newton sent Wickins a parcel of Bibles to be distributed to his flock in the village of Stoke Edith near Monmouth. The only other surviving correspondence between them is a letter written years later, in which Wickins asked his erstwhile room-mate for a further donation of Bibles.

Christopher Wren (1632–1723)

Christopher Wren, who was knighted in 1673, was arguably the greatest English polymath. He was born into great privilege – his father was the king's chaplain and Wren grew up playing with the future monarch, Charles II.

Christopher Wren is best remembered as an architect, and he designed many famous London landmarks including the modern St Paul's Cathedral, the Royal Exchange and the Drury Lane Theatre. However, he was also a skilled artist, mathematician and accomplished astronomer who was appointed Savilian Professor of Astronomy at Oxford. He was one of the earliest members of the Royal Society after it moved to London, and through his contacts with King Charles II he did much to heighten the Society's profile.

Wren conducted some of the earliest (entirely unsuccessful) blood transfusions, during the 1660s, and carried out researches into the laws of motion which later inspired Isaac Newton to conduct his own experiments. He was one of the few men respected by Newton, who publicly acknowledged the debt he owed the older man. He died in 1723 aged ninety and was the first person to be buried in St Paul's.

Further Reading: *On A Grander Scale: The Outstanding Career of Christopher Wren*, Lisa Jardine, HarperCollins, 2003.

Picture Credits

Acknowledgements

Many people have helped me see this book from concept to publication. I would like to thank my agent Carole Blake who saw something in the original manuscript and then took it to the world. I would also like to extend my appreciation to everyone at Blake Friedmann, the best literary agency in the world.

Warm thanks go out to some very good friends who offered advice about the book in its many drafts: Tim Alexander, Kevin Davies, David Michie, Karen and Julian Johnson and Jules Watson. Most of all I would like to acknowledge the huge contribution from my wife, Lisa, who offered ideas, criticisms and invaluable comments from the earliest conception of the story until the final rewrite.